Dealer No. 1

Copyright James Ross 2018

Published by **Punk/Press**

The only thing I ever got off my old man was a birthday card

when I was ten. He'd gone off when I was three and left me

and Mam and my sister to fend for ourselves. Mam never

talks about him but my sister remembers him;

'What was Dad like,' I ask.

She looks at me through dark, sleepy eyes, pushes her hair back from her eyes. Her arms are scabbed like she's been shinning up a rusty drainpipe and accidentally slid back down and scraped herself. 'Whu?'

'I said, what was Dad like?'

She smiles at me, and I suss that she's trippin' and I should ask her later when she's straight.

Anyhow, the only thing I ever got from him was a birthday card when I was ten. It said Happy Birthday Mickey! And then there was a verse inside the card that went:

Now you're ten, and how you've grown

It really won't be long

'Til you're a man, and fully grown

With arms both big and strong.

And on the front of the card was a picture, a cartoon, of a little boy wearing a hardhat and driving a tractor. But I mean, how would he *know* I'd grown? To be honest, I was surprised he knew where I was, we moved so often.

But the killer was, at the bottom of the card, below the rhyme, he'd added

Remember, no one's got your back

XX. Dad.

I'd studied this card on more than one occasion, trying to work out some depth to what he was telling me.

'Laura, what was Dad like?'

Three hours later; she's washing up. The dutiful daughter. She looked up a little, thought about my question for a second or two. Then she said, 'I love him. Still.'

'Well I hate him. What was he like, though?'

And she said, 'Stern.'

'Stern, huh?'

'I don't mean strict; more like *serious*. Like you, a bit, but smarter, taller and better looking.' Then she laughed and slapped me across the arm, 'Dry the dishes,' she said.

It's funny, I learn a lot from my sister, mainly *don't do drugs*, which I should have written in capital letters instead of italics, but never mind, the thing is, when she's not high or shaking 'cos she needs some stuff, she's really smart and, truth be told, she's the core of our family, the strength, believe it or not. Honest, she keeps us together.

There's me, fifteen, bright, got a future, they tell me, though I haven't (and I'll tell you about that later), and then there's my Mam, as honest as, and working, and sensible (though not in her choice of boyfriends or anything) and all that stuff. And then there's Laura. Seventeen. And a junkie.

But she holds the family together. Cos Mam's a flake and useless, and I, basically, am at a loose end; financially, educationally, socially, morally… I won't go on.

Laura has one thing going for her. She is honest. And because she is honest she sees more than most, so she *knows* more than most, and she holds me and Mam together.

Mam.

My mother. She is thirty seven years old and she is a flake. A total dribble. Weak as. I mean, yeah, she can be cool at times, and there are moments, just a few moments for sure, when I see her for what she could be rather than what she is, there are odd conversations when I think, oh, there you are! Then she reverts to being useless for ninety-nine per cent of rest of the time. They should do a reality TV show on my Mam – "How Not To …"

"How Not To bring up your children."

"How Not To save for the future."

"How Not To get a good job."

"How Not To attract a nice boyfriend."

She did once.

Attract a nice boyfriend, that is. And I've read all the women's magazines she buys and I knew from the off it wasn't going to last. From the moment she said to me, 'He's kind, thoughtful, good looking. He's got a good job, Pete, and a lovely car.' (A bloody good car, since you ask. You didn't? But you would have. A Kompressor. Which means Supercharger. Which also means money. German. Cool. And much more). But anyway, as she's telling me all this I'm thinking, Yeah, but Mam, you're going to fall for a skinheaded nightclub doorman or a carpet salesman called Wayne and you're going to jack Pete in and tell me 'there was no spark' which translates as, you think that love equals pain, and affection means distress and you think that being nice is the equivalent of being invisible. Which it kind of is. So just be honest. Please.

And, as predicted, Pete went the journey. Kompressor and all. And in moved Marc. Fifteen years younger than Mam. What a tosspot.

What a racket. It was embarrassing. The crime that no parent should inflict upon their children. Making *those* noises. I was thirteen, which made Laura about sixteen; she'd just failed her exams and was working in Safeway. Very content. Regular money, dreaming about her own flat. Maybe a boyfriend. And the last thing that Laura wanted was Mam and Marc doing *that* upstairs halfway through a Sunday afternoon.

Go on Mam. Be a mam. Not a flake. Don't be desperate, please.

But no.

And when Marc made a play for Laura one afternoon, just a *suggestion* you understand, she screamed the place down and Mam came dashing downstairs half-dressed and slapped Laura to shut her up and then slapped her again when she heard what she was accusing Marc of doing.

I'm not tough. Really I'm not. And I'm not pretending to be not tough so you'll think that really I secretly am tough either.

I'm just not. So when Mam took his side against Laura I couldn't drop Marc with a right hook to the jaw or a knee in the family jewels, though I really wanted to, so I just went and sat on the front step and listened to them row. It was one of those afternoons with dark and light grey clouds flying across the sky on the wind. I sat on the step of our front door watching the seagulls wheel and fly and sail on the wind. I wished I could do that.

I have this theory that, to us the world is a flat thing we stand on, but to birds it is a cliff they cling to, a huge ball and they cling to the side and then fall off and fly and glide. I'm digressing here, but I can't remember what else happened, except I know how it ended. The next morning I waited until Marc went out and then I used Mam's phone to call the police and grass Marc for the twenty grams of cocaine he had stashed in a holdall under the stairs.

Bingo. Job done.

Like I say, I'm not tough. But I don't need to be when there's five police officers and a German Shepherd dog breaking down the door and dragging Marc screaming down the path and into a van.

Anyhow, this card I got from my Dad. It said, *remember, no one's got your back*, like this was some piece of information I'd known but had forgotten, or like I already had asked someone to get my back and then discovered they hadn't got it, or something. I mean, come on Dad, I don't know who you are, or where or anything, but come on, be a dad for a minute. For as long as it takes not to write that sentence.

I was ten years old for Chrissake. Write *I miss you* or *We'll meet up when you're older* or *Stick in at school.* In fact, here's an idea. Don't send me a card. Go on. Unsend it.

But the funny thing is, daft, one-off card with a stupid picture and a deranged verse it might have been. But in the end, he was right.

No one's got your back.

Laura thinks I'm funny, that I have these ideas, I write stuff

down, and usually these ideas, she says, they leave me in a

world of my own. Just stories, she says. I know what she does,

and how bad it is for her, but I also know that quietly she's

honest and strong and the drugs weren't really her choice, but if I ask her she'll say, 'Naaah. I chose it. It's my lifestyle choice. It's my best friend. My only friend.'

And I'll say 'What about me then? Aren't we friends,' she'll say something like, 'You're my kid brother, Mick. Family's different.'

She says I have these crazes, fads, and she's right, though I think fad might not be the right word because it doesn't sound strong enough. I have these things I gets into and they become really important to me, and each one, every new *enthusiasm* is bigger and stronger than the last.

They started off when I was little, I guess, like little kid things; boys' things; dinosaurs, of course, and then Jackie Chan movies and then, weirdly, speaking backwards. Actually that was a great one, I really got into it. For about six months I spoke backwards. At school, and when I came home, I'd speak backwards. The maddest part about it was everyone began to understand what I was saying. But when Laura and Mam, and my teacher and the kids at school, when they all started answering me backwards I fell out of it and started speaking forwards, which sounded really weird at first. That was when the child psychologist got involved. And after that came social workers and stuff.

When I was ten I got that card from Dad so, to be honest, it was Dad Dad dad all the time, probably for about six months. I still bring that one up now and again. When I was eleven there was a kite festival near here, and guess what I became obsessed with? And when I got to thirteen it was cars - Evo this and turbo that and I blame Mam's boyfriend Goldfinger for all that business.

Then girls.

Well, only one girl, really. Emily.

Emily was good for me, looking back. Sensible, smart enough to keep up with me; kept my feet on the ground even when being with her made me feel like I was flying. She was a lovely, sweet girl. Don't let me make you think she was plain or anything when I talk about how smart she was, she was super pretty. Not flash or anything, a slow burner for sure, but eventually she proved she was smarter than even she looked, and when I was sixteen, just after my birthday she showed how smart she really was when she finished with me and started going out with Karl, my best friend, instead.

I understood it, well I do now. I mean I know why Emily chose calm, sensible, respectable Karl over a volatile, needy, dreamer like me. She just needed a break. I think it was too intense. But at the time I didn't understand and it turned me bitter. It seemed to me that that something had been proved right. It sounds mad but it made me feel righteous. I was filled with righteous pain and anger. Which sounds daft now, but made complete sense then.

Back then Laura would get needy and I'd say, 'I'll pop down to Balal's and get you some stuff,' and when her credit maxed out there I'd say, 'It's ok, I'll run over to Harry Welfield's and get you some,' until her credit maxed there too. And now she was on a blacklist and it's money upfront, plus ten per cent to cover the interest on the debt. When I couldn't cover the debt at Harry's I started going to Ugly Pete's, a small timer who ran his business from a squat on Mowbray Road. It was wrong of me, running these errands for Laura, I should have been at school learning to be a model citizen, but what was I going to do? I wanted to help her. To protect her. It was my job. No one else was going to do it.

And Ugly Pete took a liking to me after a while. His security, a sixteen stone Iraqi called Zuluboy, he liked me too, and they started giving me little odd jobs to do, which helped out at home, financially, and though I didn't realise it, this was my apprenticeship into the world of drugs and dealing: I watched and learned; instead of revising for exams, I was revising for a life of crime .

It wasn't a huge surprise when, eventually, I started supplying Laura myself. It just seemed easier that way. And then one day I was supplying everyone else too. Because before all the trouble with Emily, before the obsession with cars, before the dinosaurs or the speaking backwards, I'd always had this role, which was looking after Laura, being my big sister's protector. And now and again, she'd tell me about Dad, I think it was just to keep me on-side; she'd talk about Dad. What she could remember about him. 'He looks a lot like you' she'd say. But Dad was a bastard, no denying it. He left us all alone. One time she told me I had Dad's ice-blue eyes and Dad's black hair, the kind that sticks up like a brush, even when you comb it flat. And then she laughed and said, 'But you aren't stern, Mickey, not like Dad was, not really. You're gentle.'

I wasn't gentle. I was angry.

I just didn't know it.

I've been at this school for almost two years. It's a Free School, one of those the posh kids go to, and I was placed here as part of a scheme to put smart kids from rough backgrounds into good schools. Something about it being cheaper than putting them in jail later on. And amen for that. I've been in about nine different schools: we even moved away for a while, Mam had a boyfriend in another town, but when they split up, we moved back to this place, a cheap flat in the Sundered Land.

Moving from school to school is disruptive. I'd go to a new school and be six months ahead in maths, or a year behind in science, and even though I'm a quick boy, the new school would always put me in a middle or bottom set. See, they think cos you move about a bit and cos you have a social worker, you must be thick, or a bad lad or something, and they probably guess you won't be around too long, so why put you in the top set, even when you're smart enough to be there?

After a while I wasn't smart anymore. I fell behind a bit in some subjects, a lot in others. The only subjects I did well in were those that gave me portable skills. Sport. Art. Writing. And I know lots of random stuff about Diwali, Gurpurbs and Ramadan too; every school I've ever been, when they're not telling you how bad the slave trade was and how there's more to World War 2 than Call of Duty, they're trying to force that religious stuff down your throat, along with constant drugs awareness lessons in Citizenship. No matter which school I was at, they'd be giving us lessons about drugs, their effects, their history, where they come from. I learned about shamen, opium dens and hash-smoking assassins before I left primary school. I think the idea was to put us off using drugs. All it really meant was that I knew all I needed to know before I ever started selling the stuff. So it all came in handy, the stuff I learned in Citizenship, though probably not the way they intended.

Mostly, my favourite lesson is English. I love books, although in lessons only the writing bit stuck with me, grammar still gives me a 'mare, I never did my SATs, and they always want you to use more descriptive words, they call it 'figurative language' which is stupid - it's writing for non-writers. But moving around, being disrupted, it taught me other stuff too. It taught me that being smart only gets you so far, it taught me that learning to get along with people is more important. So I learned to read people quick, to fit in seamlessly, like a ghost. And that involves listening.

Like I said, I'm not tough, and I'm not really good looking, so I needed a tool to help me get *in* with new people. And I discovered that simply listening to people is all it takes. You listen; they talk. You make friends.

So, here is me, just a few years ago, with my mixed bag of portable skills, coming into year 8, slotted into set 5 of 6. No doubt followed by my social workers' reports. I read one once, a report from a social worker. Very interesting. Anyhow, they send me to a good school; it's a church school. Which is nice. And when I walk into Broadway High, I'm given a room number and I introduce myself to my new form teacher, I follow my timetable, attend my lessons, well at the beginning I attend my lessons, and I do what I have to do. But here's another thing I learned - I never do homework. The time I waste getting punished isn't as much as the time I waste doing the homework. If you want to learn at night, if you're really bored and you want to improve your education, go to the library. I do. Did, I should say, cos they closed all the libraries a couple of years ago, so I mainly hang around Waterstones, speed-read what I can, and I use the old five-finger-loan system for the rest. Take the book back when I'm done, of course. I'm lots of things, but I'm not a thief. Back at school though, you'd get into trouble for not doing your homework, especially when the teacher asks you why it isn't done and you tell them the truth, you didn't do it 'cos you never, *ever* do homework, and you have no intention of doing homework. Ever.

So then I'm in set 6 of 6. The basement crew. The window-lickers. The knuckle-draggers. Even Free Schools with church connections have them; they're like a dirty little secret. No one wants to think of them. And when you refuse to do homework, you get the Deputy Head breathing down my neck all of a sudden. But all that's just rubbish really. They talk and talk and then they give up and get you to do little jobs for them.

And I still don't do my homework.

I'm in top set for English though.

Then I met Karl on detention, and we walked up to the bus stop together and then he punched me for insulting him, and then we became best friends.

Karl says he didn't punch me, says I was just a short skinny kid back then and he wouldn't punch a little kid, all quiet and moody like I was, he says everyone was a bit scared of me, the new boy. But we walked out of school together and I started talking to him, like; 'Hey what were you on detention for?'

'Arguing with a teacher.'

'Which teacher?'

'Mrs. Robb.'

Then I just walked along beside him, doing my thing, and he sussed that out really quickly, my listening thing, and he was the only person ever called me on it. But that was later. Back then, walking out of school I was doing my thing: I'd asked him a question and then I shut up. And eventually he had to talk to me, out of politeness.

'Yeah,' he said, 'she told me to fasten my tie properly and I said I couldn't because it was in such a tight knot so she got angry and said she would do it for me and, you know how she's got those long nails, with the nail varnish?'

I nodded. I didn't, but I wasn't going to stop him mid-flow.

'Well she dug her nail into my neck so I swore at her.'

I laughed out loud. He didn't seem the type.

'So,' he went on, 'I get sent to Mrs. Prime's office. The fat bitch. I argued with her too and I think she would have sent me home but I had a scratch on my neck. They made Robb write a statement and made me write one. I think they were worried I was going to sue them or something.'

'Would you?' I asked.

'No,' he said. 'My mam is a teacher. Dad is a barrister. I'm supposed to be a good kid. We don't sue schools in our house.'

Then he started to say, 'Why're you on detention?' or something, but instead he gave me a friendly shove, or a punch maybe, and I slipped and fell down the embankment.

'Sorry man,' he said as he helped drag me back up. My knees were all muddy, my hands too, where I tried to break my fall, and I just smiled, sort of a, 'No problem,' smile.

'Honest, I really didn't mean to do that,' he said, and I thought, OK we'll agree on *that* story but we both know you did mean it. Then he took me home to clean up. Which is how we became friends.

Karl lives in a big old house in Ashbrooke, not far from where we were staying at the time, though our place was a sort of ratty, private-landlord two-room slum down on Peel Street, and Karl's was a four-story townhouse in Belle View, so I was happy to go with him for a bit, in no rush to get back home. Karl's dad, the barrister, he was home early, cooking some vegetarian concoction with rice, and he offered some to me, really friendly. So After I'd had a good wash, I said Yes Please and ate up a plateful there and then. I think Karl's dad was pleased. I never turn down food. I'm not starving or anything, I just never say no. 'I'm trying out a vegetarian diet,' he told me. 'Try and lose some middle-aged flab.' I could see Karl wanted to go but I asked his dad if he'd ever thought of becoming a vegan. He looked really happy; his face sort of lit up, at last, someone who took his food obsessions seriously. Like I say, this is just my way; ask a question, sit back, listen, and his dad was like, 'Well, I'd like to go vegan but it's so inconvenient. Not so much the leather shoes and stuff, more the why's and wherefores of where to shop, what to eat, what

to do if me and Mrs. Greener go out for a meal or even just

stop off somewhere for a coffee…'

Blah blah blah.

And then me and Karl's dad were friends too.

Which, given his job, came in handy later on.

I emailed a copy of what I've written to Miss Wright, my English teacher. This started off as just as a piece of creative writing – part diary, part therapy - part distance-learning, but anyway, the story is growing all the time. Miss Wright says that I shouldn't jump around so much. Not that it's all bad, she says. I worry a bit that this whole story might seem like an apology, or an excuse for my behaviour. It's not. It's not even an explanation. It's just a story. I'm just trying to say what happened. I wrote to people and asked them to tell me stuff, what they remembered. Some of them got back to me, others didn't. I didn't want to make this just about what *I* think happened; maybe I'll find out the truth too. But Miss Wright told the class once, one time that I bothered to attend that is, she said you can never tell the full truth, and everyone's truth is different, so even if I mixed everyone's truth together I'd end up with a whole new truth and it still wouldn't be the full story. I kind of understand that but it doesn't really matter. The simple fact of it is, this is the story you will read.

This is the truth you will hear.

My truth.

Ugly Pete's dog was some sort of pit-bull mixed with a dash

of Rottweiler: 150lb of ugly-muscled, gimlet-eyed bad attitude.

Despite this, I loved him and he loved me. Zuluboy watched

in disbelief as it dropped to its haunches and allowed me to

stroke it, a low rumble of satisfaction rolling from between its huge jaws as I tweaked and scratched his ears and rubbed the loose folds of skin around the back of its neck.

'I've known that dog three years,' Zuluboy said, 'and it still barely tolerates me.'

I just smiled at Maximus, 'He's just a sweetheart, *aren't you* Maximus?' and let the dog's muzzle slide sloppily over my face as it frantically licked me in an overwhelming display of affection.

'In my country, dogs are considered unclean,' Zuluboy continued, barely concealing his disgust at my Anglo-Saxon approach to hygeine.

'It's good for you,' I told him, 'Builds up your immune system,' and wiped my face on my sleeve, 'That's why I never get sick.' I grinned across at Zuluboy, 200lb of toughness and muscle himself, who was wiping with his nose with a tissue due to a streaming cold.

Zuluboy threw the tissue in the bin and locked the steel-framed armoured door behind me, took out another tissue and blew his nose again. 'Pete's busy with a customer. Might

be a while. Want a brew while you wait?' and when I nodded,

still stroking Maximus, he went into the back room to boil the

kettle.

'No rush,' I said to Zuluboy's back. Outside, rain was

bouncing off the streets and I was happy to spend as much

time as possible sitting with Zuluboy and Maximus before

venturing back out into the street.

Earlier, I'd left Waterstones and been forced to shelter from

the rainstorm in a derelict shop doorway on Holmeside,

counting the seconds between lightning and the thunderclaps

that followed. Cars sloshed past, people struggled by beneath

umbrellas, a fit old guy on a bike pedalled serenely through

the storm, wet to the skin, grey hair plastered to his forehead,

bike wheels going zzzhhhhhh through the water, kids dashed

out of college laughing. Across the window of the empty shop

whose doorway I was standing in was pasted a poster that

said Sunderland: City of Culture 2021, but the poster was askew and one corner had curled back on itself. I was wearing a t-shirt printed with the word *Now* and in my pocket was thirty-five pounds. Twenty-five for the heroin I was going to buy Laura, five pounds to pay off her debt, and five pounds interest on that debt. Inside my rucksack was a sweatshirt, heavy and warm, but I wanted to keep it dry for when I got home. The heating had been cut off again.

A fine mist was rising from the rain-drenched concrete, dampening my jeans when, a few minutes later I watched a blind man approach the pedestrian crossing, his white stick tippetty-tapping against the kerb and then tapping for the post on which was fastened the electronic box, with the button that he could press to change the lights and stop the traffic. Oh hell, I thought.

The man was tapping the wrong post, a newly-erected lamp-post situated right next to the crossing post, and he couldn't locate the button. The traffic slooshed by, wetting the man's trouser legs and soaking his shoes. Oh *hell*, I thought again and then, deciding I couldn't simply stand by and watch the man struggle, I stepped out into the downpour and approached the blind man.

'Afternoon,' I said to him, loudly against the crashing noise of the thunder.

'I can't find the button,' he said. 'I'm getting soaked.'

'It's ok. I pressed it,' and as if to prove him right, the lights changed, the traffic paused, and the machine made a beeping noise. I watched the blind man stepped out, watched him cross the road. 'Step is coming up,' I shouted to the man.

'Thanks son.'

The blind man stepped back onto the path and walked off, tapping his cane. A car drove by and slooshed my jeans.

'Oh, hell,' I said again.

'You're wet,' Zuluboy had said as he opened the door.

'It's raining,' I said, glancing up at the sky.

'I have to search you, little'un. Ok?'

I nodded, stepping into the doorway. Zuluboy frisked me, looked inside my bag, pulled out the sweater, shook it and then pushed it back into my rucksack. And now I was sitting waiting for a cup of tea, stroking Maximus' muscled neck, he'd climbed up onto the sofa beside me and I let myself relax in the welcoming softness of it all, my eyes drifting shut.

'I put two sugars in for you,' I faintly heard Zuluboy say, as he walked back into the room but I was going out like a candle on a windy night, cuddled up with a bloody massive attack dog on the sofa in the front room of a notorious drug-den. Bliss. I felt Maximus snuggle closer as I fell deep into sleep. Something about sharing space with Max made me feel safe.

When I woke there was a packet of chocolate ginger biscuits beside my cup, and the thunderstorm still raged outside.

It was Zuluboy talking, 'Hey, kid. Go on upstairs.' I looked up, past Zuluboy toward the stairs and nodded, sitting up and rubbing my face.

'It's ok,' I said, still half asleep, 'I've got money.'

'I know kid. You always do.'

The room had grown darker while I slept. It was October and the days were short. I stood up, pushing a reluctant Maximus from his lap, me and the dog yawning together. 'Thanks for letting me sleep.'

'I'm not a social worker kid,' Zuluboy muttered darkly, though his gentle expression made a lie of his words.

'Maybe you're a natural good guy,' I said.

The staircase was dark.

Unlit.

It was an old house. Once upon a time, maybe eighty or a hundred years ago, it belonged to a rich family but since then generations of lodgers, wasters and passers-through had lived in it, and each transient had taken away some of its shine. No-one had looked after it, and now it was condemned. The whole area was condemned. There was a patch of waste ground opposite where a row of house had already been demolished, decades earlier. There had been two murders in the last year within a mile of this house. One a racial murder following a gang-rape, the other a melee among locals that had killed a pensioner who was riding his benefits chariot – a motorised wheelchair - back from the supermarket and had got caught up in the action, veered into the road and been hit by an Uber. Somehow I doubted that ugly Pete paid his council tax.

I always felt a chill when he walked up these stairs and I walked quietly, breathing slowly, until I reached the top and paused at the steel plated door. Then I knocked, firmly. Two knocks. I stared at the spyhole, pulling my passport-photo expression. A few seconds later the door opened and a girl looked out. 'It's a kid,' she drawled.

'I'm not selling to a schoolie,' a voice said. 'Too much hassle.'

And they don't have much money, I added silently. The girl peered into the half-darkness where I stood, 'Oh, it's only Mickey Hall.' There was a pause, then the voice said, 'Let him come in,' and there was the sound of a smile in Ugly Pete's voice.

I'd had an appointment to visit the Ed-Psyche earlier in the month, but I'd ignored it; I was supposed to do some tests to determine if I was intelligent, or sociopathic, or something. To be honest I wasn't sure, they were pretty much all the same. On my way home from Pete's I passed the Education Department offices and the lights were on so I decided to pop in on the off-chance I could do the test now. Besides, I was soaking wet again and didn't want to go straight home, so the idea of sheltering from the rain seemed worth the hassle of sitting down with a social worker. I had a pocket full of stuff for Laura, but no one would be searching me. Not here. They know my rights.

I walked straight inside and pushed the bell at the front desk. A receptionist came out and took my name and I told her I had an appointment and I looked at the clock, which said, ten past four, so I told her it was for four-fifteen. She went to check, and returned carrying a slim file and said, 'Sorry, Mickey, you've got the wrong time, and day. What made you think it was today?'

I shrugged. 'Dunno.' Then I said, 'As I'm here now, so is there any chance of seeing Dr. Post?' I smiled, as though I knew really there wasn't much chance and it would be ok to be turned away, and the receptionist's expression softened, and she went into a back office. While she was in there I pulled on the heavy sweatshirt. The receptionist returned, 'You're in luck. Go on in.'

So I went inside.

'Never guess what,' I told Laura later, but she was too busy scrabbling with her kit to listen. 'Go on, guess what.'

'What,' she replied glumly, as she did her stuff.

'I did an IQ test. *And* I'm not a sociopath.'

She drew the brown fizzing liquid into her syringe.

'I got 102. On the IQ test.'

She shrugged, 'That's average.'

'That's what he said. But I hadn't done one before so I asked if I could do another one. He didn't want me too but I really did. So we did another one.' I watched as Laura slipped the needle into a vein, closed her eyes and pressed the plunger.

'And this one, I got 137. Cos I sussed out what they wanted, what I had to do. Cool huh?'

Laura lay back on the sofa, her face serene.

'If I did another one, I think I could get 150.'

Later, I sat watching TV, chewing my thumbnail, trying to get it straight, thinking, Mam said she would be back on Friday, which in reality meant anytime time between today and next week. Or never. I was feeling hungry, very hungry, so I went into the kitchen a poured myself a bowl of cornflakes. There was no milk in the fridge, so I poured warm water from the kettle and ate them like that, all soft and mushy.

This is how we get by: we live on credit and rent arrears and then eventually we max out. Then we move and start again.

Or Mam will take up with some guy and stay with him for a few months.

Then it ends and we move and start again.

One time, two or three years ago, our credit had run out at the flat we were staying at and all the landlords in the area knew our name and wouldn't rent us any rooms. So Mam had the bright idea of going to the women's refuge. But they only take battered women, so Mam had punched herself in the eye, not very hard, just enough to give her a mark, and said she had a boyfriend who beat her up and they let us in.

But not me.

'You can't stay,' the woman said to me.

To be honest, I was a bit confused, like I'd missed something, like something hadn't been properly explained. 'I'm with my mam.'

'You're a man. This is a *woman's* refuge.'

'I'm twelve.'

'We don't allow men in a woman's refuge.'

So I went to live with the orphans and the bad lads at the Care Home. At Christmas we all met up at Frankie & Benny's for a meal.

'You look fat,' Laura said and I think I did. All rosy cheeked,

'They must be feeding you up.'

They were. I asked her, 'How are you?' Which meant was she using and if so how much and did she owe money and so on and so on. And Mam was a bit tipsy but she had news about a new boyfriend with his own flat and we were all getting back together. I was pleased. Laura told me the lesbians who ran the refuge were at war with just about everyone, especially themselves, and every weekend they'd be drunk and fighting, and I knew all she ever wanted to do was fix and chill. She'd got a weekend job and that paid her way, well almost, and Mam was working too. I was a bit pensive though, as much as I loved the idea of moving back in with Mam and Laura, I guessed it would mean no more three square meals a day, like I was getting in the care home.

No more clean sheets.

So we all moved into Echo24 with Tim, the scrap gold dealer.

'Goldfinger,' I called him. He had red hair and drove an old, old Porsche. And one day I found a gun in Goldfinger's holdall.

'Hey Tim, show us your pistol,' I said one time, and Goldfinger looked up and smiled, 'It's a revolver.' Then he added, 'Don't touch it. It's loaded.' But later he unloaded it and let me play with it.

'What was it like?' Laura asked me.

'Heavy. And it smelled of oil.'

'Did you like it?'

I shook my head, 'I thought I would but I didn't. It's not like a toy; you can't play with it or anything.'

'So you're not going to play with it again?'

I shook his head; 'No, but he showed me where he hides it, down in the sub-basement below the car park, in case I ever need to get it for him.'

Goldfinger was cool compared to most of Mam's boyfriends because he just mainly ignored us all the time. He never criticized me or Laura. He didn't care, but he wasn't precious about his space either, and he was even more messy than Mam. His car had empty food cartons piled up and coke tins and things just rolling about the floor. I even think he liked Mam, she began to shine a bit in a way she usually didn't. Mam is pretty, but she's drab, and when she's not drab she's a bit brassy, but with Goldfinger she looked less harassed. Natural, almost. Then one morning, about five-ish, the police smashed down Goldfinger's door and dragged him off to jail. I remember standing in the living room in my pyjamas, yawning, muttering, 'Not another knockdown!' before pouring myself some Sugar Puffs. The quiet, law-abiding, mostly Chinese, neighbours played hell at first, but we stayed on at Goldfinger's house until he gave up the lease on his flat about six months later. No point having a lease when you're doing seven years for attempted murder.

So I was getting on, had this little job with Zuluboy and Pete and he hadn't had to change schools for a couple of years. As it turned out, I didn't change schools any more, which would have been good if I'd ever went on a regular basis. I was working weekends and things were looking reasonable. I had my best friend Karl too, and I think it was then that I stopped obsessing about cars and started noticing girls. I'm a bit of a later starter, cos I'd gotten to almost fifteen years old without really noticing girls.

Then Emily.

Bam!

And then I began attending school.

Almost every day.

Some girls are born beautiful, some grow into beauty, and some spend their entire lives attempting to paint beauty on their faces. Over the past couple of years, Emily Dunbar had grown into her beauty; her mousy hair had darkened to a rich chestnut brown, her plump face had thinned to reveal sharp cheekbones and a wide slender mouth, she had eyes the colour of unwashed denim and when she was happy she had a smile that threatened to touch both ears. I'd never noticed her before but this wasn't unusual because I was rarely in school, and Emily had grown beautiful in my absence. I was in the school canteen when I first saw her, sitting with her friends. 'Who's that,' I asked Karl.

'Emily Dunbar,' Karl said.

'Why so glum, Karlo?'

Karl shrugged, and I saw him look across at Emily, 'Hey you *like* her,' I said laughing, and then added, 'Forget about her, K, *seriously*, she's going to be mine.'

'Dream on,' Karl said, chewing his pizza.

I just grinned and stood up, reckless, then walked over to where Emily sat with her friends and just squashed down beside one of the girls. I said 'Hey,' to Emily and looked around at the other girls, smiling.

'You're Mickey Hall,' one said, and I remembered her name as being Charlotte, or Cherelle or something.

I nodded, 'True.'

She said, 'You're in my English class but you're always off school.'

'I'm always busy.'

'I heard you're a criminal,'

I shook his head. 'Nope.'

'So where do you go when you aren't at school?' she asked.

I said, 'Where do you think I go?'

She shrugged, 'Miss Wright you visit an imaginary place where you make everything in the world right again. She called you Don Quixote.'

'She did?'

'She did,' Emily confirmed, speaking for the first time.

'I'm not lying,' Charlotte/Cherelle said.

'It's true,' The other girl confirmed.

'Shove along a bit,' I said to Charlotte/Cherelle.

'You're pushing me off the end,' she growled.

The other girl asked, 'Why are you sitting here?' but by the way I was smiling across at Emily, I think they'd already guessed.

'Do you want that coke?' I asked the girl.

'Yes,' she said and picked it up, drank straight from the bottle. Then Emily glanced at her friend, back to me, and said, 'You can drink some of mine,' and she passed hers across. I took it from her, took a long, long drink before giving it back, and she took a long drink too. She put down the bottle, covered her hand, but couldn't hold back the burp, she blushed. 'Sorry,' she said, giggling.

'You didn't even wipe the bottle after him,' Charlotte/Cherelle said, with distaste in her voice, 'You don't know what you might catch.'

I gave her my winning smile and said, 'She's caught *me*.'

Emily looked at her friends, 'Yeah,' she confirmed, nodding slowly, her wide smile showing small, even, perfectly white teeth, 'I've caught Mickey Hall.' The girls all giggled together and as I waited for them to stop Karl walked over to the table; 'You ready?' he asked, his expression dark. I ignored him and looked deep into Emily's eyes, said, 'Shall I call for you tonight?'

She said, 'I've got cello practice 'til six. But I can meet you about seven.'

'Seven. Yeah. Louis' café is open 'til eight now.'

'Great. Louis. Eight.'

She smiled and I did too, and the girls all giggled again as I stood and walked away with Karl.

I saw this film on TV the other day, called something like

American Ninja Assassins 3 – Clear Target and I thought, that's

just rubbish. If the target was clear then you'd just watch the

opening credits, see the clear target, squeeze the trigger and,

pop, film over. There must be a twist, or some series of

obstacles that stop these ninja assassins from actually

assassinating their clear target. So it can't be *clear*, or the film would last, as I said, for the credits and the time it takes to pull the trigger/fire the arrow/deliver a swipe with a katana. Plus I never trust a title that's separated by a dash or a colon, like American Ninja Assassin 3 – Clear Target or *They Wouldn't Listen: The Clare Witherspoon Story* (I made that one up by the way). I'm sure you know what I'm getting at. Two titles spliced together generally means it's rubbish. You've got to have a clear, punchy title.

So this book I'm writing is going to be called **Dealer No. 1**, which is a cool title and, for a while, it was my ambition too, to be that person. An ambition that was born out of desperation, around the beginning of my fifteenth year, and grew from being a vague idea to a concrete plan by the time I broke up with Emily. But so far it could be called 'Slightly Difficult Early Teens' or even just 'Loser.'

It hasn't earned its title yet.

I thought about tarting up the story a bit, but then I thought, maybe I should just let it flow - just tell what happened - but I'm thinking film rights, syndication, financial success because, if the book doesn't work, I'll probably end up answering the phone in some call centre: *Good morning, welcome to MacBankerFone, you're speaking to Michael! How Can I Help You?* or I'll be wearing a baseball cap and asking *if you'd like fries with that?* And not in an ironic, 'Yah, just out of 'uni' gap-year' kind of way - more a real, just an inch away from the gutter and too desperate to argue, way. So I wasn't against throwing in the odd 'plot device' if it made the story better but then I sat back, took a deep breath, and thought, I don't need to insert violence, teenage pregnancies, drug overdoses and stuff, unless they actually happened.

It's all in there already there; this is my reality, as chaotic and random as everyone else's, and I was hurtling directly toward it. Because from around about this point, everything started to go wrong.

'See that?'

Zuluboy was standing at the door of Ugly Pete's den and pointing at a tall, grey, steel post at the corner of Mowbray and Toward Road, on top of which was the black bulbous glass eye of a brand new CCTV camera.

'Not good for business,' Zuluboy said. 'Evidence gathering.'

'Maybe it's just a Neighbourhood Watch thing,' I said.

'They're putting them up everywhere.'

We went back inside.

'No. They're trying to build a case.'

'You're paranoid.'

Zuluboy paused, eyes glinting menacingly, 'You do remember what it is we do for a living?'

I thought for a moment; my relationship with Ugly Pete and Zuluboy was good: I'd began doing odd jobs for them, just nipping over to the shop for them at first, buying a carton of milk or a packet of digestives for Zuluboy, or cigarette papers and loose tobacco for Pete, who was as skinny as he was ugly and never seemed to eat, just smoke his own rolled cigarettes unlike Zulu who seemed to live on chocolate digestives and coffee. Then one day Pete asked me to drop a threatening note through someone's letterbox on the way home. I think that was sort of a test, and I must have passed, because after that I started doing more and more odd jobs for them: things they couldn't be bothered doing or that seemed a bit below them, a bit demeaning for a drug dealer to be seen doing, like buying a big box of tiny little plastic bags from Wilco's or a packet of wetwipes from the Spar, I'd do them. These little jobs began to expand to fill all my available time, but I enjoyed it: if I'd been middle-class they'd have described me as an Intern. It meant I didn't get ripped off either, now that I was a sort of employee. But, I realized too that if they suddenly closed shop due to some legal technicality, like they were selling class A drugs and the cops smashed in the door and arrested them both, that sort of thing, I'd have to go somewhere else for Laura's stuff. So I thought about the CCTV for a few moments more then said, 'I can fix it.'

Zuluboy shook his head, 'You're a civilian, little Mickey. I don't want you getting in trouble for committing criminal damage.'

'I won't do any damage,' I said. 'I won't even break it. I'll just stop it working.'

Which was how, an hour later, I'd sauntered down the road, hands in pockets and my hood pulled up. I paused below the CCTV post and looked up. At this angle I was below its line of vision; the camera was 30 feet above my head, and though it had a globular shroud of darkened glass, he could see by the faint reflected light inside that it was pointed directly at the front door of Pete's place. I bent over and pulled off my cheap sneakers, unthreaded a double-length belt from the loops around the waist of my jeans and wrapped the belt around both my waist and the post. It was, in fact, two belts, Zuluboy's and my own, fastened together, and at full length it allowed me to lean back away from the post while still remaining fastened to it. I flicked the belt upwards to about chest height, grabbed the post with my right hand and climbed barefoot so that my feet were almost level with the belt, keeping my weight outwards to maintain the tension and grip. Then I flipped the belt upwards again, following with my feet. Using this technique I clambered the post in under a minute, until my head was level with the CCTV camera. Now I could lean back while staying fairly secure and use my hands to fish into my pockets and pull out the roll of bubble-wrap I'd just bought from the newsagents. I wrapped this around and over the lens of the camera until I was satisfied that the camera's view of the world was reduced to a dimpled, blurred smear of light, and then tore the end from the roll, which I let drop back onto the street. Turning back, I pulled out a roll of sticky tape and secured the bubble-wrap in place. As I tore off the end of the tape I caught the palm of my left hand on the corner of the camera, tearing the skin, which stung and began bleeding freely. Swearing quietly to myself, I pulled down the sleeve of my hoodie and pressed it into the wound. I used my right hand to pat firm the taped bubble-wrap and, job done, slid easily back down the pole, unfastened myself from the belts, put back on my shoes and walked back over to Ugly Pete's.

'You're bleeding,' Zuluboy said, and went into the back room and came out with an old dusty bandage. 'Wrap it in this.'

'Thanks,' I said, wrapping the dressing round my palm.

Ten minutes later I was walking home with thirty pounds in his pocket and a freebie for Laura.

It was quarter past eight. Louis had closed fifteen minutes ago. As I rounded the corner I saw a bus at the stop, and a figure clambering on, holding a big case. Cello case, I thought, breaking into a run leaping aboard just as the doors swished shut, thinking, if it's not Emily, if it's some biddy with her shopping trolley, I'm going to feel stupid.

But it was her; relieved, I paid my fare, and I could see she was furious as I went to sit down on the seat in front of hers.

'Hey,' I said, turning.

'What?' she said sharply, then, 'Oh god, what happened to your hand?'

I glanced down at my hand, shrugged, ignored her question and said, 'You look nice,' looking at the case, 'Practice go alright?'

She nodded cool again, studying my face, waiting for some sign of an explanation. Then I caught her gaze and held it, and she looked down, suddenly embarrassed. She has beautiful eyes, and for that tiny moment her gaze belonged to me.

'You've grown taller,' she said.

'Since this morning?' I asked, laughing, relieved more than anything that she was still talking to me.

'You were sitting down this morning.'

I got tall, I thought. When did that happen? I looked at her mouth, wanted to kiss it there and then.

'What happened to your hand?' she asked again.

'I'm glad you waited,' I said.

She glared at me, 'Are you always late for a first date?'

'This is our first date?' I said, thinking, *great!* And the bus crossed the bridge, heading north, over the river, 'Where do you live?'

'On the sea front.'

'Really?'

A few minutes later I reached for the bell, 'There's a café on Roker Avenue, we can get off here and walk. I'll carry the instrument case for you.'

She said, 'Don't you even remember what *instrument* it is?' but then she said, but then her expression softened, 'It's a cello.'

'I knew that,' I said, picking it up as the bus slowed.

'Sure you did.'

We got off the bus together.

The café smelled of grease and warmth, and I don't think it was a place she'd visit normally, but I bought her a latte and myself a coke. 'I really like this,' I told her as we sat down with their drinks.'

'You really like what?'

'This. Here. What we have. I really like it that you and me are in this café. And your cello. And I really like this song.'

'I don't know it,' she said listening to the music coming from the radio.

'My mam sings it. She loves music, my mam. She's nuts mostly, but she's got good taste in music. This one is about someone who is in love but says they aren't. But everything they say proves they are. Like me.'

She paused, latte halfway to lips, 'Like you what?'

I shrugged, like it was obvious, 'You know, in love?'

She frowned, 'No.'

I frowned too, 'Oh yeah.' Then I said, 'And no. I'm not usually late for my dates, this is my first one.'

She said, 'You are the strangest boy I have ever met.' Then she reached over took my bandaged hand; 'You need to get that cleaned up,' she said.

'This is so good,' I said again, glancing around the cafe.

'Do you always say exactly what's on your mind?'

'No,' I said, serious for a moment, watching her holding my bandaged hand, taking her hand in mine and kissing her fingertip, 'But I always try to tell the truth.'

'That is so disconcerting,' she said, taking back her hand. Then, for the first time that night, she smiled at me.

'So what do you do when you're not at school?' Emily asked. We were on our third round of drinks, well, I was. Emily had only just started her second latté. I shuffled in my seat, poured another bag of sugar into the coffee I'd just bought, 'I dunno. Stuff?'

Emily stirred her coffee, 'Mister Mystery, that's you.' She drank a sip, 'I have to go home soon,' she said, 'to turn on the oven for mum. She's working late at training course, but she's making a supper for nan.'

I said, 'Ok.' Then asked, 'Do you want anything before we go, like, a caramel slice or a cookie or something?' Emily shook her head and I went to the counter, returned with two pieces of shortbread and a doughnut for myself.

'That stuff isn't good for you,' Emily said, surveying the food I set down on the table. 'You're too skinny. Like one of those racing dogs.'

'What, a greyhound?'

'A Saluki or something.'

I bit into one of the shortbread slices and chewed, it was lovely. 'Thanks,' I said.

'I don't mean it like that,' she said, 'I just want you to be healthy.'

'Fat isn't healthy.'

'Neither is undernourished,' she said.

I shrugged, finished off the shortbread, sank half a mug of latte.

She laughed, 'Don't you even stir your coffee?'

I said, 'I like to eat the sugar at the bottom. With a spoon.'

'Yeuch,' she said, laughing. 'That's just…' she couldn't speak for laughing and then I started laughing too and we gave up attempting to finish our drinks and left the café still laughing. Home was a ten-minute walk away and as we turned the corner onto the sea front I looked at the row of tall terraced houses. She pointed, 'That's my house.'

'Nice,' I said, taking it all in, suddenly feeling greedy, not just for Emily, but for everything Emily had.

The house stood on a row, overlooking the promenade and faced out across the North Sea. It was three floors high, and I could see from the lights twinkling, that it had windows in the loft too, and a walk-in basement. It oozed quiet wealth. It reminded me of Karl's house, but even bigger and more expensive looking.

'My sister Kate lives downstairs, there. She's a student.'

'What does she study?'

'Anthropology.'

'The study of human beings and societies, right?'

She nodded, 'Yes.'

'I'm an anthropologist too,' I told her, 'I study people, too.'

'She'd *love* you,' Emily said as she opened the front door, which wasn't locked, I noticed, then the inner door, which was. Emily fished around for her key and unlocked the door. We stepped inside and I was impressed by the sheer size of the hall, it was much higher and almost as wide as my own living room. It had a wide staircase to the right. We passed a door, then another and then a third, our footsteps silent on the thick carpets, and continued down to the back of the house. There was another door and this lead into a wide, long kitchen where Emily walked over to a steel oven and opened it, checked what was inside, shut the door, turned a dial to the correct setting. 'There,' she said.

'Smells nice,' I said, then, 'What do your mam and dad do?'

Emily said, 'Mum's a social worker. Dad is a consultant.' Seeing my expression, she explained, 'He's a doctor. A surgeon.'

I looked around at the kitchen, eyes drinking everything in.

'Will you show me around?'

'These are my rooms,' Emily told me. We were on the top floor and she'd opened the door to her bedroom a crack.

'Can we go in?'

'No,' she said. 'Above here is the loft, my brother used to be up there but he moved out when he got a job.'

'Is he a doctor too?'

'No,' she said.

'A social worker?'

She laughed a little, 'No, why?'

'What, then?'

'He's a tree surgeon.'

Duh.

'I want a house like this,' I said, 'And I want children who go to university and operate on trees.'

'Expensive trees,' Emily added with a glint of a smile.

'Definitely none of the cheaper variety of trees.'

We walked back downstairs and into the kitchen. 'Sit down,' she said and stood on a chair to open one of the higher cupboards. She stepped down holding a first aid box. 'Take off that horrible dressing and run your hand under the tap.'

'Thought you wanted me to sit down,' I said but did as he was told, unpeeled the grubby bandage and, grimacing, ran it under the tap. Emily inspected the wound in his hand. 'How did you do that?'

'Knife fight.'

She ignored this and watched the water flow over my hand, then unfurled some kitchen roll and said, 'Soak up the excess blood from your hand,' handing me a wad, 'Just pat it dry, don't rub,' she instructed, and I did this while she took a clean dressing from the First Aid box and unwrapped it. 'Put it back under the tap,' she said, and I held my hand under the tap again. 'Dad gets this stuff from work,' she said, and this time she took my hand from beneath the tap, dabbed it dry herself and then said, 'Hold still.' She poured sterilizing fluid over the wound, letting it run pink and then clear, into the sink.

'He taught you to do this?'

She nodded; 'We all have to do first aid, in this family. You know, dressing wounds, strapping broken bones, the Heimlich Maneuver, that sort of thing.'

I held out my hand and she dabbed it round the edges of the wound, expertly wrapped the clean dressing round it, snipped the ends with a pair of scissors she took from the box, and then tied it together across the back of my hand. 'There,' she said. 'Feel better?'

'Feels great,' I said, meaning the attention, if I'm honest, the cut hand I could have cared less about.

'You'll need to get a tetanus,' she said.

'I will,' I said.

I think she knew I wouldn't,'

'Mam?' I shouted, walking through the front door.

'Up here.'

'Ok. Want a cup of tea?'

'Thanks Mick.'

'Ok.'

I went into the kitchen feeling pleased with myself, feeling pleased with my crisp, clean bandage. A man was sitting at the table and my heart sank, as it always did in these situations, but I said nothing and picked up the kettle to fill it with water.

'You must be Mickey,' the man said.

I nodded. Mute.

'I'm Martin.'

I plugged in the kettle and drummed up the energy to reply.

'Want a cup of tea, Martin?'

Mam came bustling into the kitchen, hiding her worried face behind a fake smile; 'I see you two have met.'

'Yeah, we've been having a good chat,' Martin told her. Then he said, 'You look lovely.'

'Thanks,' she said, blushing.

I asked, 'Do you take sugar, Martin?'

Martin said, 'No thanks, Mickey. Life's sweet enough. Just a bit of milk.'

'We met on holiday,' his mum told him, 'Martin manages a bar in Salou.'

Great, I thought.

She's fallen for a barman.

'*Managed* a bar,' Martin corrected her, 'I can't run it now, can I, now I'm back home with you?'

Great, I thought.

She's fallen for an *unemployed* barman.

And now he lives with us.

I've tried to talk to Mam about Dad but all she's ever said is, 'I made some wrong choices. Enough to fill a book.' Which is ironic, as I'm busy filling a book with the wrong choices I've made. Mam blames herself because we don't have a stable family, we don't have a normal family; she blames herself because we're never secure. And I guess she's at least partially responsible, but there's a Dad-shaped hole in that blame-equation. He walked out, not her, and all she's done is try to fix what was left behind. She hasn't done a great job, but she didn't ask for this, and she might have done a lot better if she could have shared the burden.

Mam used to give me a hug, almost every day she'd hug me and hold me at arms length, and tell me that I was a beautiful boy, but then a few months ago she did just that and then frowned, said, 'You look just like…' and then she stopped, but I knew what she was going to say and she looked really sad, so I gave her a hug, because, if I look like him, how does that make her feel? I don't know much about him but I think Dad was a hard act to follow, and I think she started going out with losers cos, after her relationship with Dad failed, I think maybe she just got used to failing relationships. Felt comfortable with them. You can only lose what you invest. You can only lose what you're worth, and Mam didn't think she was worth much. I think she tried to keep it together but she never really knew how, and she couldn't let him go, because to let him go she'd have to talk about him, talk it through with us, explain things, put everything out on display before she was able to move on, and she just couldn't go there. I think that even after all these years she's still scared of him.

And she still loves him.

And then there's me, looking just like him.

'World calling Michael Hall,' a voice said, sliding into my perfect day-dream.

I looked up, 'Sorry Miss,' and someone giggled. Miss Wright speared that person with a glare and I couldn't help smiling to myself.

'Do you think it's amusing, Mr. Hall, to drift away in my class?'

'No Miss,' I said.

'Before you left us to spend some minutes on the astral plane, we were discussing the possible reasons why Hamlet took so long to act, despite having information about his father's murderer.'

I waited for her to continue, but she didn't. I waited longer, and still she looked at me. Someone giggled again. 'You want me to answer?' I asked, finally.

She nodded.

'Oh, Ok.'

I glanced across the room at Karl, who raised an eyebrow and gave an imperceptible nod, as though to say Go for it!

I shrugged, said, 'Well, Ok,' and just went for it. 'Some people say that Hamlet's relationship with his father is oedipal, but that his uncle, by murdering his father and marrying his mother, has stolen the classic oedipal role from him, hence his inability to act.'

Miss Wright coughed, I could see she was stifling a smile. 'Go on.'

'Other people say that he just over-thinks every situation. Paralysis through analysis, as you said last week, Miss Wright.'

She gave me the tiniest wink before turning away, and I went on, 'But I think it's just Shakespeare, being contrary,' and I glanced at my notes, which consisted mainly of meaningless doodles, no help at all, 'I mean, this is the most successful playwright of his time, of all time, the richest and most successful writer London has ever known, and every play he's written contains murder and mayhem, witchcraft, violence and sex - total non-stop action and reaction - and every other play written at that time contains all that too, I mean, Marlowe, Webster, all the playwrights, they were all doing blood and thunder.' I paused to take a breath, thinking, slow it down, but get to the punchline, 'So I think,' and I looked across at Miss Wright who had walked over to stand by the window, 'I think Shakespeare just decided to write a play where the hero did *nothing*. As a challenge to himself, just to see if he could.' I almost said more, then decided I'd said enough, and sat back quietly. The class were silent too, awaiting the verdict.

Miss Wright nodded her head twice, slowly, thinking about what I'd said, then quietly she said, 'Bravo. Well argued.'

'Am I right?' I asked, not quite believing it.

'This is English,' she said, 'it's not like Maths where two plus two always equals four.'

'Oh. So I'm right?'

'Well, you're not wrong,' she said. 'It's a cogent, well-argued, thoroughly enjoyable theory.'

I sat back, relieved and let a broad smile spill across my face, though to be honest, most of my knowledge came from the hiphop revision sessions on YouTube. More fun than wading though a four hour play to discover why the Prince of Denmark hadn't done much more than talk.

'That's why you're still in top set for English,' Karl said as we walked home. 'Cos you're a bit of a genius. That is, when you bother to turn up.'

'I just like reading,' I said.

'*No-one* likes reading Shakespeare,' Karl said.

'I do.'

'Yeah.' Karl said, unconvinced, 'I think you've just got a crush on Miss Wright.'

'Peace be with you sir,' I said, as Emily approached, 'here comes *my* girl.'

Karl laughed. 'You were just *desperate* to use that line!'

I laughed, he was right. I mean, how often do you get to quote Tybalt in a normal conversation?

'You coming round later?' he asked.

'Yeah.'

'Hey,' Emily said, linking my arm, smiling at the departing Karl, 'You two having fun?'

'Just discussing Shakespeare.'

She frowned, 'You are a *seriously* unusual teenage boy,' she said, kissing my cheek.

'Michael, come on in,' Karl's dad said and I followed him inside. 'He's up in his room.'

I nodded and went upstairs. 'Pink would suit you better,' I said as I entered Karl's room. Karl looked down from the step ladder, 'Maybe,' he said. 'Or maybe that's just *your* favourite colour.'

Karl was decorating and I'd volunteered to help. It was better than sitting in the grot we lived in down on Peel Street. I pulled off my sweater, leaving only an old t-shirt and tracky bottoms. 'Where do you want me?'

'Skirting boards,' Karl said. 'Gloss paint. Tin and brush are on the table there,' he said, pointing.

I opened the tin using the butt end of an old spoon and picked up a brush, sat down on the floor and looked at the skirting boards, then I dipped his brush and began to carefully cover the skirting board with fresh paint, taking time, to make sure it was perfectly covered and there were no drips or smears. There's something magical about focusing on a simply task like that, and doing it well. An hour passed during which time we painted and chatted, one of is occasionally breaking off to change radio station or go downstairs for a snack.

'This room's the wrong shape,' I said, looking around.

'What's the right shape then?' Karl asked, stretching up to paint the ceiling.

'Square. That's the right shape for a room. Or rectangular. This is all sort of odd and stuff. The ceiling slopes down over there, the room has a bit that kicks out over there, and then you have this alcove here. Odd shape.'

'You finished?'

'Ten minutes,' I said, looking at the length of skirting to complete.

'I mean finished criticising my room.'

'I *like* this room,' I said, 'it's quirky. But it's got a lot of skirting board for the amount of actual space it occupies.' I counted, 'A square room would have four lengths of skirting, maybe five, because of the door, but this room has eleven. Eleven! It's shaped like a maze.'

Karl's dad knocked at that moment, and came in with a tray holding two steaming bowls of pasta, 'Here's some fuel,' he said, setting the tray down on the table top.

'Thanks,' I said, meaning it; he's a good cook.

'There's more in the kitchen if you want it.'

'Should have had some meat in it,' Karl said later as we finished the pasta, sitting on a dust-sheet that covered bed.

'Naw. It's really nice.'

'You always say that.'

'We did a good job,' I said, nodding at the paintwork, and Karl agreed, wiping his mouth.

'We'll finish this and then we can straighten the room.'

'You straighten the room,' I said, 'I'm going downstairs for more of your dad's pasta.'

We celebrated finishing the painting by going for a wander into town and then walking down the High Street, stopping to buy a pizza. 'I used to live over there,' I said to Karl when we reached Echo24 on the way back. 'Bout three or four years ago.'

'How many houses have you lived in, altogether?'

'Dunno. Dozens, maybe.'

'I've lived in the same house all my life.'

'I can't even understand that,' I said. 'You've always had the same room?'

Karl nodded.

'Weird.'

'It's normal,' Karl said. 'That's a nice apartment block, mind. A lot of people have invested in property there.'

'We lived there with mum's boyfriend, Goldfinger.' We stopped and sat down on a wall opposite, sharing the pizza, 'He was ok. Left you alone.'

Karl nodded, asked, 'How you getting in with your mum's new boyfriend?'

'He's a creep.' I took a deep breath and let it go slowly, 'They've only been together a month and now he says he wants to "be my dad"' and I made the inverted comma sign with my fingers.

'You don't want that?'

'I've got a dad,' I said and Karl knew the subject was closed. We sat eating for a while longer, then Karl pointed out a Ford Mustang that was pulling out from the basement garage. It looked great and it sounded fantastic, like a grumbling roar.

'Goldfinger had a Porsche, used to park it down there,' I said.

'But it was a wreck.'

'It was a Porsche,' Karl said, as though was argument enough.

'He had gun too.'

'A gun? Goldfinger?'

'Yeah, a Magnum.'

'You ever fire it?'

'No,' I said, 'But I know where he stashed it,' and I pointed at the basement garage, 'Down there. In the sub-basement, behind some girders.' I paused for a moment, thinking, 'I bet it's still there.'

'Wow.'

We stared at the entrance to the basement garage, a scary thought stirring inside both of our heads. 'Possession of a firearm gets you three to five years,' I said.

'It might not even work now, anyway,' Karl said.

'We won't bother finding out, huh?'

'No.'

I remembered Goldfinger cleaning and oiling the gun and then wrapping it in cloth and sealing it in a ziplock bag, with a separate bag for the bullets. 'It'll still work, probably,' I said.

We both stood, the thought of a handgun so close at hand

spooking us both, and Karl went to put the empty pizza box

in a bin. 'You meeting Emily later?' he asked.

'Yes. It's our two-month anniversary.'

'In another fifty-nine years and ten months it'll be your a

diamond anniversary,' Karl said.

'Sixty years.' I said, breaking into a broad grin, 'I'm looking

forward to that already.' Then I said, 'If sixty years is diamond,

what's one year?'

'Paper, I think.'

'Paper? What's two months?'

'Paper cut,' Karl said, laughing.

'Paper bag.

'Filing paper.'

'Toilet paper.'

Still riffing on paper-based anniversary ideas, we walked back

through town laughing.

Over the next few weeks Emily and me got into the habit of meeting after her cello practice and going for a coffee, and then back to her house to hang out, chat and just be together until around eleven when I'd leave her at the doorstep to walk the two or three miles home. And this had been a special night, two months together.

She is *sooo* nice, I thought, and really pretty. And sexy, but I

didn't want to dwell on that because she'd made it clear that

subject was out of bounds.

I live in hope though.

She's from a nice home too, I thought, so when we have kids

she'll know how to bring them up because, to be honest, I

don't really know how to. I know how not to, obviously.

I watched as a Hell's Angel pull out from a side street. I saw

that he'd left the side stand down on his Harley, or it had

flopped down more likely (it was tatty-looking, a rat bike held

together by bailing wire and desperation) and I watched to see

what happened next - watched him lean into a left turn, saw

the loose stand dig into the road, and the bike juddered,

taking the rear wheel off the ground for a moment,

threatening to topside him, but then the Angel deftly kicked

his foot out and the stand flicked back up into place, and he righted the bike as he accelerated in a loud roar and black cloud of exhaust fumes.

He impressed me with this display of instinctive skill, the Angel and his bike were one unit, there was no gap between them – despite the age of both the biker and the bike they were in a state of grace when they were together. As I turned away I felt like I was in something of a state of grace myself: I'd spent a wonderful evening with Emily. I can't tell you what we said or did, nothing much probably, but just being with her was enough to make me a better person. I headed toward Sinbad's Kebab Korner to reward my improved self with a large Doner. Five minutes later I stepped back outside chewing on the meaty goodness, checked my watch – almost midnight – I still felt like I was floating on a cloud as I walked home back across the bridge, through town and up Stockton Road.

I turned into Alice Street and then left onto Azalea, my shadow flitting between the patches of light shed by the few unbroken streetlamps still standing, taking a circular route home, in no rush, passing along the top of the park where the statues were then slowing down when I got to the top of Peel Street and I saw Martin sitting in the front seat of a battered pickup parked outside the house, talking to someone. I couldn't quite put my finger on it, but something felt wrong; my spidey-senses are pretty-well attuned to dodgy situations and dodgy people and I didn't feel too happy with the cameo I'd just witnessed. But I passed him without stopping and went to the front door, let myself inside and told myself not to jump at shadows.

Mam was still up, watching TV, a copy of the Daily Mirror in her lap. 'Hey,' I said, glancing at the lurid headlines in the newspaper.

'Have a good night son?' she asked.

'Where's Laura?' I asked, remembering I still had the stuff I'd picked up for her earlier, worried she'd be upset about it being late.

'She's asleep, I think.'

'Ok.'

I went upstairs and knocked on her door. No answer, so I knocked again, but there was still no reply. Not a sound. I pushed open her bedroom door a little asking, 'Laura?' Silence, and now I was getting a little worried, so I pushed open her door, and in front of me was my worst nightmare. She lay sprawled across the bed, head lolling, eyes rolled back in her head, foam coming from the corners of her mouth, her breathing labored and rattling at the back of her throat. An empty syringe lay on the floor beside her, a dark pearl of blood on her forearm. 'No!' I heard a voice shout, a howl of anguish that I didn't recognise as my own, and I was already pulling her up into a sitting position against the wall, checking her airways and then listening, head against chest, for her heartbeat. It was labored and sluggish, like it was trying to pump mud. She was dying.

'Mam! Mam!' I screamed, 'Laura, *No!*' and all I could do was hug her in despair, just hold her close as Mam ran upstairs, screamed something, and then ran back downstairs to phone an ambulance.

I think I was still holding her when the paramedics arrived; it felt like they'd come in seconds, or years, I couldn't tell, time had just stopped. 'Come on son, we've got her now,' one of them said. Gently I laid her head back against the pillow, stood back and allowed the medic to take over. In less than a minute she was in the ambulance as it sped away, as they pumped her chest to restart her heart, the lights flashing, the siren blaring.

Martin said, 'She'll be alright. I'm sure she will.'

I jerked upright, determined to neither cry nor fall asleep in front of Martin. It was five am. The hospital waiting room was quiet, strip-light bright, and the chairs were hard plastic and uncomfortable, but the urge to just let everything go and fall asleep was overpowering.

'She was just trying out this new stuff,' Martin said. 'My mate's a dealer. I get discount, see? And of course, you hadn't delivered, so I stepped in.'

I ignored him, my mind curiously softened by fear and fatigue.

'She'll be alright,' Martin said. 'She's just not used to the quality of the stuff I gave her. It wasn't an OD. Just a miscalculation.'

He turned to face me, his face growing redder, and said, 'Your mam's worried sick, you know, going out and getting her stuff like you do. I'm not saying she's blaming you or anything, but you just don't know where this stuff is coming from. At least with my mate there's ...'

'Afghanistan.' I said, remembering something I'd learned during Citizenship lessons. 'It's most likely coming from Afghanistan; ninety per cent of heroin imports come from there. It goes out through Iran. The amount dropped while the Taliban were in charge but ever since the country became a democracy the Warlords have increased the amount produced.'

Martin looked confused, 'Yeah, but my mate, he's ...'

'Afghanistan.' I repeated, then closed my eyes and went to sleep.

Martin shook his head, 'Dunno 'bout that. My pal gets it from a guy he knows who works on the railway, who gets it from someone who works on the Eurotunnel...'

I couldn't hear him. I was already dreaming.

I was jogging.

Jogging the two miles out of town and up Strawberry Bank to Tunstall Hill, climbing the steep hillside, and when I reached the top the steady wind cooled the sweat on my brow. From here I could see for miles: the town to the North and west, the ocean like a grey stripe to the east; the countryside behind, the turbines of the Nissan plant like huge white gulls wheeling on the wind. I unfurled the kite. It was made from a silk sheet and cane struts with plastic joints, tethered by two thin nylon cables. I built it when I was ten, for a school project and Miss Whinn, my teacher at the time, had been impressed with the patience and the skills I'd shown to build it, she told me I had a good chance of winning the school craft competition, or at least getting placed. But I'd left the school before the competition, before my SATs, and my third school in two years became my fourth. And about three months after I started at the new school, a teacher had passed on a note from Miss Whinn: *Dear Mickey, how are you? Hope the kite is still flying. I think the best place to fly kites around here is on Tunstall Hill. Plus it's a great view.*

I'd crumpled the note and thrown it away. But I remembered her advice and now I was up on the hilltop, about to fly the kite. I locked the spine in place, splayed out the ribs into an X shape, then clipped on the two cables, fastened on the long, red-feathered tail I designed myself. The kite had a Chinese dragon painted on it.

'Where did you find that design?' Miss Whinn had asked, 'It's beautiful.'

'I saw it in a book,' I said.

'You like books?' she asked.

'I go to the library every day.'

The wind was blowing strongly across the hill, blowing to the south, toward the sun. Good, I thought, taking out the two cables, one in each hand and spooling out four or five yards, then walking backwards to the brow of the hill, until the cables became taut against the wind and the kite shimmered against the tension, lifted for a moment then nosedived back into the ground. I wiggled the cables until the kite lifted again, stepped forward with the wind at my back allowing the tension to slack a little, spooling out more cable as the kite lifted away from the side of the hill, letting slide more nylon cable, until the kite was hanging in the wind thirty or forty feet above the side of the hill. Gradually, carefully, I let out more cable, more distance, more flight time and the kite really began to fly. As I got comfortable with the strong, dipping wind I began to make the kite do stunts, dodging and diving, tail whipping, dragon's face leering at the sky and then the ground beneath, until after about twenty minutes the kite was at the end of its leash, fifty meters or more above the hill, but three hundred feet above the fields below the hill; the kite's responses were lazier as the cable had lengthened and I drew it inward a little, wrapping the cable hand over hand until the kite became friskier, lively. This is it, I thought.

This is it.

This is now.

My soul was flying alongside the kite.

There was a moment when the wind and the kite harmonised perfectly and I *knew*, I just knew what I had to do: my fingers relaxed and the two handles dropped to the ground at my feet, their weight keeping tension in the cables as they were dragged away across the grass, keeping the balance as the kite drifted through the air leaving me behind, the dragon face leering as it flew further and further away, disappearing toward wispy clouds. I watched it for a few moments longer, watched it flying away, balanced perfectly, perched on the wind. Then I turned and walked back down the hill. 'Come on, sleepy head,' said a kindly voice, and I opened my eyes to see a policewoman looking down at me. I rubbed my eyes, discovered I was lying across three chairs in the hospital waiting room. The kite fading from my mind as I focused on the Sergeant standing beside her who didn't look quite as friendly.

I rubbed my eyes, 'How is …'

'She'll be fine,' the policewoman said. 'I'm more worried about you at this moment.'

I looked round. Martin was gone. I checked my watch; it was almost half past seven. Morning. 'Can I go and see her?'

'Not yet, sonny,' the Sergeant said.

'Mickey,' I said.

'Not yet, Mickey,' the policewoman said, her voice still kindly. 'She'll be asleep until at least lunchtime.'

She seemed nice for a police officer. Maybe she was the good cop, or maybe she was just new to the job.

'It's fortunate that you found her when you did,' the Sergeant said. 'The crash team say they lost her a couple of times. Another five to ten minutes and she'd have died. As it was, they had to give her a full oil change.'

I sat up, groaned at the thought of Laura needing a complete transfusion to clear her body of the toxins, put my feet back down on the tiled floor, saying, 'She'll be in withdrawal when she wakes up,' my mind numb, working on autopilot, 'and she'll need her stuff,' and without thinking, my hand reached for the drugs in my jacket pocket.

They say that there are certain points in your life when you do something, or make a choice, and everything changes. The world turns and you find yourself in a place you didn't expect to be.

This was one of mine.

I was tired, and I reached for my coat without thinking, and the police Sergeant must have read my mind because he had my jacket in his hand before I had even properly stretched out my arm, and he was telling me something official-sounding even as he checked my pockets. He found the drugs I'd bought for Laura the day before, found them straight away, it's not like I was trying to hide them or anything. Then he read me my rights. This might sound cool and dramatic when you're watching TV but it's pretty horrible when you're in a hospital waiting room with ordinary people watching and looking daggers at you and it's for real and even the nice policewoman is starting to act like you're kiddie-murderer or something. All of a sudden I was a suspected criminal, a possible drug-dealer, and all my running around and keeping it together was falling apart in front of my eyes, just like the kite, it was flying away from me. And what really hurt most, what really twisted the knife, was that they suspected me of being responsible for Laura's overdose. Fortunately, although he was pretty formidable looking, the Sergeant did it by the book, called social services and arranged an interview for later.

In the meantime they cuffed me and took me down to the station to wait in a cell.

I spoke to the social worker, and then a while later Karl's dad arrived, which was extremely weird but very welcome, and I heard raised voices between him and the duty sergeant before they both came in to speak to me again.

'Am I under arrest?' I asked.

'No,' the sergeant said, glancing at Karl's dad.

'They'll need to interview you,' Karl's dad said.

'What are you doing here?'

'Your mum called me.'

'I can't pay you,' I said.

'You can owe me,' he said.

So I was interviewed, and I pretty much told them the truth; I *did* have drugs for Laura, I *wasn't* involved in her OD, I *wouldn't* be prepared to testify against the dealer I bought the drugs from. I made a statement to that effect, they bailed me pending further investigation, warned me I could be facing a custodial sentence, and then I was back on the street again, just standing there, Karl's dad next to me. I remember he turned to me, studied me, his face going through different expressions 'til he found one that was stern enough. But really he just seemed a bit tired, and a bit sad. 'Mickey,' he said, 'I know you were telling the truth, as far as you're told us anything, and I can pull some strings and get this sorted out quickly.'

'Thank you.'

He ignored that and continued, 'But if you really think you can hold this thing together, if you really think you can save your family, save Laura, all by yourself, and yes, Karl explained what you do for her,' he shook his head, sad, 'if you think that, you're mistaken.'

'Everything will be fine,' I said. 'We don't need anyone else's help.'

I must have looked defiant or something, because he sighed as though he'd made this speech a thousand times before and said, 'Listen to me, Mickey, and listen well, because I'm throwing you a life-line here. When everything falls to pieces, when it all goes wrong, when you've *finally* hit rock bottom, you come and see me. We'll fix it. Properly.'

'No one helps me,' I said. 'Not ever.'

'I just did.'

I ignored this. 'I don't need help.'

He reached into his pocket and gave me a card with his name and number on it. 'You're lucky I was already there, seeing to another client, when your mum called me. If you need me, you can contact me on this number.'

'I won't get in trouble.'

'Yes,' he said. 'Yes, you will.'

We walked to his car and he drove me home.

Karl's dad is really and truly one of the good guys, but it didn't sink in then, it didn't really occur to me then how good a person he was, because, as soon as I got out of his car and said goodnight and thanks again, all I could think of was I needed to go straight round to Ugly Pete's. Laura would need

some stuff when she got out, the cops had taken my stash, and

I wasn't going to let Martin supply her again.

For a while, maybe three or four months, nothing much happened. It's like when we studied History in Year 9 and learned how at the beginning of the Second World War the French, Germans and British all declared war on each other and then sat back and did nothing for six months. People called it the phoney war, the fake war, the Bore War, because nothing happened - they just stared at each other across No-Man's-Land, with their rifle safety catches on.

This was my phoney war.

Mam didn't do anything totally flakey, like run off to live in Turkey again or become a nun or anything, and Laura was holding it together, with a little help from me. I was making some money doing odd-jobs for Ugly Pete, and I even went into school now and again, though that was mainly to stop Mam being taken to court. And of course, I was seeing Emily. You know when some people just 'click'? Like they're two parts of the same whole? When the things they have in common are sort of like they'd arrived by chance at the same party at the same time and you can't tell if it's coincidence or pure magic. Or when the differences between them are just things to laugh about? Emily and me laughed a lot.

After a couple of months I even took her home; I introduced her to Laura and they seemed to get along really well. Mum was out but that was a relief, really, 'cos she'd have been too desperate, too eager to please.

My odd jobs for Ugly Pete and Zuluboy meant I had money to take Emily out, and they weren't really illegal, just a bit of running and fetching, and this kept me in ready cash, because Ugly Pete always had cash to spare. So I thought everything was fine, which was stupid of me really. I let down my guard. I thought that everything was going to be alright, that this was how it was going to be from now on. Emily and me. Me and Laura. Mam. All good. All as it should be, almost like in a normal family. For a few months I managed to forget that out there across No-Man's-Land, Life had me in its sights, and it had an itchy trigger-finger.

I was at Emily's house one teatime and they invited me to stay.

Her dad was tall and thin and he had round glasses, like a

hippy John Lennon type, but the way he spoke he just came

across as really smart. Like, if there was an intelligence scale

with Martin at the bottom and Karl's dad in the middle,

Emily's dad would be at the top. He just oozed smartness. But he was kind and he listened too. At one point we were chatting about life and about careers, and he said it was easy, having a plan, 'You take what you want, then pay for it,' and Emily glanced at me and then sad, 'Daad! It's not that easy,' and he said, 'It's never easy when you're a teenager, but it gets easier as you get older.'

She just laughed again and went back to eating. It was weird, this big house, dad was obviously dead smart and they weren't short of cash, but their meal was sort of scrambled eggs on toast with some weird vegetables. I'd have preferred a Big Mac.

'So where'd you get that wisdom? Daddy-school?' Emily said.

He smiled at me and then said to her, 'It's an old Spanish folk-saying.'

'He once told me my reat grand-dad was Captain of the titanic,' she said to me,

'so I usually take what he says with a pinch of salt. Especially the life-wisdom he gives me.'

But I sort of knew what he was saying, even if she didn't, and it was aimed as much at me as it was her, and he was right, I guess, because it sort of means that the decisions you make about your life have to be accounted for. There are consequences. Every time you make a decision, it's like taking a loan from the bank of life. The things you do have to be accounted for, debts have to be paid in full. So even though Emily didn't get it, I did. And even though I think it was more for my benefit than hers, I think she lived the advice. Looking back, she was ambitious, she had plans. She was almost sixteen years old, with her whole life ahead of her. There were things she wanted to achieve. When people saw her they saw this quiet, hard-working girl from a good family, who got good grades and would probably go to Uni and maybe become a doctor like her dad. Well, yes. But they didn't see the other side of her, the part of her that made her own decisions; made her own choices. And when they did, they were shocked. I was shocked too. Because when she decided

to do something, she did it.

Like her dad said: Take what you want, then pay for it.

And she was all good with that.

'Laura,' I shouted up the stairs, 'I got takeaway.'

The two chip shops nearby were having a chip-war and both had discounted their stuff and added free extras to the menu in an attempt to undercut the other. It was madness, but it meant I got us both a good tea for the little money I had spare.

I went into the kitchen, turned on the oven, gathered up the old newspaper on the table and threw it in the bin. I shared out the chips: a plate for me, a plate for Laura and a plate kept warm in the oven for later. It was all part of my master plan to feed her up, get her healthy again, and so far it was working. Laura had shown no sign of after-effects or complications from her overdose beyond a low-grade tiredness that came and went. She even joked that the transfusion had left her feeling stronger, less addicted, though I knew that she said that mostly for my benefit.

'Laura!' I shouted again.

'Give me some,' a voice said.

I turned to see Martin. 'You still here?'

'I'm not going anywhere son. Come on, share out your chips'

I thought for a moment, about what had gone before, and something cracked a bit inside me. 'No,' I said.

His face went dark and he made a grab at the plate, lifted a fistful and stalked off into the living room. I followed him. 'If you want chips you have to pay for them. I can't afford to feed you too.'

'Chill out kid, we're all one big happy family now,' he said, scoffing the chips almost in one mouthful, 'Here! Give me some more,' and he made a grab for the rest of the chips that I was holding on my plate. In the struggle that followed the plate fell to the floor and the chips spilled across the carpet. Both of us stared at the spilled food for a moment. Then Martin straightened up and then backhanded me across the face, knocking me back, and I tripped on the low table and fell to the floor. '*Stupid*!' he shouted, 'Look what you done. You stupid, *stupid* boy. If I'd paid for those chips you'd be getting more than the back of my hand.'

I glared up at him, could feel blood at the corner of my mouth where my teeth had dug into my lip, 'You are temporary, Martin the ex-barman. Very temporary. So enjoy my food while you can.'

He leaned over and slapped me again.

'Scrounger!' I hissed.

Martin threw a punch this time and I ducked it. Seeing red, I leapt up and grabbed Martin by the throat and screamed at him 'You're getting a FREEBIE cos you're LAZY and USELESS!'

His next punch caught me in the stomach and I fell back to the floor coughing but still shouting insults. He kicked me in the face. 'Eat your chips!' he yelled, 'GO ON! EAT THEM!' and he picked up a handful and threw them at me, dashed into the kitchen and returned with the rest, Laura's portion, and the ones I'd put in the oven for later. He threw these at me too, knelt down and ground them into my face, and I was still stunned by the blows, my nose bleeding, ears ringing, but I managed to look up and shouted, or tried to shout, but it came out like a croak, 'At least I PAID FOR THEM! More than you. LIVING OFF A KID!' and then I was shouting at myself because Martin had stormed out, punching a hole in the door as he left the room.

A while later I was still sitting there, fingers nipping the blood flow from my nose, other hand gathering the chips back onto the plate, scraping the grease from the carpet with my fingernails. I didn't want Mam to know what had happened, so an hour later I'd cleaned everything away and my nose, though a bit swollen, was no longer running or dripping with blood. I went into the bathroom, stared at myself in the mirror and said quietly, 'I'm still here. I didn't walk out. I stood my ground.' But I knew the ground I'd stood was worthless; a cheap, tatty flat with old furniture and a flimsy door that'd now need to be repaired, or the landlord would either charge us or chuck us out. And worst of all, I was still hungry.

I felt hollowed out.

I felt as thin and worn out as the t-shirt I'd just used to mop up the bloodstains from the floor. Nothing was going right and I knew with a sudden clarity that nothing ever would. No one would make it right for me, or for Laura. Like Karl's dad said, I was desperately trying to hold things together, and I just couldn't. It was impossible. I went into my bedroom, blew the blood from my nose onto a tissue, binned it, pulled open a drawer and picked out the birthday card I'd got when he was ten and sat down on the edge of the bed. 'You were right, Dad,' I whispered bitterly, 'I don't know how you knew, but you were *so* right,' and wishing desperately it wasn't true, 'No one's got my back.'

I reached into my pocket. 'I got something for you.'

She put down her hot chocolate, her lips rimmed with

whipped cream, and I picked up a napkin from the tray and

gently wiped her mouth. She smiled, but her focus was

already on what I had for her, an eyebrow raised in

expectation. I put down the

napkin on the table top, oblivious now to the noise and bustle of the other people in the café, my eyes level with hers as I reached into my pocket and took out a small box. 'I had it made,' I said, giving it to her. She took it and opened it, took out a wad of purple tissue, unfurled it in her hand, to reveal a small, heavy shape in silver. I leaned in, 'It's a yin. Half of the yin/yang sign.'

'Yes, it is,' she murmured as she studied it, tiny, but she could feel the weight of it, rounded and heavy in her hand.

I'd found a silversmith, working from a room in the arts centre, and had her make it, asked her only that it be heavy and small and half the yin/yang sign, leaving the artist to interpret the final design, which was, I could see, beautiful.

'There's no loop, to wear it,' she said, meaning, on a chain.

'You don't wear it,' I said. 'Just keep it somewhere. Safe.'

'Where's the other half?'

'I have the other half.'

'Where?'

'Safe,' I said.

She looked up from the gift, a calm, sure, wide smile forming on her face.

Later, we walked barefoot along the beach, holding hands, fingers talking quietly, the sun hanging midway down a mild blue sky. She glanced over at me, brushing away her hair, and then looked back at the footprints we'd left behind, trailing back along the beach to the distant steps that led down from the cliffs. She dragged on my hand, pulled me to a stop and turned me to face her, looking grave, and she said, her voice quiet and soft, 'You have hidden places, Mickey, you have fortresses and you hide your feelings and you stay safe from the world, and you stay there forever.'

I looked at her eyes, the colour of faded jeans, 'I never lie to you,' I said.

'Only because you never tell me anything,' and her eyes were sad in the bright sunlight. I stroked her face with my fingertips.

She shook her head, 'Forget it. I didn't mean that.'

'Sure?'

'Yes.'

She looked down, and I looked away into the distance of the beach and the pier a mile away, my hand squeezing hers and I knew she loved me then, more surely than I ever knew before or after, and I knew she was right, but if I ever told her the things inside me, it'd make everything real, too real, and my heart would break into pieces, so instead I pulled her close and hugged her and then we began walking again, and I saw a single tear that had bled onto her cheek. 'Sure?' I asked again, wiping it away with a fingertip.

'Yes,' she said again, blinking, and smiling. She punched me lightly on the chest, 'Come out come out, Mickey Hall, wherever you are.'

'I'm here now,' I whispered back to her, holding her gaze, drawing her close, and she held me tight in return, and I knew she was thinking, *No you're not. Not really.*

So I kissed her.

She held me tighter still, drawing me close, until we broke off their kiss and something soared inside me and I began to dance with her, we began to dance to a slow, gentle beat that only I could hear. Our feet drifting together in rhythm, hands holding, eyes connecting, two souls in union, dancing on the soft sands, until after a while we stopped, and she rested her head against my chest.

Gulls wheeled above.

Part Two

'Hey boy. Hey Maximus…'

The dog limped across the yard, whimpering a little, looking

liked he'd been beaten or whipped. I bent to stroke the back of

his head, gently, my fingers avoiding the wound where his ear

had been torn, looking over the cuts and bumps that he'd

suffered. Someone had given Maximus a kicking, and looking at the bite marks, they'd had a couple of dogs with them too. I know this might sound harsh, but when I got to Ugly Pete's place and saw the state it had been left in, with the doors kicked in and the windows smashed and the place trashed and Pete and Zuluboy gone, I was almost relieved to see that Maximus was still there, that he was injured, that he needed my help.

It gave me something to think about instead of how I was going to look after Laura now that the only dealer left in town who'd give us a line of credit had, it appeared, gone out of business. I'd been feeling low recently, deep low. So having someone else to think about gave my mind a rest. I'm not sure that's the right reaction, but that's how I felt.

The day had started pretty normal: Martin had been out of town for a couple of days so things were quiet at home. It had broken out into almost open warfare with me and him, and he wasn't slow in giving me a slap now, but I didn't care, hardly felt it, I despised him so much. Anyway, with him gone I didn't feel confined to my own room, and Laura was mooching around watching TV, between shifts at the supermarket.

'Make me a cup of tea, Mick,' she said. She was flicking through the channels, a little bored, a little wired, and I sort of guessed toast and tea wasn't going to fix it. 'Here,' I said a few minutes later, holding out the tray.

'Put it on the floor,' she said, and I did.

'You got much money?' I asked.

'About seven quid.'

I did a quick calculation. With the cash I had saved there was enough to keep her alright for a couple of days. 'When do you get paid?' I asked.

'Next week.'

I sat down beside her and sighed. She rubbed my hair, 'What's up Mickey boy?'

I took a deep breath. 'You ever thought of just giving up?' I said.

'Giving up what?' she asked, but then she must have realised so she put her arm round me. 'Are we broke again?'

'I'm broke,' I said, 'and I'm tired, Laura. Tired of finding money, or credit, or things to sell, just to keep you addicted.' I looked at her in the eyes. 'Sometimes I just feel like I'm *helping* you stay unwell.'

She sighed. Looked away. 'I never asked you to help me, Mickey.'

'It's part of the deal though, isn't it? We're family. We look after each other.'

'You look after me, you mean.' Her face softened and she wrapped her arm around me, 'Come here, little brother,' and she hugged me tight. I felt like crying, felt like giving up. I was so worn out with running flat out just to stand still. I closed my eyes, and didn't cry. I just breathed slowly, feeling the love that connected us, feeling safe for just a few precious moments. She kissed the top of my head and said, 'My tea is getting cold,' and so I sat up and made some space for her.

'Want me to go round Pete's for you?' I said.

'Good lad,' she said.

And an hour later I was standing in Pete's place and it was empty and it had been trashed. I went upstairs and it was worse. Someone had battered down the armoured door, taking the door-frame and a part of the wall with it. Paraphernalia was littered about, needles, empty baggies, old takeaway cartons. I went back downstairs and the rooms were even worse, which was when I heard a noise in the back yard and I went out back and found Maximus all cut and battered and bitten. Walking him gently into the kitchen, I took off my t-shirt, pulled my sweatshirt back on and then tore the T into rags, and then ran some water and used the rags to clean his injuries. I spent a half hour dabbing his wounds clean of muck and dirt and he sat patiently while I did, only shivering a little or whimpering when it hurt him. I unfastened his collar and shoved it into a pocket while I cleaned away the dried blood around his neck and throat. He was so patient and brave, and I think that's when I decided I was going to keep him.

'Good boy,' I whispered. 'Good boy.'

I asked him 'Where'd Pete go?' and his eyes rolled at the sound of the name. 'And Zuluboy?' This time he barked. 'Yeah. Zuluboy. Where'd he go?' He sat quiet while I worked and I told him, 'Well, I think they might not be coming back, Max, so we're both out of work. You're staying with me until I find out what to do with you, ok?' He barked again, and licked my hands, and so the deal was sealed. For the time being at least, we were a team. I finished cleaning him up and took out his collar to fasten it back on, which is when I noticed a bit of paper stuck on the inside. A yellow post-it note that I peeled off, unfolded and read, and it was from Zulu.

To me.

'Mickey,' it said. 'We had to close down the business.' Zulu's writing was neat and methodical, written in a slow hand. 'I don't know what has happened to Pete but I'm pretty sure

he's not coming back. I'm not. I couldn't take Max with me.' I

turned over the note. 'If you read this, he's yours. He never

liked me anyway. He loves you. Check the CCTV camera.'

I turned it back over. Nothing else. Check the CCTV camera, I

thought? For what, an action replay? I went into the yard,

raked about until I found a piece of rope that I could use for a

leash. 'Come on, boy,' I said, tying it to his collar.

We stepped out of the front door and it was sunny and bright.

It was almost lunchtime and I had eleven pounds in my

pocket, Laura's seven plus some of mine. I was feeling a bit

rebellious. Maybe I'll blow the lot on dog-food and a MaccyD,

I thought, we're both hungry enough. We deserve a treat. As

we passed, I glanced up at the CCTV pole where I'd wrapped

bubble-wrap round the lens just a few months ago. It was still

there, mostly. Then I took a second look and saw that just

below the lens was hanging a separate piece of bubble wrap

that looked like it had almost dropped off or maybe had just been stuck on afterwards. It was more like a package, about the size of the palm of my hand, all bubble-wrapped and swinging free almost ready to drop. I looked around. The street was empty and dusty, with papers and bits of old pizza cartons from the takeaway at the end of the street blowing about in the mild breeze.

With no belt to help me, the shin up the smooth pole was harder but I took off my shoes and socks, grasped the pole and began squirming up. At the top I grabbed the package, tore it free and shoved it into a pocket, then slid down. I quickly put my shoes back on and walked away, along Toward Road and through the park. I sat down on a bench near the bandstand at the far end and opened the package.

It was cash.

I counted it. Fifty ten-pound notes.

And dope, too. Enough for Laura for a fortnight or more.

If a cavalry band in full plumage had trotted onto the stand and started up playing Mr. Sandman I couldn't have been more stunned. And the thought of Zuluboy hauling his bulk up that same pole had me smiling to myself. There was another note inside, in that same steady, determined handwriting: 'For Mickey. To help look after Max. And stuff like that.'

I sat on that bench near the bandstand for a while, rereading the note in the sunshine, in the park, with my new dog, with ten day's supply for Laura and with enough money to get by nicely for a long while. A feeling began to wash over me, a feeling of contentment, or maybe just a lack of fear, which was a much better feeling than happiness to be honest.

I started to laugh to myself. I felt bulletproof. For the time being at least, things were going to be alright. I could switch off the warning siren that rang in my head most days. I had enough money that I could make things start to work for me. It gave me breathing space. Room to manoeuvre.

Anything was possible, I thought, and I sat there feeling *so* happy, *so* relieved. The way you feel when you watch a movie and the hero suddenly arrives to kick the bad-guy's arse. I wished it could have just stayed like that. It didn't, of course, but for those few minutes, life was perfect. Then I stood up, took Maximus by the lead and went home, still smiling.

She was sitting on a swing, her feet trailing, looking up me as I sat on the crossbar of the frame. It was lunchtime. 'You going to tell me how you got that face?'

I smiled, shook my head. 'S'nothing.'

'Was it Martin again?'

I shrugged.

'He's always hitting you,' she said.

I said nothing.

'You make it hard for me to care for you, when you don't tell me things,' she said, lifting her feet to let the swing take her back and forward. She said, 'I can tell you're upset, but when I try to talk you just give me the big Everything is Alright smile.'

I looked down and gave her the big Everything is Alright smile.

'That's the one,' she said.

Suddenly I dropped backwards, hanging onto the frame only by the crook of my knees, and she took a sharp intake of breath as I swung backwards and then rocked forward, back, forward again. I hung there swaying for a moment or two, arms hanging down, then reached up and levered myself upright and dropped to the ground.

She said, 'Come here,' and when I did, she kissed me, her fingertips touching the bruises on my face.

I flinched.

'We should go back at school,' she said. 'Get some lunch.'

'You go. I'll catch you later.'

'Skiving gain?'

I nodded, like it was standard.

'Alright,' she said, and she looked almost glad to be away from me. She stood up, brushed invisible particles of dust from her skirt, said to me, 'You're barely even here today.'

I tried to smiled but then just looked at the sky, 'Classes start in twenty minutes. That gives you time to walk back, even eat some lunch.'

'What will you do?'

But I was looking over, across the park to the gates, behind the health centre, to where some Asian kids were selling all sorts of illegal stuff from a beat-up BMW.

Emily followed my eyes, 'You're not using, are you?'

I shook my head. 'I'm not into that stuff. Never will be.'

My mind was busy and at first I didn't notice her walking away. I turned to see her almost gone, 'Hey, I'll meet you tonight,' I shouted, 'after Cello?'

She paused, then shouted back, 'I can't. I'm revising for the exams.'

'Oh, alright.'

I looked back at the older kids in the car, watching the teens and schoolies queuing up, and when I looked back she'd gone, but I was already thinking, there isn't a huge market, but it's steady. The same kids returning every day for enough to get them through the afternoon. Kids with money. They all had money to buy. One of the gang selling the stuff was a big guy, really big, the muscle of the outfit I supposed, while another stood at the end of the road watching for any police who might approach. The road they were parked on was a cul-de-sac, a dead end, so any cars would have to come from that one direction. The gang were pretty secure. If someone approached who was tougher than they were, they could just drive away. And if the police came, the car was parked right next to a drain, with a missing cover; they could dump their stuff in seconds. I could see the strengths of their operation. That's how it's done.

I thought of Ugly Pete's arangement. Of Zuluboy and Maximus. You need some muscle, I thought, and mobility too. Pete wasn't mobile, which was a weakness, made him a sitting target. And you need time to get rid of the evidence, if absolutely necessary. Then you're safe. Then you get rich.

All you need is muscle and mobility and a get-out plan. And it's good if you have absolutely nothing to lose.

A series of lightbulbs were switching on in my head.

One, by one, by one.

It seemed like all my life I'd been buying stuff from low-lifes, or had been forced to hang around with Mam's lowlife boyfriends. Maybe I was a lowlife too, I thought. Probably was. Sitting there on a park swing studying criminals instead of sitting in class studying for my exams. I took off my blazer and shoved it deep into my rucksack, then I stripped of my shirt and tie to reveal a grubby t-shirt beneath, shoving the shirt and tie into the rucksack too. The t-shirt had a picture of a Minion on it, but it was worn and thin and I could poke my finger through the Minion's eye. I shivered in the breeze. Yeah, I thought, when it comes to low-lifes, I've got the t-shirt.

It was Chloe who told me.

She wasn't called Cherelle or Charlotte, but she was Emily's friend at school, and one day, a long time after everything had gone bad between us, I bumped into Chloe in town and she took a lot of pleasure in telling me how it started, one lunchtime in school. I don't think she liked me at all, she was one of those possessive friends that girls sometimes have.

'Being with Mickey,' Emily had apparently said in the lunch hall, 'it's like, well it's sort of like eating a feast, but only being allowed to chew on one side of your mouth.'

This was a week or so after I'd found Maximus at Pete's, and like most days I hadn't turned up for school. Chloe-not-Cherelle/Charlotte, had frowned. 'That's a strange way to describe a relationship.'

'I mean, it should be wonderful,' Emily said, 'it *is*, but it's sort of frustrating too.'

'He's just a kid, you know,' Chloe said. 'Girls mature quicker than boys.'

Emily nodded, 'I know, but it's not that. He's really smart and sensible.'

'He's a madman.'

'Yes, that too, but in a really cute way,' Emily said, blushing a little. The lesson bell rang. It was just after one o' clock as she walked into the classroom and sat down. Karl came bustling in, books falling out of his rucksack, and sat down at the desk beside her. 'Hey,' he said, taking out his pen and pencil case.

'Hey Karlo.'

He blushed. 'You done that essay?'

She nodded, 'Most of it.'

He took the pile of books from his rucksack and organised them into a pile, blowing air through puffed-out cheeks. 'Me too. Spent all of last night working on it but it's not quite finished.'

'Want to come over to mine tonight and we'll work on it together?' she asked.

His face pinked. 'Sure.'

Emily looked back toward the teacher who was about to start the lesson. Karl watched her for a while longer, then looked down at his books.

That's what Chloe told me, that's how it began. Innocent enough. But I don't think Chloe was telling me to make me happy; she had that hungry look some people have, like she'd never be satisfied, never be happy with anything, so making someone else miserable would have to do.

While all that was happening at school, I was back at the park again, this time with Maximus, watching the kids buying from the dealers in the BMW. I watched them until lunchtime was over, had been watching them on and off for a few days, and I knew the pattern. The schoolkids were gone now. There'd be a few sporadic deals done over the next hour, then the gang would drive off.

I climbed down from the climbing frame, picked up Max's lead and mooched across the park to the road. 'Hey,' I said, approaching the BMW. I popped the last chunk of chocolate into my mouth, glanced down at the empty bin liner that lay in the oozing black water of the drain, almost submerged and barely visible, but not sinking any further.

The big Asian kid nodded. 'Nice dog.'

'Yeah.'

'You're here a lot.'

'Now and again.'

'Not go to school?'

'Truant.'

The big kid nodded approval, like being a truant gave me a sort of passport into the underclass. Which it probably did. He gave me a quizzical eyebrow.

'Ain't buying,' I said.

'Then keep walking, bruv. No offence.'

'None taken.'

As I passed the car I bent to stroke Max's head, the windows had been coated with some sort of one-way stuff but it didn't work too well and I could just about see inside. I'd done some asking around and he knew the names of the two guys sitting there. 'Come on boy,' I said and kept on walking away from the car, seeming in no rush, walked round the corner and along the street. I stopped and took out my phone, dialled a three-digit number: 'Hi, yeah. No I don't want to give my name,' I said, adding dramatically, 'They'll kill me.' I grinned to himself, stroked Max's ear. 'There's these kids, outside my school, well just nearby, and they're selling drugs.' I listened, nodded, waited while I was put through to a different number, 'Yeah,' I said again, 'I want to report some drug dealers, selling drugs to kids near my school. Yes, I know their names, and I've got their car registration number. I wrote it down.' I hadn't, I just had a good memory.

'No, I won't give my name,' I said. They could try and trace the phone, but I'd bought it off a lad at school who'd nicked it out of a handbag in Sainsbury's. It was going in the bin straight after. 'I'm scared,' I added, in a pitiful voice, grinning even more now, not scared at all. I listened to the police officer at the other end of the line then gave him the exact details: names, number plates, full description of the kids in the car. Explained that they'd probably drop the drugs into the drain if they were raided but that it looked like the drain was blocked and they might be able to retrieve the evidence. I knew the drain was blocked of course because, the night before, I'd come down and pushed four bin liners into the empty drain, making sure that nothing that was dropped into the drain would sink, poking the bags with a stick so that they barely appeared above the surface of the inky water. 'Gotta go,' I said, suddenly, 'I think they're after me, one of them has a machete!' and I hung up. Then I walked back toward the park and sat on a swing with the dog and waited.

Within ten minutes three police cars and a van came hurtling round the corner, sirens going, lights flashing, and I watched the big muscular guy run over and drop a carrier bag, no doubt full of their illegal stash, into the drain, saw him look down in panic, reach in and start pushing with his bare hands, trying to make the contents sink, but he probably couldn't push it down past the multiple bin liners that floated there. I was smiling as the big lad kept on trying to sink the evidence until he was grappled away by two officers. I watched while the whole crew was taken down. I just sat and enjoyed the show, every moment, rocking back and forward on the swing chuckling to myself for a long while after it had all died down. An hour later and the street was quiet. I doubted they'd send forensics. CSI aren't going to roll across town for three Asians in a ten-year-old beemer with four bags of weed and some ecstasy. Gradually the smile faded from my face and so I walked over to where the car had been parked and waited. 'Where's the bad boys gone, Max?' I said, and the dog looked up at me, but didn't answer.

I must have stood there a good hour and a half, maybe close to two hours. Then the car approached. A big grey car with two men inside. It passed me, turned and drove back out of the street. Five minutes later it was back, and it rolled to a slow stop.

A window slid open.

'Nice dog.'

'Yeah.'

A pause.

'You waiting for someone, kid?'

'Yeah.'

Another pause, then 'Who you waiting for?'

'You,' I said.

'We've never met,' the man said. The window slid up again. I watched as the two men talked. One made a call on his mobile. More talk, then the window slid down. 'You see a BMW here, earlier?'

I nodded, 'They got busted. Taken away.'

'Does the dog bite?' the man asked, reaching out of the window to stroke it but Maximus instantly bared his teeth and growled and he took his hand back.

'Everyone but me,' I said.

'Bordeaux mastiff,' the man said. 'Tough breed. I knew a guy who had one. It never liked anyone. Not even the guy who owned it.'

I said nothing.

'Wouldn't be the same dog, would it?'

'No.'

He paused, looked at Max for a few seconds. 'Looks the same. I saw a dog like that take on two pit bulls like it was nothing. Bit me too, when I tried to pull it off one of the pit bulls' throats.'

When I didn't reply, the man sniffed, glanced across at the driver, looked back at me, 'So what do you want from me, kid?'

'I want to work for you,' I said.

'Doing what?'

'I don't need a BMW,' I said. 'I just want to make money. Lots of money.'

The man's face became set, stone hard, 'You think you can just turn up with a hand-me-down dog and get a job working for me?'

'Yes.'

The man paused and studied me for a bit. I kept my expression blank. 'I'm Andy,' he said, finally.

'Mickey.'

'Apart from a big dog. Mickey, and a perfectly ordinary desire for wealth, what else have you got that qualifies you for my line of work?'

I'd prepared a speech for this moment. I would argue my case, persuade whichever men turned up in their big car to employ me, to not beat me up and not kill my dog, to give me a chance to earn money. I'd spent an hour earlier rehearsing it, but instead I decided to ditch the speech and go for honesty. 'I'm not tough,' I said, 'but I'm smart, and I think ahead.' I paused. 'And I've got nothing to lose.'

Andy looked thoughtful, nodding to himself. 'You rehearse that speech?'

'I had a different one all ready, practiced it over and over, but I decided not to use it. Made that one up just then.'

He nodded. 'You get on well with people, Mickey? Good communication skills?'

'Good enough, yes.'

'Good enough.' He nodded to himself, chewing over these words. 'You don't need to be tough, not with that dog. Smart is enough.' He turned back to the driver, a question on his face, the driver nodded.

'You prepared to do whatever you have to do?' he asked, turning back.

I nodded.

'Say the words,' Andy said.

'I'm prepared to do what I have to do.'

'You're not a grass?'

'Never.'

Andy looked across at the driver. 'Tomorrow,' he said, turning back again to me.

'Ok.'

'I'll make you rich, Mickey,' and when he smiled I half expected a forked tongue to flick out from between his lips. The window slid up, then stopped, wound back down. 'By the way,' Andy said, 'did you have anything to do with what happened earlier?'

'No.'

Andy smiled, and now it seemed more like I was watching a leopard, baring its teeth. 'I like ruthlessness Mickey,' he said, 'it's an effective business tool. But be careful who you use it on.' He looked at the dog, 'Or it can come back and bite you.' He held up his hand to wave goodbye, and I noticed the fresh pink scars of a recent dog bite across the palm. The window slid shut and the car pulled away.

And just like that, I had a new career.

It didn't feel good. I thought it would, but it didn't. I felt like I'd been teetering on a precipice my whole life, and just then I'd stepped off, stepped into the void. This is a bad thing I'm doing, I thought. I know this is a bad thing. But bad things are all I understand.

'Come on,' I said to Max, and as we began to walk home the bad feeling had gone; already I was thinking, to make this work, I need a crew.

I wasn't naïve enough to believe I could just arrive at the park the next day with a bagful of mixed stimulants, opiates and hallucinogens and hope I could make my fortune; things would go very wrong very quickly. But all my days spent watching TV at home instead of studying at school meant that I knew how to work a 'cut-out' system, and I understood the importance of security before I ever began selling. And I knew I had to keep track of the money, because if I didn't keep track of the money, or if I got into debt with my own supplier, it'd lead to nowhere but dark places.

So I needed muscle and runners, and I needed a bookkeeper.

And I knew just where to find them.

Oscar was waiting for me in the deli with a large pot of tea to share, and a sandwich each.

'Nice one, O,' I said, sitting down, pouring myself a cup, and tucking in.

Oscar waited for me to finish and then said, 'I've got last week's takings.'

'You paid the lads?'

Oscar nodded, 'Paid the crew, paid Andy, took my cut.' He pushed a fat envelope across the table, 'The rest is yours.' I nodded but didn't move to pick up the envelope.

I met Oscar three months ago, just before the start of the Easter holidays, at the start of my new criminal career. He had just transferred into our school. I saw him sitting alone in the canteen; a neat, bespectacled boy with a rucksack fastened tightly across both shoulders, and I'd recognised a fellow misfit when I saw one. A few days later I'd learned of Oscar's special skill with numbers and had made a special effort to befriend him, persuading a group of boys not to beat him up and thereby earning myself a new friend. Oscar was slight and quietly nervous with a sharp, inquisitive face. He was also, by his own admission, Aspergic.

'So you like to tell the truth, no matter how ugly it might sound to people,' I asked him, a couple of days after my first meeting with Andy. 'You can't tell lies?' when Oscar had explained his condition.

'I like to tell the truth,' he said. 'Sometimes people find it uncomfortable. But I find it difficult to know how to do the stuff other people do, you know, when they say things they don't mean. It upsets me. So I don't do it.'

'That's good, really, I suppose,' I said.

'Is it?'

'Yeah. It means you can be trusted not to lie. And I need someone I can trust.'

'You can't trust anyone,' Oscar said, 'People can be mean, even when they think they aren't,' and I had to agree with that, 'But I try and tell the truth, no matter how awkward it might be.'

'I like you more with every passing minute,' I said. Then I asked, 'And you're good at maths?'

'Yes.'

'Square root of one thousand and two?'

'To how many decimal places?'

'Two.'

Oscar pushed his glasses back onto his nose, a thing that Mickey picked up he did when he was thinking. 'Thirty one point six five.'

I sat forward, 'I won't tell you you're a genius, 'cos you already know that. But I do have a business proposal for you that would mean you get to do what you're good at and earn lots of money.'

'Is it legal?'

'No.'

'How much money?'

'Lots. Lots and lots.'

Oscar thought for a moment. 'Lots and lots of money?'

'Yes. Think of the computer you could buy. Maybe a VR set. Your own mainframe.'

Oscar looked almost at me for a few seconds. 'Ok,' he said.

The other three members of my crew were comprised of the front row of the school rugby team: Lance, a fourteen stone ever-smiling loosehead prop, Gabriel, the tighthead prop, bigger than Lance but not as happy, and Knud, the team hooker, short and stocky with a shaved head and missing front teeth. All three were strong, fit and fearless, in Knud's case, quietly deranged, and in Lance's case, possibly brain-damaged by too many slam-scrimmages and head-on open-field tackles. To me though, they were quality because they'd already worked as a team, and being rugby players, they respected the chain of command. In rugby only the Captain is allowed to speak to the referee, so with Knud being the hooker and school captain, he was the spokesman for the three of them. I only had to keep Knud happy and they were all happy. And I gave Knud lots of money for simply being Knud, so everyone was happy.

A couple of days after I took on Oscar as my accountant I found them in the derelict subway opposite the demolished council estate, a prime place for school slackers. Gabriel and Knud were avoiding their compulsory Citizenship lessons, smoking cigarettes, and Lance, though temporarily excluded, had put on his uniform, walked down to school and joined them, as he did every day, at the subway. He was hanging by his heels from a rail in the ceiling.

'Hey lads,' I said.

'Reet,' Knud muttered.

They stood, or in Lance's case, hung, ignoring me for a while and I leaned against the wall at the end of the subway, watching the students in the distance head toward school.

'You Mickey Hall?' I turned to see Knud speaking to me. I nodded and Knud said, 'Thought you'd left.'

'I sort of have,' I admitted. 'Only come here to check out the trade.'

'What trade is that,' Knud said, though I guessed he had an inkling already. I just stood, pushed my hands in my pockets, smiled and said, 'You lads want to earn good money? Regular good money?'

'Doing what?'

'Just being yourselves,' I said, looking them over; eyeing their scars, bruises and the muscles swelling beneath their ill-fitting uniforms. 'Doing what you enjoy doing best.'

Knud grinned. 'We can do that, can't we?' turning to Gabriel, who nodded and stubbed out his cigarette. They all looked up at Lance who closed his eyes and started humming a tune to himself. 'Yeah,' Knud said, turning back to me, 'We can do that.'

The waitress brought us over two more slices of caramel shortbread. Oscar stared at me as I ate one. 'Don't like caramel shortbread?' I asked and when Oscar shook his head I said, 'How can you not like it?'

'The sugar makes me go all hyper. I can get really angry. Sugar-fury.'

I leaned over and took it off Oscar's plate, 'I'll have it then. I go the opposite way. Hunger-rage.'

Oscar giggled at this. 'I've never heard that, but I know what you mean.'

'See you're getting better at the humour thing.'

'I'd like another sandwich now.'

'Sure.'

After lunch they sat by the indoor fountain, watching the people go by. I asked him, 'Are we good?'

Oscar nodded, 'Yes.'

'The crew happy?'

'Yes. They like getting paid.'

I'd quickly worked out a system designed to keep myself away from the action as much as possible, with the crew doing the spade-work and Oscar as his never-tell-lies middle-man and accountant. Despite Lance, Gabriel and Knud being twice as tough as me, I had the people-skills, and that was gold in this business, and I had contact with Andy, and therefore the merchandise, and so I was the one who ran the outfit.

Because I never really went to school, I held our patch, like some old general I'd read about had said: winning was mainly about holding the ground, so I did; I was on-site every day. I had the crew change their location daily though, sometimes twice daily, and each time I would stand at the previous location and point the customers toward the new place, taking payment in advance and handing out a numbered, colour-coded raffle ticket as proof of payment. The raffle tickets I'd bought in a pack of one thousand from a thrift store. By the end of the month I was onto my second pack and would be visiting the store again soon.

I was solvent, and that'd happened quickly: within a week I had more money than I'd ever seen. I'd bought an iPad and had Oscar set up some weird intranet system with me and the crew, cos I'd equipped them with cheap burner phones; old-school Nokia bricks. All told, things were running smoothly, which worried me, but not as much as the money made me happy. My ability to chat to anyone, or rather to get others chatting to me, meant I was making new contacts daily, which meant more money and, to my mind, increasing the distance between me and destitution.

Walking through town a few days later I spotted a new shop called Cakeaway. The chalkboard outside said it was an 'artisanal bakery' and boasted of using only organic and vegan-friendly products for the best quality, hypo-allergenic cakes and pastries in town. I picked up a leaflet from a pile in the doorway. Then I went in a bought a selection of products for the crew. They weren't keen.

But my mind was on other things.

'Two jam doughnuts, half a dozen cream eclairs and a raisin swirl. Deliver to 9 Mason's Avenue, 8pm tonight. Looks like they're off raving.'

'Reet. On it, boss,' said Knud.

It was the third order that day. The website Oscar had put together (on my instructions, naturally) was working like a charm. On the face of it, Cakeaway had some new competition: Sunderland Sweet Treats promised "hand-crafted, classic baked goods with a modern twist, all ordered from the comfort of your living room". But those in the know were in on the secret: each delicious cake on the site corresponded to something a bit… less legal. I got the automated messages generated by the site, organised the merchandise and the boys did the rest.

Business, which had been steady up until that point, had gone geometric. I sold to teenagers outside of school, I went to the Uni and sold to students, went into the old people's home and sold cannabis to peoples' grans, all the while handing out freshly printed flyers for the Sunderland Sweet Treats page.

By May I was supplying party drugs for stressed professionals, cannabis to despondent mothers and delivering horse steroids to bodybuilders. In other words, the website idea had worked. On one occasion, I turned up at a School Reunion party for a bunch of over-forties with a supply of recreational drugs, mainly ecstasy, poppers and acid, all stashed safely inside the handlebars of my new BMX, only to discover that the buyer was my PE teacher, Mr Guy.

Another time I'd delivered to a party with an aspirin bottle full of cocaine and a strip of Viagra, plus four ounces of skunk and a handful of ketamine tablets, and only later did I recognise a couple of leading councillors from an article in the local daily that Mam read every evening.

That made me smile.

On some level, I knew that I was doing wrong, and that it couldn't last, but I was on a helter-skelter of deals and profits, and the blur of movement and the whirl of sales pitches and deals closed was my own, very new, very addictive drug of choice. If I'd been a trainee stockbroker or a young businessman, I might have been seen as a wonder-kid, a boy genius, someone who spotted markets before they existed, someone who created markets simply by thinking them into existence.

But I wasn't. Deep inside, I knew what I was: a grotty, cheap drug dealer, way down the food chain. Worse still, I was making new Lauras. knew all this, and part of me wanted to get off the merry-go-round.

But I wanted the money to keep coming in too.

And there was a lot of money.

Toward the beginning of the summer holidays I'd made more than I'd thought possible to earn in a lifetime. At school, the rugby team had ended the season on an impressive losing streak after the entire front row stopped attending after-school practice. Or matches, for that matter. Oscar was put forward for his A Level maths exam four years early, with the possibility of a fast track to Oxbridge. Emily was studying hard and didn't have much time to spend with me, but to be honest I hardly noticed, I was so busy with the business.

On the last day of the school year, Oscar arranged a sit-down and when I asked him how the business looked, Oscar paused, gave it a moment's thought and then he said: 'We need a bigger crew.'

They say that everyone has their drug of choice. For some people it's power or success or sex or, if you believe the gossip magazines, just being *adored*; for others it's heroin or alcohol, and for others again it's adrenaline.

Me, I'd discovered cash.

Cash was my drug of choice. Cold, hard cash, and the security that I thought it could buy me and my family. After a lifetime of not having any I'd discovered an easy way to acquire it and I began to spend most of my time doing just that, or thinking of ways to get even more.

But it wasn't the money itself. Never having had any money when I was a kid, I had no taste for *things*: gadgets, toys, bikes... whatever. Ok, I'd had a kite once, when I was a kid, a nice one with shaped like a dragon, but that was more about what it *did* than what it was. And what cash did for me was make my family secure. It meant that we could pay our rent, cover our bills, buy decent food, nice clothes, and we weren't going to have to move out in the middle of the night to escape an aggrieved landlord or an angry ex-boyfriend.

On that particular subject, Mam was still with Martin, which I didn't much approve of, though I always think 'better the devil you know' and all that, and me and him had reached a sort of unspoken non-aggression pact: he didn't bother me and my 150lb fighting dog didn't bite him. At first he tried to persuade Mam to make me get rid of the dog, but even she recognised when something was not negotiable, and Maximus was absolutely not going to leave my side any time soon. So generally, Martin and me agreed to disagree, we rarely spoke, we didn't argue, and if he came into a room, I left.

And vice versa.

Pretty soon I stopped using the living room altogether, which was ok; I like to read books. A lot of the time I wasn't even running my operation, I was just sitting in my room reading. They'd closed all but one of the libraries in town, but I didn't even have to borrow from Waterstones; I could actually buy books as I had so much money now, though I still preferred to borrow them.

I also discovered that there was a whole genre of books about how to persuade people to do things that they didn't always want to do. Books on the psychology of selling, of winning and of using others to get what you want. I read them all: Dale

Carnegie, Sun Tzu, Machiavelli, all the classics. Funny thing was, the things they said, most of it I was doing already. Schooling was pretty much irrelevant by this point, though you could argue that my education in the ways of the world was picking up speed . The summer holidays had begun, I was heading toward my final year, I was almost sixteen and there was nothing that school could give me. Nothing that made any sense. Nothing apart from Emily, that is.

Thing is, the drug side of it, the dealing, I knew it couldn't last and I knew it was wrong. But that just made me work harder, knowing that it'd stop at some point. I was like a squirrel, vacuuming up as much money as I could and burying it for when we'd needed it, for when our luck ran out. I was making more money than I could count, buying anything and everything wholesale from Andy, then selling it to on to people stupid enough to buy it.

I knew the whole deal was going to implode on me at some point but I just hoped to have saved up enough money by that point. Enough money for what though? Simple truth was, I didn't know, at this point just the having was enough. Maybe enough money to keep us alright until I could officially leave school and could get a job. I didn't care what sort of job, anything with a regular, dependable wage, I'd do it. But until then, I was doing this.

'Well, what do you think?'

'Let me get in first!'

I stood and held open the door to let Mam and Laura step over the threshold. We'd rented, actually I'd rented, a ground floor apartment on Christchurch, a much nicer street that was on the other side of the park. It had a large living room, a fully-equipped kitchen, two bedrooms, and a couple of basement rooms thrown in for free. Laura'd had to sign the lease papers because I was still technically a minor, but I'd paid six month's rent upfront, cash. I watched with pleasure as Mam and Laura walked from room to room checking out their new home. Mam turned and said, 'But what about our furniture? From our old flat?'

'It was a furnished flat Mam, we didn't own the furniture in the first place.'

'It was all grotty anyway,' Laura said, giving me a wink then turning back to say, 'Bagsy this room for me.'

Mam asked, 'Where's your room Mickey?'

'I've got the basement,' I said, grinning from ear to ear, 'I can keep Maximus out of your way.' Then I asked, 'So you like it?'

'It's lovely.'

And it was. Large airy rooms, freshly painted the previous weekend by me and the new crew. New furniture. Bought cash, again. I'd even bought Mam an Ikea newspaper rack to put at the side of her chair to stack her tabloids. 'Well, I'll leave you to it,' I said, 'I'm going to meet my pals in a bit.'

Laura followed me downstairs to my bedroom. 'This your den?' she asked.

'Like it?'

'I love it.' Then she said, this house has lovely bones,' and she tapped a wall at the back of the room; it sounded hollow. 'Someone's boarded over the fireplace alcove.' Then she said, 'I've got something for you, here,' and handed me a cardboard tube. 'I bought it about a week ago, when I knew we were moving.'

I opened the tube and took out a rolled up calendar. On each page there was a month and a picture: 'Where's this for?' I asked.

'It's a Greek island. Paxos. Near Corfu; I always wanted to visit it. It's an academic calendar, so you can keep track of your studies. Your exams are in less than a year.'

I said, 'I want to come with you, to Paxos, when you go.'

'You'll need a passport.'

I'd never been abroad. I held the poster against the wall to see where it looked best, and Laura took a lump of blu-tac from her bag, 'Here,' she said.

'No, here.' I wanted to stick the calendar so that I could see it when I was lying in bed.

We stuck it up and stepped back to admire the view.

'Thanks,' I said.

She said, 'Maybe we'll go there next year.'

'Yeah. Maybe.'

We went back upstairs, the dog following behind. 'How can we afford it?' Mam asked, to nobody in particular when we were all together again, but I said nothing and Laura went to check out her new room. A few minutes later I left the house, walked down the street and hopped on a bus that took me over town to the Bridges where I dropped leaflets for Sunderland SweetBreads in a couple of charity shops and a vegetarian cafe, popping into my favourite bookshop and returning the novel I'd read back to the shelf I'd borrowed it from, complete with helpful review on a post-it note on the inner leaf. Then I went and dropped leaflets at the Citizen's Advice, Centre and the Museum. Outside the museum there was a poster for Sunderland City of Culture 2021, but someone had written over it in spray paint so that it read ~~Sunderland~~ Squanderland City of Culture 2021.

When I got home Mam was in the kitchen washing up, 'Hey you,' she said.

'Hey,' I said.

'He's not in,' she said, racking the dishes.

I looked at her as I did about once a year, as a real human being, not just my mam. I saw her as a person, 'How are you today?' I asked her.

She hung the dishtowel over the edge of the sink, 'You're very formal.' Then she put her arms around me, hugged me tight, in a way I couldn't really remember. hugged me said. And when she let go she said, 'I'm good.'

'I'm glad,' I said. 'I'm taking Max for a walk. Do you want to come?'

'Give me a minute.'

So ten minutes later we were back out on the street, heading toward the park, Max on one side, Mam on the other, linking my arm. 'When did I start having to look up to you?' she said. 'When did you get so tall?'

'It's a boy thing,' I said, and she ruffled my hair, laughing to herself.

'This might sound stupid,' she said, 'but there's no manual you know. No one to tell me how to bring up a son. One day you're a tiny thing in nappies, screaming to be fed and changed, the next day you're little bundle of energy and running around with a kite, and the day after that your taller than I ever will be, almost fully grown, a man.'

'You're the best mam I've ever had,' I said, and she punched my arm, mock indignant, then put her head against my shoulder as we walked. 'I'm a screw-up,' she said sadly. 'I'm pretty useless.'

'You're my useless,' I said.

'That'll have to do,' she whispered, 'I suppose.'

We paused at the park gates, looking up into the clear night sky. Stars twinkled, the breeze was cool and a few clouds drifted across the sky. Max whined and I said, 'Once round the park?'

'Definitely,' she said.

We pushed through the gate and walked up the bank to the park.

And you're back in the room.

I don't know what had lulled me into this false sense of
security.

Probably the rhythm of the thing, the same business, night
after night, week after week, everything just rolling on

unchecked. Maybe it was the run of good luck we'd had (ok,

punctuated by the odd threat or the even rarer straightener

dealt out by Knud or one of the boys, true), but mainly good

luck and good news. And, of course, lots of good money.

Maybe I'd just gotten lazy.

I'd forgotten that life had given me the gift of fear. I'd

forgotten to carry that gift with me. I'd messed up. And now

there was a smackhead with stinking breath and mottled skin

and a knife to my throat. One moment your mind is idly

wandering down a variety of paths.

Next, you're back in the room.

Or in this case, a rainswept, cobbled alley behind Oddies,

which for those who don't know is a pub in Millfield. A pub

whose bright welcoming lights reflected against the glittering

broken glass and the grime and the filth out here on the street.

I was standing next to Oscar congratulating myself on doing

well, and the smackhead had emerged out of the shadows,

asking for smack, obviously, and I'd told him the party line that I didn't hold that stuff, but I could pass him on. I did the recreational stuff: cocaine, ecstasy, E, roids, poppers, that sort of thing. Smack was Andy's. He told me that every smackhead earned him three or four hundred a week, and they were his customers, not mine. Loyal customers. They were his for life. Every one a devoted follower; an acolyte. A permanent earner. They supported his lifestyle. So I told the smackhead I'd pass him on. And then, like someone flicked a switch, the smackhead was in my face. One second he was not there, and then, click, he was, and I felt the cold sharp steel at my throat. The sudden cold sweat at the base of my spine. The thumping, turgid beat of my heart.

He whispered, 'Call in your little gang, and tell them to bring everything, all the drugs, and all the money, or I'll cut your throat til I hit bone.'

'Mickey.' Oscar said, his voice rising in panic.

'Shut it, Doctor Logic,' the smackhead hissed, or your friend here is going to bleed out all over this lane. 'Maybe we'll film it,' he added, his voice leering. By *we*, I guess he meant the other two who'd drifted out of the shadows to join him. He too had a crew.

'It's ok, Oscar,' I said. My heart was beating like a mash-hammer in my chest and my throat was dry, but I felt strangely calm, detached, and I felt that detachment growing with each moment and my heart began to slow as the surge of adrenaline changed gear, gathered and focused by some quiet intent I hadn't even realised was there. Slowly I lifted my phone to shoulder height, so he could see it, I said, 'I'll need to look at it, to text the right people,' and maybe he'd made a mistake too, maybe when I switched it on the light from the phone blinded him from seeing into darkness for a moment, because you can't see from light into dark, and I could hear the intake of breath from his partners, and he turned to look at them and instead he looked straight down the barrel of my gun, the one I was holding in my other hand. Pointed at his temple. I leaned in, against the blade. 'I. Don't. Care.' I said, very slowly.

'What?'

'I. Don't Care.' I repeated slowly, pushing my throat against his blade so that I could feel a tiny trickle of blood running down my neck. 'We can both die now,' I told him. 'Or we can both live. And if we live,' I said, 'then we'll do a deal, because I'm in the business of doing deals.' I studied his eyes, and they were confused, like a rat in a trap. 'I do deals,' I said. 'I'm Dealer Number One.' I paused to let this sink in, then continued, 'We can deal, or we can die, and either way is good by me. Because,' and I eyeballed him now to show I was sincere, 'seriously? I don't care.'

'Uh huh,' he said, my gun nuzzling his earlobe. And I could smell the piss he'd unloaded onto the cobbles.

I felt completely detached. I was watching a movie. 'Step back,' I said, leaning further in, feeling the blade against my neck quivering in his hand.

See, the thing is, in business you don't ask someone to do

what they won't or can't do at that moment. That makes you look weak. So I didn't say Drop The Blade, cos he might not have, and then I'd have lost my power over him and he might have began thinking I didn't mean it and done something stupid. And the thing is, I did mean it. At that point, I really didn't care.

But equally, I don't like stupid.

'Step back,' I said again, and he did, slowly, knife still at my throat, but the pressure easing, my gun tracking him until it was at arm's length, then the knife was away from me and he stepped back enough so I could put the stare on him. I don't know where it came from, but I knew how to do it. It felt natural. I said, 'You want to do a deal, we'll deal,' and my voice was dead calm. 'You want to come back another time, give it some thought, that's cool. But if you bring a knife to a gunfight, next time, I'll leave your brain on the cobbles.'

One of his friends, the smart one, said 'Come on Hoops, we'll come back later.'

Right, I thought. And the offer will still be on the table.

Hoops nodded, said, 'No harm intended.'

'God loves a tryer,' I said.

He gave a weak grin. 'No hard feelings?'

'None.'

And they were gone.

I watched them ghost down the alley, their feet flapping, almost silent in their tattered snidey Converse, and I felt the adrenaline dump as my legs went heavy, my hands began to shake, the thunder of my pulse began bouncing round my head.

I let out a long slow breath, and then I began to laugh. Maybe I laughed for the joy of being alive, for having taken a risk and have it pay off. Maybe I laughed because, for those few moments, all the worries and cares in the world hadn't mattered. All that had existed in my world was the smackhead, his blade and me. And it was like a relief from pain; a relief from care, from duty and obligation, a relief from love. Just that simple focus on the *now*. Or maybe I laughed

because, if I hadn't, I too would have wet my pants. I dunno, I

just kept on laughing. I laughed so hard it doubled me over. I

laughed so much it took a long while before I realized that

Oscar was standing in the darkness of the alley, crying.

Don't laugh, but I'd begun going to church. I'd been thinking

of going for some time. The nearest church, the one next door

to where I lived, had become a Sikh temple and that was

maybe a step too far. I wasn't even religious, had never been

Christened or anything, couldn't ever remember being inside

a church, and I'd never been at school for the Christmas or

Easter services they held in the local church, but I wanted to know what they were like inside, and St. Ignatius was close to where I lived.

I walked up the worn stone steps and pushed the heavy door. It gave. I couldn't believe you could just walk straight in off the street. That was strange. Bit risky. I wondered what their insurance bill was. I laughed to myself as I considered whether they'd be insured against acts of god. I stepped inside and it was cool, and quiet, and there were rows of empty pews that smelled of wood polish, so I edged along one pew near the back and sat down on one near the wall just next to a pillar, and crossed myself. I'd seen movies and I knew that was what you should do.

'Well,' I said to God. 'Here I am.'

God stayed silent, so I stayed silent too. Then after a while, speaking quietly I said, 'I'd really like it if you could show me a way out of this situation, God. I've heard you listen to sinners. You like to give them a fresh start and stuff.' God continued to stay silent, so I just sat there in the cool quiet of the old stone church. After a while I went on, voice almost a whisper, it didn't seem like the place to raise your voice. 'I like this place, God, but I'd like it more if you could give me some guidance. Anything would do.'

From a side door a priest stepped out. He stood and watched me, wary at first in case I was a vandal or a drunk, then I think he was just curious. He didn't speak to me but just watched from a distance. I ignored him, kept on with my quiet conversation. After another ten minutes or so I stood and said, quietly, 'Well it's been nice talking to you. I'll come back, if that's ok.' I edged along the pew and walked back down the aisle toward the door. As I reached the door I saw a small wooden box and on it was the words: All Donations Welcome so I took out a wad of twenties and tried to shove it into the slot. It wouldn't go so I split the wad, shoved half in and then shoved the other half in.

Then I left.

'I thought I was the one who was always side-tracked,' I said.

'My mind on other things; but today it's you.'

She looked up, smiled at me, 'Sorry, I've got revision; we have a maths test tomorrow.'

'Another one?'

'You should try it,' she said. 'Tests and stuff, you'd probably do well.'

'Want another milkshake?' I asked.

'No.' She shook her head, 'You'll make me fat.'

I sat back, studying her, 'I don't think I can make you anything,' I said.

She reached out across the table to rest on hand in mine; her fingertips cool from the tall, cold glass. She held it there for a while. Her eyes rose to meet mine. 'You can make me shiver,' she said, her voice soft.

'Really?'

She blushed and looked away. 'But shivering won't help me pass exams,' she said after a while.

I threaded my fingers into hers, drew her hand toward my mouth and kissed her fingertips in turn: index, middle, ring, pinky. I said, 'We'll have more time when the summer arrives.'

My lips felt the coolness of her fingertips.

She nodded.

'Yes.'

My business model:

Mondays to Thursdays

- Crew 1

- Overheads £240/week

- Income – minimum of £600/week (maximum of about £2,500)

- Wholesale - £200-500

- Profit range £160-£2260, mostly toward the top end.

Fridays and Saturdays

- Crew 1&2

- Overheads £340/week

- Wholesale £700-1000

- Income – minimum of £800 (maximum up to £3,000)

- Profit range £1160-£2660, mostly toward the top end.

Sundays off, unless there's a party or something, which there often is, and I'll deliver myself.

- Overheads nil

- Profits insane

That's not an exact description, obviously. It's tough to keep track of everything, to be honest. And that's why I have Oscar.

He told me later that he studied me for a long while. Couldn't stay in Sunderland at that time, was too well known, so he stayed in Newcastle, twelve miles up the road, lived in an apartment on the quayside, sat in riverside cafes, had meetings, would watch the sunset with a glass of wine in his hand, pondering. Mulling things over. Me, in particular.

I was a kink in his plan.

He was tall and lean, with unruly black hair that stuck up a bit at the front and was showing a few strands of grey at the temples which was probably due to the stressful nature of his business. He wore quietly expensive suits, off-white linen shirts, and dark laced boots. From a distance he might have resembled a curator from the Baltic art gallery across the river from where he was staying, or a successful middle-brow author or perhaps a retired games designer, enjoying his millions, definitely someone employed in the creative industries, someone with a bit of wealth. He didn't look what he was. I've been with him quite a bit now and every now and again I see a woman glance in his direction, though he never seems to return their look. On closer inspection though, his sleepy expression revealed a quiet, steely gaze. He had icy blue eyes beneath his long lashes, and his gaze pierced as it scanned the people and the passers-by.

He was always thinking.

Planning.

For he was not, as I immediately discovered when we finally met, a wealthy, retired games designer or a middlebrow author, or an art curator. He was a predator. He was a shark in human form and he preyed on people who were themselves sharks, who were themselves dangerous, and yet were unlikely to ever take recourse in law.

His business model, quite simply, was to locate and destroy other criminals, and strip them of their worth, their wealth and their affluence. So, as long as he was more dangerous than his prey, more swift and more deadly, with everything to gain and nothing to lose, he was able to conduct his business model extremely successfully. And he was about to head back to his home-town after a long absence, about to execute a final bit of business. It was his last big job and then he was going to retire. A multi-millionaire already. With lots more to come. But I was the fly in the ointment, something to take care of before he could take care of business.

And he had a crooked smile, just like his son.

Have you ever walked into a door? I mean, *really* walked into

one? You turn, start walking, and a door just springs at you

out of nowhere, and because you're not expecting it, it seems

to actually attack you. It's the

shock that's worst, that sudden BAM! And then you're on the floor watching stars float around the room. And the mad thing is, the door was actually there all the time. You just didn't see it.

This is how it happened to me: I was on my bed in my room, just looking up, staring at the poster Laura had bought me of the tiny Greek Island of Paxos, studying it, I'd just filled in the passport form she'd given me, and was imagining us being there next year, on a tiny little dot on the Ionian sea, a dozen miles south of Corfu. An island of olive groves and history, as it said on a little box-out on the left side of the poster. Maybe we'd buy a little café, Greece is a cash economy, I could probably afford to buy something, we could live there. Staring at it gave me a feeling of comfort somehow. A feeling that things would work out ok in the end. Just then Laura knocked and came in. 'Hey bruv,' she said, 'Not in school?' I shook my head and she said, 'Mam'll get taken to court again.' 'If we get a summons I'll go back for a couple of weeks.'

She sat down on the edge of my bed and I was expecting some lecture about my future or something but instead she said, completely out of the blue, 'Hey, guess what?'

'What?'

'I think I'm going to get clean.'

This was a surprise, to put it mildly. I tried to process this new information. Laura'd been addicted as long as I could remember. All I could say, a bit stupidly, was 'Why?'

She looked around my room, 'All this,' she said. 'The money, the stuff you're doing, everything we've suddenly got; it makes me feel uncomfortable. It's wrong.'

'But why?' I said. 'Why now?'

'I made you do all this, Mick. You do it to look after me, I *know* you do,' she said when I went to protest, 'and I want you to stop.'

'So you're going to get clean? For real?' My voice was rising, giving away just how excited I was.

She nodded. 'For real. I've been to see a counsellor, today. I told him what I wanted to do. He said that there were different ways to get clean, slow withdrawal, methodone, which is yeuch, but I said I just want to stop, go cold-turkey.'

'That's supposed to be horrible, sis.'

'It's not,' she said, and when I looked at her sort of puzzled she said, 'I've done it before. I came off it for three or four months a few years ago, way before you started buying it for me.'

'I didn't know.'

'I know you didn't. Then I started using again,' she said, 'I don't know why. Because I had no reason not to, I suppose.' She took my hand in both of hers, they were shaking and very cool, 'But I've got a reason to stop now, haven't I? You looked after me for so long, and now I'm going to look after you.' She paused, picked up the forms I'd just completed, studied them, put them down again, said, 'I just needed a reason to stop, Mickey, and you're it.'

I sat up, unsure of what to say, still not really able to grasp what she was telling me. Her eyes were bright, too bright. She spoke again. 'All you have to do is stop the dealing.'

I guess I should have felt happy. Elated. Relieved. Or at least not quite so anxious; my big sister getting straight, all the worries and cares taken from my shoulders. But all I felt was flat, deflated, like I'd been training for years to run a race I really didn't want to run and I'd gotten in the best shape of my life, and only now, when I'd finally got my feet on the starting blocks, I learned that someone had cancelled the entire event.

'But we need the money now, Lau,' I said.'

'No, we don't need the money. That's just it. I've been offered more hours at work, I'll save a fortune by not buying the junk, the rent is paid up-front until after Christmas, and you can get a job as soon as you leave school. Plus whatever you've got stashed,' and she gave me a funny smile, as though she knew my secrets.

'You've thought this through.'

'I have. And I haven't used since yesterday.' She was smiling, proud, tears in her eyes, her voice almost pleading as she said 'Let's do it, Mickey, let's be a normal family. Let's both of us give up the drugs. No addictions, no dealing, no awful things ever again.'

She wrapped her arms around me, rested her head on my shoulder, 'Please bruv, let's just do it. Martin leaves you alone now, Mam and him get on, and I've looked at the money for this place, if we save the pennies we can just afford to live here, forever, like a normal family, and I'm really good at managing money when I set my mind to it.'

'We've had practice.'

'We have,' she sniffed. 'It can only get better.' She smiled, 'Hey, we're a proper family now, we've even got a dog.' I hugged her back then, as what she was suggesting gradually seeped into my brain; she was coming down, fast, and the words were rushing from her, 'What do you want me to do?' I asked.

'Just stop.'

'No, I'll stop if you want me to, you know I will, it's over as of now, I mean about you going cold turkey?'

She sniffed back tears, 'It's not too bad, you know. I had the flu once, and that was worse. I just needed a reason to stop.'

'Can I get you anything?'

'Maybe later. Peppermint tea. And aspirin. Tell me you'll definitely stop though. If you stop, I can stop.' She was laughing through her tears, a weird mix of emotion had overcome both of us, and that sold it for me. She was committed to this, so I was through. My career dealing drugs was officially over. I felt a weight lifting from me and I said, 'Yes,' then repeated it, 'Yes! I'll give it all up, if you do.'

'I will,' she said.

We hugged again. She shivered and shivered and shivered again. 'Here,' I said, almost leaping off the bed, 'Here, climb under my quilt, I'll go and get you some tea.'

'And aspirin?' she said, as she dragged herself beneath the quilt.

'Yeah, that too.'

Maximus chose that moment to pad through the open door into my bedroom. 'Want someone to keep you warm?' I asked her and Laura, who'd burrowed herself up to her neck beneath my quilt looked over at Max and giggled, 'He'll squash me!' but she let Max lie beside her on the bed and I went to make her a pot of tea, knowing that, finally, Laura and me and Mam were going to be safe from harm.

I took her the tea and stayed with her all the rest of the morning, and then all through the afternoon, letting her sleep when she could, bringing her hot drinks and painkillers when the chills and the aches really kicked in, a cool damp cloth for when the sweats began, I went to the shop and bought her a magazine that she didn't read, I heated a tin of soup that she didn't eat but said smelled lovely, and generally hung around making sure she was ok, until finally it was starting to get dark and she said, 'Go and have some time to yourself, I can manage for a bit.'

'Are you sure?'

'Yeah. The next few hours are going to be a solo flight.'

'Alright. I might go over and see Emily.'

'How is she? You never mention her now.'

'She's great. Studying like mad for her exams'

'So should you.'

'I'll be back for midnight.'

'K, Cinderella,' she murmured, eyes closing, and turning to face the wall.

It was dark when I left the flat, I'd left a small lamp on in my room to keep Laura company but she said to leave Max too, and that was cool because it meant I was able to jump on the bus rather than walk so that I arrived at Emily's about a half hour earlier than arranged. I didn't quite recognise the emotions that I was experiencing but I was beginning to understand that whatever they were, they felt good; maybe this was normal, I thought. If it was, I liked it. I was going to change my life, I *had* changed my life already, in my mind. I was going to go back to school, spend the last five or six months studying hard and I was going to have future where Emily and me would get married and live in a big old house and have children who performed surgery on trees. Everything had changed for me at that moment, and all for the better. 'God,' I said, looking toward the stars, 'Thanks for your help.' I meant it, and I was smiling to myself. And then I turned the corner, and I saw them together, standing at the gate.

Emily.

And Karl.

And they were kissing.

That door, you see. I just didn't know it was there, until I

walked right into it and BAM! Everything had changed again.

She told me later that she felt bad for what happened. Not just that she betrayed me, but that she never really liked Karl that much anyway, not in that way. So, she said, she kind of betrayed us both.

Karl was safer, he was reliable, and he liked her. He was *like* her too, they were from the same sort of background and they had a lot in common, and he liked her, a lot. With me I think she always felt that I liked her when I had the time, that I really *really* liked her, when there was nothing else on my mind. But Karl doted on her all the time.

And he was there.

It started out innocently enough, with them revising together a couple of nights. Then he started popping round two or three times a week. Then one week they went out to watch a movie together. I'd bailed on her again, had some sort of scheme going on though I can't remember what it was now, so when Karl asked if she wanted to go to the cinema with him she just said yes.

Then he kissed her.

We were barely sixteen, the three of us. What did I expect, marriage vows? None of it was forever. She started seeing Karl, and I think that she was hoping that I'd either wake up and claim her back, or just not notice and let Karl fill in the space I'd left in her life.

Madness.

And then I walked around the corner and saw Karl kissing her goodnight and I know she saw me just standing there, like I'd been frozen under the streetlights. I even saw her push Karl away, heard her shout for me to stop and wait. But by then I was already gone.

And that was it.

Part Three

I peeled off twenty-pound notes from the wad and handed five to Knud, who said, 'Not bad for a couple of hours a night,' grinning as he shoved them into his pocket. I nodded, grinning too, but more at the fact that for two or three hours work a night, Knud and the lads could have earned as much working in MacDonalds. without the risk of physical harm or a lengthy criminal record either. I'd taken the time to read up on some of the studies on low-level drug-dealing and I knew that it paid really badly for the runners and the bottom-rung soldiers. Working for me wasn't much better than being an intern for some multinational, just doing it for pennies and hoping to get a foot onto the corporate ladder. The crew got about hundred pounds a week each, in cash, more if there was a rush, and Crew Two got slightly less. I let Knud worry about that, paid him extra to run the second crew, but my weekly earnings, after the last two or three months of hectic selling and hard graft, were easily into four figures every week. I was, as far as I could tell, rich.

'I love capitalism,' I said to no-one in particular.

Oscar frowned as he wrote down the figures in his notebook.

'Money creates money,' he said. 'It's a phenomenon.' Then he said, 'We have three parties tomorrow night, plus one not confirmed.'

'Can you get onto it?'

'I'm not a great salesman,' Oscar said, 'And they like to deal with you.'

'Ok, I'll call them.'

Oscar took out his new phone, we'd switched burners that day, and sent me the number. The FB page, Sunderland Sweat Treats, complete with price lists, images of succulent cakes and treats, plus quotes from satisfied customers, was a raging success. We could barely keep up with demand. If you knew the code, you could look on the FB page, message us with an order from the menu. The fact that the FB page had the artwork and photos from a real cake shop in town just made it more fun. Business was booming. I dialled the and listened for a reply, walking into the mid distance as he began speaking,

'Sunderland Sweet Treats– tasty treats delivered to your street!'

I'd made that up myself.

After a couple of minutes chat and friendly negotiation, I returned a minute or two later with a big smile on my face.

'New contract,' I said, 'worth six hundred pounds. I'll have to call Andy for more stuff.'

'I can do that,' Oscar said that.

'Great.' I gave him the list, then I asked, 'Have you made those extra donations?'

Oscar said, 'Yes. I set up an online account so it's all completely anonymous.'

I had a thought, fished into my bag, 'Here, I've got something for you.'

'What is it?'

'It's the original episode of Doctor Who.' I said, 'The one they put out the night Kennedy was shot, so they redid the entire episode the following week.'

'Oh,' Oscar said.

'I know you've got it,' I said as Oscar pushed his glasses back on his nose, a sure sign he felt uncomfortable, 'But this disk comes with all the extra camera shots that they didn't show on the night, but they kept them on film. They were only rediscovered about six months ago.'

'Really?' Oscar's face lit up.

'So you like it?'

'Aw, thanks Mickey!' he said, taking the DVD from him. 'I really like it.' His voice was loud. When Oscar was happy his voice rose from a nervous whisper almost to a shout.

An hour later I was at home, lying on my bed, staring at that picture of the Greek Island, imagining I was there. I closed my eyes and pictured myself sitting astride a bodyboard, floating in the warm, pale blue waters of the Adriatic, maybe a mile off the coast, just close enough to see the beach and the holiday villas and the vines climbing up the side of the hill above, but completely free, just drifting on a calm sea. Safe. I smiled to myself: Laura was clean, the rent was paid, I had a stack of cash and I intended to give up the dealing before I left school. Life was good. For a moment I thought of Emily, but then shoved that thought out of mind mind. Forget her, I told myself, I hadn't seen her in a couple of months now, through the simple expedient of not attending school, and that was all good with me but still, if I'm totally honest, I went to sleep thinking of her, and in my sleep I talked to her, told her what I'd done and what I thought, told her my plans, and when I talked to her the smile didn't leave my face because I was with her again.

One night I woke, still smiling from some fading moment, and I heard something, so I went to the window and looked out onto the street where a car sat, engine purring, but I couldn't make out the figure in the driving seat. I closed the curtains, went back to bed and dreamed some more.

'That car's here again,' Knud said.

'I see it.'

We stood and watched it for a while. 'Police?' Knud said.

'In an M5? Doubt it.'

He shrugged.

'He's not hiding.' I bent down and stroked Max's muzzle.

We watched on and off for the next hour, and at some point the car had gone. Thing is, you can't be deal drugs without it having some repercussions, or without people trying to take over your patch. A couple of months ago a crew tried to muscle in. They got me when I was alone: five of them, really gnarly chavs, all grubby white tracky bottoms and bad teeth. But then Knud arrived and gave their leader such a resounding headbutt it almost gave me whiplash just to witness it – they had to carry him away, holding him by a limb apiece.

Squads like that are easy to deal with really, you just have to be prepared. Wary. And violent, if necessary. If the police don't arrive with three dogs and an armed response team there'll always be some other crew, tooled up and prepared to get all mentalist, who want to take you down. I'd watched the Sopranos and Game of Thrones, and I'd studied Macbeth and Sun Tzu, so I was well-versed in the dynamics of treachery and survival. I'd learned from the Asian gang not to be conspicuous and not to be anywhere near the drugs, if possible. Andy had warned me that there was always another crew on the make, always another crew ready to make a bid for the throne, and to let him know if anyone turned up who acted or felt wrong. I knew the dog only took me so far in terms of safety. And in the absence of steel doors, which hadn't worked out too well for Ugly Pete anyway, I needed some extra insurance. Which is where Goldfinger's gun came in handy. I always kept it handy, for that moment when it might get serious.

The first week I began dealing I'd walked across town to the Echo24, quickly checked no one was paying me any attention, and walked down the ramp to the car park beneath the Thai restaurant, then down the stairs to the sub-basement. It was empty but lit by strip lights and I could see oil-stains dotted about the concrete floor. My footsteps echoed as I marked the route to the rear, where spare building repair equipment and stacks of random boxes stood, and where Goldfinger had stashed his gun, once upon a time. I wondered briefly if he was still in jail. If not, it might not be there. It was a huge open space, and there was a pickup truck parked at the back in its own bay, and I climbed up onto the rear bed of the truck and then reached up and pulled myself up to the steel girder, feet wrapping around it as I slid my way into the hidden alcove. The concrete was dry and dusty, a couple of bricks piled up, rubble and weirdly, an old tennis racket. You wouldn't know this place was here if someone didn't tell you, so how did a tennis racket get here? I pushed the rubble aside and found the canvas sack, hefted it, felt the weight, and then unzipped it to confirm the contents.

I took out the gun.

Three pounds of hardened steel with a knurled wooden butt. It felt good in my hand. Ergonomic. Crafted. Cold. I opened the cylinder of the revolver to check it wasn't loaded and then I aimed at the tennis racket, said, 'Bang! I whispered, then laid it down carefully. A fist-sized drawstring-bag chinked as I took it from the sack. The bullets. I counted twelve of them. I don't like violence. I'm not tough and I'm not trying to be, but who needs to be tough when you have a gun in your hand? God made men, they said, but the gun made them equal.

I packed everything back in the bag again, shoved the bag into my rucksack and clambered back down into the basement, walked out the stairs and then the ramp, out of the building, past the lovely smell of Thai cooking from the restaurant there, across the roads and back through town. That night we'd arranged to meet in the park and the crew were there, dotted about, and Oscar was sitting on a swing. He said, 'You're late.'

'I've been arranging some extra security.'

'Expecting trouble?' Oscar asked, pushing his glasses back on his nose and looking round to see where the boys were.

'My whole life,' I said.

I sat down on the same pew I used every time I visited. I was never sure what to say, I felt like I'd backed out of the deal God had given me. 'I'm trying to do good things,' I said. 'But I guess that no excuse.'

God was silent as usual, but I thought maybe he was listening.

'My plan is to get out of the business in six months or less.

When the summer arrives, this is all over.' I sat quiet, listening. Then I said, 'I know that's not good enough.' I frowned at a thought. 'Maybe,' I said, answering an internal voice that was asking me if I was committed to giving it all up, and asked me why I didn't consider just stopping now. I nodded and said, 'I'll think it over.'

On the way out I dropped a wad of cash in the collection box.

I took out the gun, checked the load and shoved it into the

back of my jeans. Oscar watched my, his lips silently

calculating something or other, and asked, 'Is it heavy?'

I shook his hips a bit, 'Yeah. Feels like it'll slip down my

trouser leg.' A little embarrassed, I took it out and shoved it into the pocket of my hoodie instead. I'd been carrying it all the time lately; had an ominous feeling of something about to go wrong. I was used to the weight, and to the feeling of security it gave me. But it was awkward.

Oscar was staring at something behind me.

I turned.

'Hello,' she said.

'Hi.'

I kept my voice cool but my heart lurched.

Emily.

'I haven't seen you since…'

'No,' I said. 'I've been busy.'

'So I hear.'

She looked at me and she tried to smile, but I kept my face closed off, my expression blank.

'You look *stern*,' she said. Then, 'Do you hate me?'

I wanted to tell her that what I felt for her was the opposite of hate, but I didn't, I just shrugged and said, 'No.'

'I'm sorry,' she said.

I nodded, asked her, 'Why did you come?'

She said, 'To tell you to stop this, Mick.'

'Only my sister calls me Mick.'

'Alright then, *Mickey*. I want you to stop.'

'Stop what?' but I knew exactly what she was saying.

'Stop all *this*,' she gestured around at the lads, his crew, 'Come

back to school. You're the smartest kid I know, and what

you're doing is just wrong.'

'What about us?' I asked.

'It's not about *us*, Mickey, it's about you.'

It *is* about us, I wanted to shout. You've hurt me and I'm

angry and this is all I can think to do to make you hate me

even more than I want to hate you. But all I said was, 'Well

then,' as though that was an end to it.

'I can't deal with you,' she said quietly, fierce. 'Not like this. I

can't fix you, I can't *save* you. Only you can save you. Don't you see?' Her eyes filled with tears. 'Please stop doing this

Mickey. It's so wrong.'

'*I'm* wrong,' I said.

'But you don't have to be.'

'Yes I do. I was born wrong.'

You *proved* it, I thought. You chose the nice kid, not the

wrong'un.

'Are you doing this to get at me?' she asked.

Yes, I thought. I'm absolutely doing this for you. Because you

hurt me so much, all I can think of is to do this.

'No,' I said.

She stared at me for a few moments, then turned away, head

down, and I watched as she walked away, watched her walk

all the way along the street. I knew she was crying, at least,

trying not to cry, I knew her that well. She reached the corner,

didn't look back as she turned out of sight. I watched the

empty space where she'd been for a while, then I reached into

the pocket of his hoodie, felt the comforting weight of the gun, smiled my Everything Is Alright Smile at Oscar and said,

'How's business?'

Oscar thought for a moment. 'Business is good.'

I think I impressed Andy.

He'd taken a bit of a risk taking me on like that, and I knew

that he knew, or at least strongly suspected me of the

takedown of the Khan crew, and the fact that I simply stood

there and waited for him, or whoever it might have been,

because I really didn't know who it might have been or how they'd have reacted, he knew that took foresight and it took guts. Looking back, I think I was mad, or maybe just desperate, but Andy thought I had what it took. And I discovered that I had a way of doing things. I had commitment.

So he gave me the job, watched over me for a few days to make sure I didn't flake out, and then left me to it. I was just a street-level seller, after all, one of his stable, though I ended up earning him more money than all the rest put together. I did well, got my little crew together, and the business blew up big time. I made a lot of money for Andy. Almost as much as I made for myself. Within a month business was booming, within three months I'd got it running like a well-oiled machine, I'd just be standing on the side-lines like an orchestra conductor, keeping everyone in time, everyone moving to the beat, servicing my little empire. Maybe it was a sign, the way I kept myself insulated from the cut and thrust of the business so early on, the methods I employed to keep everything sterile, Andy thought it was good business but I knew I just didn't like it, not really. I didn't really want to be part of it. He thought it was my management style, thought I was destined for big things, but in reality I was shy of it. The websites, the raffle tickets, the constant movement; I didn't want to be there. My habit of moving the crew round, which is a smart thing to do so long as the customer knows where to find you, different venues, unpredictable, it became my USP, part of the fun. A customer told me it was like the raves back in the '90s; Andy said that was back when he'd cut his teeth in the business, you never knew where it was all happening, then someone would whisper a venue, then everyone would know. I think the idea that I did that naturally, it charmed him. And the cake cake-delivery service, he thought that was funny. 'It's a moveable feast,' I said to him one day when he was dropping off some stuff.

'Yeah, and I suppose you're the Chef?' he said.

'Not the Chef,' I said, 'I'm the Number One.' We both watched as, over the road, another deal took place, and then I turned back to him with a happy grin on my face. 'I'm Dealer Number One.'

I glanced past him at a poster on the wall that someone had doctored. It read **Sunderland: ~~City of Culture~~ Sweet Treats.**

When it ended, it all ended so quickly and none of us saw it coming.

And really, Andy should have recognised me for who I was. He should have known.

Not just how I looked, but my *style*. He should have recognised me for the son I was. Because he knew him, he knew my Dad. Knew him from way back.

The last time we were together, long after we'd split, Emily

told me about a conversation she'd had with her parents.

Her Mum said she had to think of me as her first bad boy.

'Hopefully your last, too,' she added.

Her dad looked up over his breakfast.

'He isn't a bad boy,' she told them both. 'Not really.'

'They never are. Not really,' her dad said. 'But if he's doing bad things, what does that make him?'

And there was no answer for that.

What I was doing was generally known, if you wanted to know; what I sold was for sale, if you wanted to buy, and even knowing me made you seem cool, if you wanted to seem cool. In my absence I was becoming a bit of a legend.

Rumours spread of my exploits. I could get you anything. Could get you any*one*.

Some said I even delivered drugs to some of the teachers at school. That I had a BMX with the handlebars stuffed with two kilos of Skunk. I lived in a Georgian Townhouse that I'd paid for, cash. Apparently I owned three BMWs. I was becoming a celebrity outlaw: Robin Hoodie.

But Emily knew that most of this was just rumour built on rumour. That it was desperation disguised as success, the way some chavs put a big chrome exhaust onto some old banger of a car. She said she thought I wanted to be happy in the same way that someone might want to win the lottery, knowing they probably won't - sort a theoretical happiness that I was sure existed but wasn't sure how to go about getting it.

But really, she said, being sad was all I knew.

She told me she spent the next two or three months at home, not going out, in her room mostly, downloading music, doing all her schoolwork, and her grades improved to where they should have been all along, better even.

Her iTunes collection was becoming huge, both because she was living like a hermit, not seeing anyone (including Karl, my anger had killed that stone dead), and that left her revising for her exams like the A-grade schoolgirl she was.

Then winter came properly, it got really dark and cold, and all that stuff, and we didn't send each other cards. And then it was the Christmas holidays and our exams were only five months away and both our futures beckoned.

She kept on studying.

I kept on dealing.

'Well,' Mam said, 'This is nice.'

Laura carved the turkey as we sat around a table that was groaning beneath the weight of more food than our family had ever seen in one place outside of Aldi or Lidl where Mam usually shopped.

Even Martin seemed in a mellow mood, probably because I was paying for it all and he wasn't. He popped the cork on the bubbly and poured us all a drink. I shook my head, as he reached toward my glass, sticking to juice. One thing I'd learned is that I didn't like drugs, not even alcohol. I was becoming a puritan on that topic, which was deeply ironic. But Laura was clean, had been for a few months now, and I'd promised her I was giving up the business before my exams.

'You could still pass,' she said, later, as we watched a Christmas movie. 'Four or five months of hard revision and you'd ace them.'

'I could,' I said, thinking about it. 'I could.'

The truth was, I couldn't see the point. I was making more money than anyone I knew, including the Head Teacher of the school I never attended. The idea of giving that up to study and, maybe, in twenty years time, being able to earn about a tenth of what I was putting by right now seemed stupid. Beyond ridiculous.

Mum and Martin were sitting on the sofa and I was squashed onto the armchair with my big sis, feeling cosy as toast. 'It can't last,' she said quietly, 'You get successful enough and someone will decide to take you down.'

'The police?' I scoffed. 'There's not enough of them to run a Lollipop Lady to work.'

'I'm not thinking of the police,' she said. 'And I'm keeping my end of the deal,' she added, her fingertips playing with the ends of my hair.

She was. And I wasn't. So I reached over to the table, 'Here, let's pull a cracker.'

Martin switched channels.

'Turn that back!' everyone shouted, we'd been watching Home Alone. A family favourite. Sheepishly Martin turned it back, 'I was just going to watch the Queen's Speech,' he said.

'Hark the Royalist,' Laura muttered, giving me a wink and wrapping her arm round my shoulder. I studied her wrist, stroked her forearm with the tip of my thumb: clean and unmarked. A few faint scars but that was ok; I wasn't worried

about me so long as she was safe.

That was good enough for me.

I'd spent the week between Christmas and New Year touring

the estates to sell a bags of New Year's Eve goodies to chavs.

The estates were full of them: houses stripped bare, no

furniture except a widescreen and a tatty sofa, the stench of

unwashed skin and no one cared, cos skunk smelled so strong

you lost the ability to smell anything else, including yourself, or the three pitbulls you own that shit all over your living room carpet. These houses were so awful they made our grotty flat seem like a palace. But they had money, and they had FaceBook, so they were customers.

The last call of the day had tried to bargain me down but ended up buying more and paying more than he ever intended. One of them had to get off the settee and go out and get extra money. As I chatted with the main guy he told me to take a seat, offered me a cup of tea, but I'd said no. The house was so filthy I didn't want to touch anything except with the soles of my shoes, and I left as quick as possible, promising myself a shower as soon as I got home.

I hopped the bus back into town; I wasn't so rich not to take advantage of my student bus pass. Besides it had been snowing the couple of days earlier and the roads were slushy and cold. The bus was warm and quiet and I sat near the front so that I could peer forward and see what was going on ahead through the falling sleet. At one stop an old lady got off the bus and I went to help her down with her bags, and then went and sat back down. At another stop a man got on, I glanced up but didn't stare; some sort of student in a long coat, winter scarf, battered briefcase on a shoulder strap.

'Mind if I join you?'

I looked up again. It took me a few seconds to make the link between a face I'd known well and the person with that face who was now sitting next to him. 'Zuluboy,' I whispered.

Zuluboy smiled, 'Actually, it's Suleiman. Zuluboy was just a nickname.'

'Right.' Zulu Boy. Sulei Man.' I made the link. 'Of course.'

Suleiman settled into the double seat, taking up at least two thirds of it. He said, 'And how are you doing, little man?'

'I'm fine,' I said. 'You've changed, Zul... I mean, Suleiman.'

Suleiman smiled broadly. 'You think I look different?'

I nodded. 'You look like a teacher.'

He nodded. 'Correct. I lecture now. Classics and middle-eastern studies.'

'Weird,' I said, letting out a low whistle from puffed cheeks.

Suleiman raised an eyebrow. 'Does that seem incongruous?'

'It does, a bit.' I asked, 'How is Pete?'

Suleiman shook his head, his expression growing sombre. 'I like to think he got away. But I don't know.' And then, changing the subject, 'How's the dog?' he asked.

'Maximus is fine,' I said, 'Getting a bit fat.'

Suleiman smiled. 'You got my message then.'

'Yes. Thank you. I'm grateful.'

'You're welcome.'

We sat together for a while in companionable silence until Suleiman reached up and pressed the bell for the next stop.

'So when did you become a lecturer?' I asked.

'I was a professor at the university of Baghdad. Came here when the insurgents decided they didn't like intellectuals questioning their decisions on who to kill and who to let live. But when I came here I couldn't work for a number of years, until I got my passport...'

'So you worked for Pete.'

He nodded. 'Regretfully, yes. All those years of wrestling and boxing as a youth, stood me in good stead.'

Suleiman sighed, then stood up as the bus slowed down.

'You got your passport then?'

Suleiman nodded. 'And a job. Now I'm British, like you.'

'Congratulations,' I said. Then asked, 'Look, Zu, Suleiman, how did you get out? Out of the business?'

Suleiman studied me for a second or two, said, 'I just stopped.' Then he turned toward the door, said something to the driver. He turned back to Mickey and said, 'Have a successful New Year.'

'You too,' I said, watched him as the bus slowed, watched the doors shushed open, watched Zuluboy recede into a memory as Suleiman stepped down onto the street and strode away into the crowds.

Late January in Sunderland.

It doesn't get any colder than this I thought. Not a bright hard

fresh cold of deep snowdrifts and pale blue skies, more like a

grey, damp chill that burrowed through your clothes and into

your bones. I shivered again, pulled the zipper up on my

jacket, pulled my hoodie tighter to my face. Sometimes being a criminal wasn't much fun. Come to think of it, it was rarely fun, it was just the rewards that were good.

I tried not to think of the downside to being caught by the police, checked my phone again. The crew were late, they'd been persuaded, more like begged, to play an away match, just to rescue the honour of the school team, who'd lost every match this season so far, and they weren't due for an hour. Oscar was seeing a specialist at the hospital about his Asperger's syndrome. So I was alone and I was cold and I didn't like it. There was a stash, cut into tiny shares and secreted around and nearby, all I had to do was take the money and point out the location. I looked up as a car slowed, drew up beside me, and watched as the window wound down.

'What you selling?' the man inside asked.

'Nothing,' I said, ever careful of a police sting. 'But I could make a call and maybe find something.'

'You could make a call, could you?'

I shivered, there was something about this man I didn't like. I shrugged, 'Do you want anything?'

The man stared at me. 'Do I want anything? Are you asking me a philosophical question?'

I felt a rush of bad adrenaline. This man was wrong. He wasn't buying, but he wasn't leaving. 'Is there anything you want?' I asked.

'Is there anything I want?' the man asked. 'Another existentialist question.' His eyes narrowed. 'You're quite the philosopher.'

The car door opened a crack and I panicked, turned to run, but all of sudden someone was behind me and I found myself gripped by strong hands, holding me face down toward the ground, then spun round and facing backwards in a headlock, what the professionals call a 'guillotine' and being reverse-frogmarched toward the open car door. I tried to reach into my pocket for Goldfinger's revolver but a hand gripped mine, prised opened my fingers and took the gun from me.

'Nice toy,' the man said. Then, 'Get in,' and I was pushed into the rear seat. The door shut and I tried to open it but it wouldn't open from the inside. The man who'd grabbed me, a burly thug with a shaved head who looked about forty years old, had climbed into the passenger seat, he nodded to the driver and the car pulled away smoothly into the road.

'Who are you?' I asked.

'We're corporate asset-strippers,' the driver said to me in the mirror, grinning across at his co-driver. 'Now put your seatbelt on.'

The burly one nodded, 'Safety first,' opened the glove compartment and stashed the gun.

'Always,' said the driver, glancing down at the gun and then in his mirror and giving me a wink that wasn't friendly. 'If you try anything stupid, we'll beat you into mince. Understand?'

I looked away, nodded, the adrenaline had subsided and been replaced by a sickly knowledge that this wasn't going to end well. I was about to speak again but the passenger turned on the radio, fastened his seatbelt and slumped back into his seat. After ten minutes of driving he half-turned in his seat, his sharply broken nose silhouetted intermittently in the passing streetlamps, 'We're going to see someone very important, and you had better behave yourself, or you *will* get a slap.'

I sat in the back seat, the fear growing into something I could barely control now; this wasn't like having a row with Martin or negotiating a better cut with Andy, these guys played for keeps, I could tell. Not fifteen minutes ago I'd just felt cold, and now I felt sure I was going to be murdered. As my imagination began to play games with me I suspected that I was being taken somewhere to be tortured first, and then murdered. 'I don't know anything,' I pleaded. 'Nothing. Just let me go and I'll stop. I promise. I'm still at school.'

The man turned back again, 'Well, you're about to take a final examination, son. So *behave.*'

'We're almost there,' the driver said some minutes later and flicked the indicator to turn left, pulled the car in behind a warehouse-turned-apartment block still mid-transformation, then stopped, ratcheting on the handbrake. The burly man looked back and said to me, 'If you try and run away, son, I *will* catch you and I *will* break one of your arms, ok?'

I shivered, sick with fear.

'Ok,' I said quietly.

'Think this is a game? You think you can mess with us and nothing bad will happen? You think you can carry a piece but it won't come back on you? You're with the big boys now,' the man said grimly, 'So you'd better man up.'

We got out, the man gripping my arm at the elbow. The driver walked to a steel door, spoke into an intercom and a moment later a buzzer sounded as the door unlocked. We stepped inside, the door slamming closed behind us, and ascended a stone staircase.

At the top of the stairs we walked along a narrow corridor and then came to an iron-bound wooden door. I saw that it had a spy-hole and opened outwards. I was getting sick of doors with spy holes and steels frames, doors that opened outwards. The driver rapped at the door and we waited. A few moments later the door opened by a man who was so tough-looking he made the guy who had a hold of me look like a nun by comparison. 'This him?' he asked, giving me a good look-over. The driver nodded. 'Has he seen the picture?'

'Yeah. Seen the picture, wanted to see the kid for himself.'

I wondered who 'he' was. And why the big grudge against me?

'I'm just a schoolkid,' I said to the man at the door. The man looked at me again, frowned in a way that turned his face into a weathered rock of scars and fissures, said, 'Schools out, son. Come with me.'

The driver said, 'Oh, and he had this,' taking Goldfinger's revolver from his pocket and handing it over.

'Some schoolkid, huh?' The man took me by the shoulder and pushed me through the doorway. I stepped awkwardly inside and the door shut behind us, leaving the two men who'd caught me outside. The new man, now holding the gun, walked me along another corridor, 'This used to be a warehouse,' he said in a tone that had suddenly turned conversational. 'It was part of the shipyards. Now they're busy turning it into apartment blocks.' We turned a corner and the floors and wall were covered in thick polythene sheeting, I gave out a whimper of fear, almost wet myself, and the man turned, looked down at the polythene, then down at the gun he was holding, for all his tough look his face softened a little, and he said, 'You've seen too many movies, kid. In here.' He motioned me to go first, and I pushed at a door, legs shaking with fear so bad, fear of the unknown fate awaiting me in the next room. He stepped inside behind me.

The room was dimly lit and there were three men sitting at a table, coffee cups, a couple of empty pizza boxes and loose papers were strewn across it, a radio was playing quietly in the corner of the room.

One of the men had close-cropped hair, and tattoos were visible where he'd rolled up his sleeves, the second was taller, lean-built, with a shock of dark hair, greying at the temples. The third looked to be Indian, had pitch black hair and was wearing a pale blue polo-shirt and chinos. The crop-haired man glanced over, and the Indian glanced over too, but nothing was said. The man with the shock of black-tinged-with-grey hair looked up, stared at me for a long moment, stood and walked over. He stopped a pace away and stared at me, his pale blues eyes piercing and hard, and then he nodded, as though confirming something to himself. He looked me in the eye, face intent.

'Hello,' he said.

I stared at him.

'It's been a long time,' the man said and turned to the others, put his arm round my shoulder.

'Lads,' he said, 'I'd like you to meet my son. Mickey.'

Part Four

It's always been Laura and me.

One time back when I was a kid, just after the talking

backwards phase, we'd gone to the seafront together for

something to do. It was the beginning of summer, we'd done a flit a few nights earlier cos Mam didn't have the money to pay

the rent and we'd got a couple of rooms above a takeaway

close to the beach. So I was 'between' schools - in the way that

most of the population of Marley Potts estate are 'between'

jobs – and so one morning Laura and me decided to go to the

sea front.

The tide was out so we walked along the beach until we

reached the fairground, and we walked in through the gates,

attracted by the loud music and the smell of hotdogs and

candy, and we stood and watched the rides. Watched, mind.

Rides you pay for, but watching is free, but we had almost as

much fun from watching the rollercoaster and the dive

bomber and the dodgems as we would have from riding them.

Fairgrounds are best at night, when the lights and the noise

and the smells and the happy crowds can make you feel like

you're in a magical world, but during the day they're a bit

seedy, a bit worn-out, you can see the rusted bolts holding the

rides together, the candyfloss machine seems like it was

rebuilt from parts off an old washing machine, and empty wrappers and random bits of rubbish just float around on the breeze. But despite it being a chilly October morning, it was the fairground, and I was spellbound by the rides.

I liked the waltzer best.

In the weird way that my mind worked back then the waltzer seemed the most mathematical of rides. The cars spun on their axis, but the axis itself moved around the floor of the walzter, and the floor of the waltzer was also tilting on its all the time, while spinning slowly in the opposite direction to the cars, so the movement of each car seemed jerky and erratic, unpredictable, but after watching for a while I knew each car followed a clear and certain route.

Laura decided she had enough money for a hotdog and went off to buy one, but I stood where I was, transfixed. I locked my gaze onto one empty seat in one of the waltzer cars and tracked its movement, trying to measure the path of this individual seat, imagining that I was sitting on it, my gaze locked onto that empty seat and my mind calculating what I'd experience if I were sitting there, my head spinning in time with the waltzer car itself. In my imagination, I also attached a sparkling, golden star to the seat and followed the glittering elliptical trail it left as it moved through the air, one part of me imagining the sparkling movement of the star from where I was standing, the other part of me imagining myself sitting on the seat, and a third part of my mind again mapping the route of the star and me both as we spun.

Swamped by all these theoretical possibilities swirling around my head, I closed my eyes and let go.

I woke up some minutes later with Laura and a concerned-looking fairground barker standing over me, asking me if I was alright, the barker offering me a glass of juice as I sat up, groggy. Somehow, I'd fainted, the movement of the waltzer and my own focused imaginings had unlocked my grip on reality and I'd gone out. 'Dropped like a stone,' Laura told me as we walked home, sharing the hotdog, smothered in mustard and ketchup, which is free, so why not ladle it on?

'What happened?' she asked me.

'I stepped outside.'

'Outside of what?' she said, rolling up the now-empty hot-dog wrapper and dropping it into a bin, putting her arm around me and giving me a squeeze.

'Everything,' I said, 'outside of everything.'

'Everything?' She gave me a shove and called me stupid, but then she hugged me tighter as we walked, laughing to herself.

'I liked it,' I said, laughing too.

That was sort of how I felt now, that giddy rush, that sickly, head-spinning disorientating shift in my world as I attempted to track the careering movement of the waltzer. That was exactly how I felt now. Except this time I didn't like it. I didn't like it at all.

And no one was laughing.

As I looked round the room, bewildered, the tension in the room seemed to fade, the other two men at the table briefly grinned to each other, then at me, both saying a brief 'Hello'. I stood for a moment, trying to process what was going on.

'*Whu*?' I said, and the man, who seemed to be in charge of everyone in the room, looked at the gun in the tough-guy's hand and asked, 'This his?'

'Yeah.'

He looked back at me, a strange look on his face, 'I'm in the middle of a meeting, so go and get yourself a drink.' Then he spoke to the tough-looking man who'd brought him, 'Where's Lisa?'

'She's upstairs, I think.'

'Tell you what, go and find her, ask her to maybe take Mickey for a bite to eat. We've still got stuff to talk about, and the boy looks hungry.'

'Ok.' The man turned to me, his voice gentler now, more someone's rugged uncle than a thug with hurt and pain on his mind, 'Come with me young'un.'

'Oh, and put the gun somewhere, will you? Someone might get hurt.'

The two men at the table chuckled at this.

'Yeah.'

I followed the tough-looking guy, staring back at the man who was now sitting at the table again as though that whole scene hadn't just happened. We left the room by another door, walked up a wider concrete staircase, through a door and into another room, this one a spacious, more comfortable-looking living room. The man said, 'Lisa?' and a moment later a woman of about thirty came from another room, drying her hair with a towel.

'Mick asked me if you could look after the kid until he finishes the meeting.'

Lisa paused about ten feet away, studying me intently, her hazel eyes sharp but with a gentle twinkle of kindness, she wrapped the towel round her head in a sort of turban, 'Hello Mickey,' she said, 'Pleased to meet you.'

'Hello,' I said.

'I'm Lisa. I've heard all about you.'

My mind had gone a complete blank.

'Do you want to go for a bite to eat while we wait for your Dad's meeting to finish?'

I considered that word for a moment. *Dad*. Chewed it over. I nodded, still unable to speak. Lisa looked at the burly man. 'Harry, you've scared the boy,' she said, before looking back again at me, 'Don't worry, you're totally safe with me.' And looking at her, her bright eyes, the humour and kindness in them, I believed her. I needed to believe someone.

Harry coughed, 'I'll leave you to it then,' and left the room. I stood silently, still trying to work out what was going on, only the warmth in Lisa's eyes stopping me from running away, somewhere, *anywhere*, but here. She went over to a fridge-freezer and took out a bottle of coke and a couple of bars of chocolate. 'It's all we've got, I'm afraid. Your Dad has a sweet tooth. We mostly order in, or eat out. We move around a lot.' She frowned a little to herself, 'Hey, why don't we go and get a cheeseburger or something? As soon as I dry my hair and get some shoes on.'

Only then did I notice she was barefoot.

'So do I,' I said.

She smiled, 'So do you what?'

'Have a sweet tooth. Like, like my…' I paused, unable to say the work *Dad*.

'You're the double of him,' she said. 'I could be looking at a photograph of him from twenty years ago.'

'More like twenty-five,' I said, with a shy smile.

'Yes,' she smiled back, 'more like twenty-five,' she put the bottle and chocolate onto the bench top, 'You're tall like him too,' and I was about to say 'I've grown, the last few months,' but she'd gone back into the room she'd come from. I stood for a moment before hunger got the better of me, then tore open one of the chocolate bars and ate it in seconds flat, before opening the can and drinking most of that in one long gulp. Then I sat down in a comfortable chair, relaxing little and blew air out through pursed lips.

Lisa made me up a spare bed. 'We don't normally live here,' she told me, 'But our apartment is being redecorated. It's just about finished. Tomorrow, I'll take you to see it. There are a couple of spare rooms, you can choose one for yourself, if you like.' She gave me an apologetic smile, 'In the meantime we're sleeping here.'

'Ok,' I said. 'Ok.'

She shut the door and left me alone in the room where she'd made up the bed, using an old iron-spring cot and a cheap mattress. At least the quilt appeared to be new. I switched off the lights, undressed and then sat on the bed with my feet on the floor staring into the blackness. I wonder what I'm supposed to do now, I thought. There's probably a template for how to behave in this sort of situation, I'm sure lots of people are snatched from the streets, meet up with their long-lost father and spend the night sleeping in a camp-bed in a grotty room in an old warehouse.

I lay back on the bed, pulled the quilt across me and closed my eyes. In the darkness my mind wandered for a bit but then I slept, dreamt that I was flying a kite but the wind caught it and snatched it from my hands and I was running around trying to catch hold of the end of the string which was dangling in the air, tantalisingly close, just out of reach. I was running downhill, too fast, getting faster, knowing if I kept running I wouldn't fall, but if I kept running I would go too fast and when I *did* fall…

I woke to the sound of people talking in the next room and soft light oozing through the heavy wooden shutters. I climbed out of bed and pulled on my pants and t-shirt, and padded barefoot across to the window, the concrete floor was gritty and cold beneath my feet, and with some effort I managed to unhook the shutters and drag them open to let in the light and look out through grimy windows onto the world. The room I stood in was two or three floors above ground and looked out onto the river that flowed only a footpath's distance from the side of the building. The river curled away downstream to my right, two or three small boats bobbed at anchor, and across on the other bank were other run-down buildings, some in quite a state of disrepair, and further down was some sort of new industrial estate. One building opposite was being renovated and was heavy with scaffolding, workers and the faint noise of machinery drifting across the water. I pulled on my clothes, sat down to pull on my socks and fastened the laces on my sneakers, and opened the door into the room where Lisa was sitting having breakfast.

She looked up. 'Morning Mickey, hungry?'

'Yes,' I said, not even realising I was until I said it.

'Ok,' she was still eating, 'Sit down and I'll fry you up something.'

'No, eat your breakfast,' I said. I'm used to cooking for myself and to my eyes, the only unusual thing about this kitchen, apart from it being plonked in the middle of a dusty room in an old warehouse, was that on inspection it appeared to have a fully stocked fridge. Even now, when I was earning good money, the sight of a well-stocked fridge-freezer brought me a feeling of complete pleasure.

I squatted down and had a good rake through the food, deciding in the end that I was going to have a double egg, double bacon sandwich. I glanced over my shoulder to see Lisa watching me with amused eyes, she said, 'You're used to looking after yourself.'

I nodded.

She put down her knife and fork, carried her plate over to the Belfast sink that stood against the wall in the corner, ran it under a tap and placed it on a wooden shelf. Then she came over to where I was fetching a box of eggs and, gently but firmly, took them from my hands and said, 'This is my kitchen, so sit.'

I sat.

I watched her make my breakfast. It felt good to watch someone cooking for me. Sometimes Laura would cook, but mainly I was my own chef. Always had been. And now here was someone volunteering to cook for me. Of all the things that had happened over the last twelve hours this was the strangest because it was the only thing I could compare to my previous life. I think, for the next few years I counted my life pre and post-Lisa's fry-up. It was only small thing, but it had momentous implications, someone looking after me that first time. 'Where's Dad?' I asked. The word felt dry in my mouth, but that could have been the dust and grit that seemed to coat the surfaces inside this building.

Lisa turned to me, a smile on her face that didn't fully mask the apprehension. 'He's got a meeting this morning. An important one.'

'Is it dangerous?' I ask.

She turned back to the frying pan. 'What? No. Just a meeting.'

I knew she was lying but didn't know what else to say so just asked, 'Does he do a lot of dangerous things?'

'Why do you say dangerous?'

I thought of the men who lifted me, they weren't accountants or doctors, they weren't builders or veterinarians or postmen; they were thugs. 'I guessed,' I said.

With her back to me she gave the slightest of nods. 'He's going to retire soon. This deal will be the final one, we're going to make a killing, he says. Then we are retiring.'

'Lots of money,' I said.

'Yes.'

'Where are you going to live?' I asked.

She used a spatula to transfer the eggs and bacon to a slice of bread, looked at me and I said, 'Ketchup please,' and she poured on some ketchup from a bottle and then placed another slice of bread on top, sliced it into two and handed it to me on a plate.

'Eat up,' she told me, 'And don't worry about your Dad, he's Teflon, like this pan. Nothing sticks to him.'

'I'll wash,' I told her between bites.

'My kitchen,' she repeated, looking round, 'I'll wash. You dry.' Then she sat down opposite me. 'I'll take you to see the apartment this afternoon and you can see how we really live.'

I nodded. The fry-up was good, and like I say, the events in my life can be divided by that meal, before and after, but at that moment it was merely delicious, too good to waste time speaking when I could be eating. I wolfed down the food and she sat opposite, watching me.

A couple of hours later one of Dad's business partners arrived. The one who'd driven me in the car, he picked up a bag of things, said a quick hello and goodbye to Lisa and gave me a wink before leaving. It was weird, I'd become a member of the club, I'd passed some sort of initiation test without even knowing. Lisa watched him go, studied the door for a couple of minutes after it closed, then said, 'Negotiations continue.'

'Negotiations for what?'

She went to the window and said, 'Look over here.'

I went and looked out of the window. 'All those buildings, your Dad either owns or is part owner of them all. Apart from that one,' she pointed at the building where work was being done. 'And he needs to buy that to complete his business plan.'

'Sounds like he's playing real life Monopoly.'

'He is. We own all the key buildings on either side of the river for four hundred metres, apart from that one. It's all about the real estate.'

I studied the buildings, then the land behind them where the ground rose up above the river. I looked at the roads to either side, then thought for a moment. 'Someone wants to buy this land,' I said. 'For a development.'

She turned to me and stared,' Did your Dad tell you that or are you just a smarty-pants?'

'Top set,' I told her.

'In what, Monopoly?'

I nodded and she gave me a conspiratorial grin as though to say, *ok*. She said, 'The council, in partnership with the European Union, are planning to build a bridge over the river. It's part of the drive to increase business, reinvigorate the docks…'

'City of Culture.'

'That too. A thriving business life leads to more money for culture. So they say.'

'It's an artery, I said. 'The bridge.' I studied the waste ground either side of the river, 'Or maybe more like a coronary bypass.'

'Now you sound like your Dad. What it will be, is the best bridge on the river for transporting goods, mainly Japanese cars, of which this town produces half a million a year. They need to buy the land below the bridge and either side, to clear the site.'

'So why's that guy renovating that building?'

'He'll get a lot more for it if people are living there.'

'So he renovates it, lets the properties and a year later the government gives him a massive amount of money to sell up.' She nodded.

'But if the site was derelict it wouldn't be worth as much.'

'For every pound he spends he's likely to get fifty back.'

I said, 'If you own all the properties, you can hike the price.'

She nodded again. 'We'd own all the land. We've already put in development plans, not real ones, just good enough to hack the price up a few thousand per cent when we own it all.'

'You'd be like a cartel. You could dictate the price.'

'That's the plan.'

'I thought he was a rival drug dealer,' I told her.

She shook her head. 'No. You *were* going to get taken down though. When your Dad heard about that he stepped in and lifted you himself. To keep you safe.' She pursed her lips, 'I'm not sure how much I should tell you but amongst some old friends of your Dad's there's a turf war going on. You and your schoolboy friends were only a small part of that; a lot of the main dealers were replaced a few months ago. Things went quiet but they're going to kick off again soon. So your Dad snatched you out of the way.'

'What about my crew?'

'They've been warned off.'

'It's like the tide,' I said. 'Someone builds castles in the sand, then the tide comes along and washes it away. I took over Khan's business, I built a better sandcastle, then the tide comes in and someone takes over my business.'

'Not yours. Andy Logan's. You were just a franchise.' She looked at me. 'Logan had guys like you all over the place; miniature dealers who worked through him.'

'He gets a slice from every dealer and doesn't have to do any work,' I said.

'He can't. Not now. He's dead,' she told me. Her voice flat.

'Andy? I...'

'Nothing to do with your Dad,' she said. 'He's into real estate nowadays.'

I felt sad more than shocked. Andy, I hardly knew the guy, but he'd played fair with me. If selling drugs to a fifteen-year-old to sell onto other kids can be defined as anything approaching fair.

I said, 'Don't suppose you ever heard of a guy called Ugly Pete?' and was about to continue but she said, 'You need to forget about all that life Mickey. And keep clear of the new guys. They're bad people, and I mean seriously bad. Way beyond the point of just needing to be. The business has always been unpleasant, but it's going to get a lot worse. Meth is coming, and you *really* don't want to be part of that.' She shook her head, almost as a way of stopping herself from speaking further. 'But you're safe now.'

I said, 'How long has Dad known about me. Did he keep track of us?'

'As long as I've known him I knew he had two kids. But he stays away. If people could track you down they'd maybe try and get to him through you.'

I thought for a moment. 'I need to phone my sister.'

She looked as though she was going to argue but instead she just nodded. I went into the room where I'd slept, picked my phone from the table and tried to call Laura. No reception. I looked at the walls; they must have been a metre thick. Solid stone. Built a century before people had mobile phones. I pocketed my phone and went back into the room where I found Lisa washing the dishes.

I dried.

I said, 'It's a bit of a shock, this whole situation. I mean, meeting my Dad, finding out he knew where I was all this time. And Andy, dead.'

She nodded. 'Mick says life is like a game of Jenga. People pile things on top of other things, they build homes, get jobs, they buy and sell, they live their lives thinking it's going to be the same forever. They forget how precarious everything is beneath them. They forget that even as they're building things up, time is undermining everything. Then one day something small happens, way down below where you think the solid ground is, and the whole things comes crashing down. One minute everything is fine, next thing there's a total landslide of events.'

'He sounds like a barrel of laughs.'

I polished the last dish, washed my hands and dried them on a paper towel, threw it into the bin from about ten feet away, a looping arc that saw it plop into the bin without touching the sides.

'Three points,' she said.

'I need to go home and check on everyone,' I said.

She said, 'Let me check with your dad, first. But it should be ok.' She smiled at me and I could see why Dad liked her, she was lovely; she gave off a feeling of calm. And her eyes were kind. She said, 'Tell you what, let's go for a drive first, do a bit of shopping. Then I'll drop you off.'

'I'm not sure about these jeans,' I said.

Lisa had taken me shopping, which was a surprise, and she helped me buy clothes which were a lot more expensive than I'd ever bought before. 'I feel a bit of a toff.'

'Don't worry,' she said, 'You're still the waif you've always been, just a better-dressed version.'

'Is that the smooth-talking that won my Dad's heart?'

She smiled, 'Believe it or not, he pursued me.'

'How did he win your heart?'

She paid at the desk using a platinum card. Then she gave me the bags of clothes I'd just bought and as we walked away she said, 'I'm not sure he has, yet. He's still on probation.'

I looked at Lisa. Dad must be about forty, which is pretty ancient, but Lisa didn't even look thirty. I couldn't be sure how old she was and didn't want to ask, but she looked about the same age as my English teacher Miss Wright, and she's only twenty-seven. Lisa is slim and pretty and really looks like she's got her life together. The only question mark I'd raise is her relationship with my old man, which is a bit dubious, but maybe she has a thing for bad guys. Or maybe she just has a thing for my Dad.

'How'd you two meet?' I asked.

'A long story,' she said. 'I'll tell you some time.' And with that we left the shop, walked to the car park. As we walked she said, 'I want you to be careful, Mickey, for the next few weeks, keep your eyes open and if you see anything that feels dodgy, don't stop to think, don't try and work out some sort of complex scam in that complex head of yours, just turn and run.'

I tried that when Dad's crew caught me, I thought. It didn't work. 'Did he tell you to tell me that? Dad?'

She nodded.

'I guess he understands dodgy better than me.'

'He understands dangerous better than anyone I know,' she said. 'Try not to worry too much though, there'll be someone keeping an eye on your home.'

I thought of the BMW that I'd seen parked outside of my bedroom window a few weeks ago. Wondered how many nights it had kept watch over me and Laura and Mam.

We got into her car and she took me home.

She dropped me at the corner of the street and I walked to the front door, let myself in, juggling shopping bags and door key and was just about to go down to my room when Laura burst out of the living room.

'Where the hell have you been?' she shouted, and then she threw her arms around me, hugging me tight. I let her hug me, then let her continue to shout at me too. 'We were totally worried sick! Where have you been?'

'Shopping?' I said.

'Jesus Christ Mickey, even Emily came round. Everyone was at their wits' end.'

I was dumbstruck. Emily? 'What's happened?'

'Oscar saw two guys drag you into a car, yesterday.'

'That was just, erm…' I ran out of words, not sure how I'd explain the events of the last twenty-four hours.

'Are you in trouble?' she asked, her voice frantic. Then a pause, 'You've been shopping? We're all sitting round thinking the worst and you go *shopping*?'

'Will you let me explain?'

'Yes,' she said, 'But I'd better call Mam. She's off to the police station to report you missing. And Emily; I'll call Emily. Unless you want to?'

'No! No...' I said hurriedly, 'You call her,' a combination of embarrassment over how Mam had probably behaved in front of her, God knows what had gone on in my absence, plus my own still-simmering hurt, there was no way I wanted to speak to her.

'Hey,' I said to Laura before she disappeared to make the calls.

'What?' she stopped and turned. 'What is it?'

I looked at her. 'I saw Dad. That's where I was. With Dad.'

And just like that, Laura's face fell.

She stared at me for a few moments, then without a word, she turned and went into the living room, leaving me standing in the hall with my shopping bags wondering why exactly *nothing* in my life made any sense. I took a deep breath and went down into the basement, dropped my bags, went back upstairs and into the yard to pet Maximus. He was sun-puddling in a shaft of light, eyes half open, one ear tweaked toward the door as I stepped into the yard. He gave a little whine, half a bark really, and turned his head. 'Hey, Max,' I said, squatting down beside him and stroking his ear. He rolled onto his back, legs waving in the air, tail flicking, mouth open, panting as I scratched the folds of skin around his neck. 'I'm sure you're part bulldog,' I said. 'You're all wrinkly and your face is a bit flat. Someone said you're a canary dog but you're not a canary dog. You'd be all yellow.'

Max didn't take this as an insult.

'Want to go for a walk?' I asked and at the sound of this word he was wide-awake and leapt up ready to go. We went inside and I took his leash from the coat hook, fastened him up but before we went out I went to the toilet and took Goldfinger's gun from my pocket. Dad must have left it lying on the kitchen workbench so I'd re-appropriated it, dunno why. It was no use to me, but I felt some sort of ownership, it was part of my history, not his. I'd carried it round with me on my shopping trip with Lisa. I lifted the cistern and dropped it in, bullets and all. If nothing else it'd help save water. I put back the lid and washed my hands. Then I went back into the hall to collect Max.

We left the house together, walked out into the front street, ambled slowly to the park and then I let him go for a run. The day was still short and it was growing dark when we got back and I didn't bother going into the living room to speak to anyone, but as I went downstairs Mam's boyfriend Martin collared me. I heard his footsteps behind me and turned. 'Hey,' he said. 'You. Sackless. I want a word with you.' I stopped and waited until he got really close, listened to him while he tried to tell me off for worrying his gravy-train, my Mam, unnecessarily. I let him go on for a minute or so, spittle flying in my direction as he tried to assert himself in some meaningful way. 'Are you *listening* to me?' he shouted.

'Don't try to be my dad,' I said. 'Cos you're not.'

'I'm the closest thing to a dad you've got, you ungrateful little shit.'

I shook my head. 'No, you're not. And if you don't step away now, my dog is going to bite you so bad you'll need an arse transplant.'

He looked down at Maximus, whose jaws were only inches from his buttocks and as if on cue Max began to growl, low, in the back of his throat, and he teeth began to bare. I looked at Martin and said, 'If you speak to me again, I swear, this dog will tear off your arse cheek.'

He backed off.

I went into my room, sat down on my bed. I wondered where my Mam was when Martin was doing all this. I wondered why she let it happen. I couldn't think of any reason why she would allow it, other than she was useless. Great taste in music, if you like trip hop and acid jazz, and pretty too I guess, if a bit faded, sort of like a paper poppy a few days after Armistice Day.

But otherwise, useless.

I went up to the bathroom, undressed and took a shower, went back to my room wearing only a towel and dried myself off, then changed into some of my new clothes. In one of the bags was a new phone that Lisa had bought me. The only number stored in it was her number. I texted her: *can you come and pick me up.*

She texted back minutes later: *you ok?*

I replied. *No.*

She replied: *half hour.*

I was sitting on my bed waiting for Lisa, staring at poster on the wall. The Greek island of Paxos, the text told me, is much smaller than its neighbour Corfu, and the main source of income is mainly through the growing of olives and a small but enthusiastic tourist industry. There are only two very small tourist centres on the island, which measures less than twelve miles in circumference and only has a couple of beaches. My bedroom door opened and Laura came in. She sat down on my bed. 'Panic over then,' she said. 'You're safe.'

'I'm retired too.'

She raised an eyebrow. 'You see Dad once and then retire from your criminal activities.'

I nodded. 'He only got involved because some people were going to do me over.'

She shook her head, 'What, like, does he read the Criminal Gazette or something? Or is he a twat by day and a superhero by night? How did he know what you were doing?'

'He keeps an eye on us.'

She shook her head. 'No,' she said, voice flat. 'No, he doesn't.'

'He does.'

'He hasn't done a very good job then.'

'I'm going to see him,' I said. 'I'm going to spend some time with him.'

'Don't involve me, Mickey,' she said. 'Please.'

'Why not?'

She looked incredibly sad. 'Thing is, this is just another one of your mad schemes. Like the kites. And the drug-dealing. Then Emily. Now it's Dad. And in three months when he lets you down what'll it be then?'

'He won't let me down.'

'He's been letting you down your whole life.'

'Not this time.'

'You don't know him.'

'I know how he feels about me. About us.'

'There's no *us* in this, Mick.' Then she straightened up and said, 'Let's not fight, bruv. If you want to go and be with Dad that's ok. I'll square it with Mam. It's not like you're invested in this place,' she said. 'We've moved so often that everywhere probably seems temporary.'

'Why has she not come to see me? She sent Martin to tell me off.'

'I dunno,' Laura said. 'She's just staring at the TV, won't even come into the hall.'

'She's useless,' I said.

'I think she's scared,' Laura said.

'Of who, me?' Then I realised who she was scared of. I stood up and Laura said, 'Look at you, all smartened up and things. You've even had a haircut.'

'Lisa took me to this place.'

'Lisa?'

'Dad's girlfriend.'

Laura nodded, eyes a little downcast. Then she looked up again, forcing a bright smile, I recognised it. The Everything Is Alright smile. A family trait. 'You look really handsome.'

'You like it?' I said, pulling on a jacket Lisa had persuaded me to buy, using Dad's credit card.

She nodded, still sitting on the bed, looking over at me as I opened the door, 'You're all *new* Mick.'

'Will you look after Max?' I said.

She nodded. 'Sure. Keep in touch.'

I nodded and left the room containing the only three things I really loved and could rely on: Laura, Max, and my Greek Island poster.

Lisa was already waiting out on the street, her car idling when I got there. I climbed in and she looked at me. 'You ok?'

I nodded, smiled. 'I'm all new,' I said.

I nearly believed it, too.

Life with Dad.

It was different.

After that first night, and a couple more squatting in that

warehouse, Lisa drove me to their apartment, their real

apartment, over in Newcastle. A real city, I'd said, and she laughed. Unlike Sunderland.

I told her the logo I'd invented. "Sunderland: Built by Monks. Full of Drunks. City of Culture Twenty Twenty-One." Lisa laughed at this. She was a Doncaster lass she said, but she got the rivalry between Sunderland and Newcastle, said for her it was Donny and Sheffield. Everywhere across the north, towns were rivals, she said, like pit dogs, fighting over scraps, while down south the real money and the real decisions were being made.

Then she explained about her and Dad; they were just hanging round the derelict quayside warehouses while he closed the deal, and some evenings when he worked late they stopped over. They liked to keep mobile, but they had apartments dotted around and this one we were going to was their main one in the north-east. The deal was closed, she told me, only needed a couple of signatures. Dad would be in later so I had time to settle into my own room before he got there.

We drove across the swing bridge and arrived. It was really, really nice. Right on the river; an old building, a big arc of apartments. Lisa parked and we went inside, pushing through old carved doors with stained glass that gave the entrance a hue of many different shades of light. There was a broad staircase to the right, with a dusty old carpet running up the centre; a chandelier hanging down from the middle of the ceiling. To the left an old fashioned lift with the iron cage door you had to drag across before it worked. It smelled of oil and iron and polish.

We went up to Dad's apartment, which was on the top floor. Actually, it seemed like it was most of the top floor, which impressed me. Lisa showed me round, pointed out the various rooms, let me choose a room from the three available and left me there to make myself at home. The entire place had just been redecorated. My room had a double bed, an iMac, a TV with every conceivable channel and movie available at the flick of a remote.

I know, I checked.

After half an hour of scrolling through what the TV had to offer, I used the iMac to check up on the dozens of orders for Sunderland Sweetmeats already backing up on the FB message page. They say rust never sleeps, and as far as selling drugs, that's absolutely true. I looked at the page for a few moments, then scrolled through the options and closed down the page.

I heard noises in the living room, it sounded like Dad had returned with some other guys. I stayed in my room, caution getting the better of me, but then there was a knock on the door. 'Come in,' I said, and Dad came into my room. He was holding a tray that held a plate piled with bacon sandwiches, and a mug of tea. 'Thought you might be hungry,' he said, setting it on a table by the TV.

I didn't know what to say. 'Thanks,' was all I managed.

'Lisa made it,' he said and he paused, studied me, but I didn't look at him. He said, 'Come and join us in the living room. Eat your sandwiches first. No rush.'

'Thanks,' I said again, and he left the room. In a drawer I found a hard drive packed with movies so put one while I ate my sandwich. After thirty minutes of watching Jason Statham kicking increasingly unbelievable arse I took my now-empty tray out and went to the kitchen to wash up, ignoring the four guys chatting in the living room. As I ran hot water to wash the dishes, the Indian guy who I'd first seen with Dad came in.

'Hey, Little Mickey,' he said, and that reminded me of Ugly Pete and Zuluboy, which made me feel sad and upset. I think tears came to my eyes 'cos the Indian guy put an arm around my shoulder and said, 'I've got two boys, you know, a little bit older than you.'

'So?' I said, and sniffed.

He gave me a squeeze with the arm round my shoulder. 'It's tough for boys, 'cos we don't show emotion, right? And all this is a massive shock to you.'

'Right.'

'That's what mums are for, eh? Getting upset.'

'Yeah,' I sniffed again. 'Boys don't cry.'

He grinned at that, 'Right. Boys don't cry.' He left go of me, 'I'm Raj by the way. Come and join us. Here, I'll dry,' and he took the towel and helped me wash up. He reminded me of Oscar, but with better people skills.

'Are you an accountant, Raj?' I asked.

He frowned, 'How'd you know that? Did Dad tell you?'

I shook my head. 'Just a wild guess.'

We walked back into the living room, 'You're very perceptive,' he said, and smiled again, 'So is your dad. That's why he's so successful at what he does.'

'What does he do?' but by then we were sitting down with the guys and one of them was saying, 'So I put the gun barrel in his mouth and asked him, if he wanted to live, could he recite the Lord's Prayer?, him being a Welshman and probably a bit more religious than me.'

Dad winked at me as I glanced across at him. He looked at the guy talking and said, 'Sounded convincing to me.'

'Naah, I couldn't understand a word. Well, maybe one word in three or four.' He mimicked the guy, 'Ah ahtha, a-oed e aye ame.'

They laughed.

I smiled a bit, just to show good face. The guy talking looked at me and said, 'We were inspired by you, Junior. Your gun. The hand-cannon. We used one just the same. Very visually effective. Real visceral impact.'

'That was my feeling too,' I said, which got a chuckle.

'I prefer a five-seven', Dad said.

'Tart's gun,' the guy said.

'I haven't got hands like shovels, Teez,' Dad said, and grinned, 'Anyway,' he said, 'After the negotiations, we got the contract signed and witnessed, as per. So we now own all the buildings on either side of the site of the proposed road-bridge for three hundred yards in each direction, apart from two that we're still negotiating. And the Government is going to start asking for estimates in about three months.'

'So we get the final sigs and start building in a couple of weeks,' the Indian guy said. 'Don't have to do much, just start work to show good faith. Send in the plans, they don't even need to be approved, and then hand in the books with our proposed investment and business plan.'

'How much will you make?' I asked.

The room went quiet and everyone turned to look at me. The Indian guy went to speak but Dad said, 'We're looking at just under ten million, Mick, for an outlay of less than one million.'

'A one thousand per cent return,' I said, impressed.

'What did you make with your schoolboy scam?' Teez asked me.

I thought for a moment, 'About eight hundred percent per day,

Give or take.'

Teez grinned, said, 'Hey, this kid is making more than us.

Sign him up.'

Dad said, 'He's already signed up. Aren't you, Mickey.'

I nodded.

The night dragged on and when the guys began to open cans of beer and Dad went for a bottle of bubbly I made my excuses and went back into the bedroom, and just lay there listening to them celebrating their business deal. I've had time to think since then and I've realised that, obviously, not every business deal is criminal in nature, but I think they all depend to some degree on someone taking more than they actually deserve, or earn. There's no such thing as a win-win deal. Someone always wins more than the others. I suspect that Dad made a lot more than the rest. Even in his own home, amongst friends, he was quiet, a little withdrawn, but the other guys seemed to give him respect.

'Why do the other guys give Dad respect?' I asked Lisa,' the next morning over breakfast.

'He's got the vision,' she said. 'The attention to detail, the management skills. The charisma.'

'I thought you had to be tough too,' I said. 'To lead a gang.'

Toast popped up and Lisa took it out and began buttering it.

'Your dad can be pretty tough when he needs to be. But he's smart enough to not use that part of him, not when he's got other guys to do it for him.'

'Like Teez.'

She nodded. 'Teez is tough but not so smart. He's not stupid mind, and he wouldn't be happy if you acted like he was. But he's loyal to your dad. They've been friends forever.'

'Reminds me of Max.' She raised an eyebrow and I said, 'I have this big dog, Maximus.'

'Oh yeah, I heard. Skinny kid with a big tough dog. Running the show. That's what your dad said when he first saw you.'

'When was that?'

She paused. 'Look, speak to your dad. I could tell you all this, but speak to him first. If there's stuff he leaves out, I'll fill in the gaps.'

I realised that I hadn't said much to Dad, nor him to me. I thought of Raj, Dad's Indian accountant, and what he said the night before, about it not being easy to show emotion. 'I will,' I said.

'Good lad.'

I thought of Raj telling me that was what mums were for. Lisa seemed very maternal. Maybe she could help me. 'I don't know how though,' I said.

'How what?'

'How to speak to him. Will you tell me how to speak to him?'

'Sure,' Lisa said. 'Course I will,' and she gave me a hug. Not like a hug from Laura, or even Max, but it was nice. She smelled nice and she was pretty and kind and I thought again, what are you doing here with Dad?

The next morning I woke feeling more comfortable and content than I could remember. It wasn't that I felt like I'd arrived at my spiritual destination, or that I'd found my place in the world, it was just that I no longer had to be on my guard. I no longer had to be on permanent lookout for everyone and everything. I didn't know

Dad beyond the few words we'd spoken but I could see he was someone who would do all the things I'd been used to doing since I was old enough to realise there was no one else to do it. Now there was someone else. Of course, I should have thought a bit deeper, and realised that the reason I'd spent my life on edge and stressed was precisely because he hadn't been there doing it for me. For us. But at that moment I just felt safe.

And that's all I'd ever wanted.

After a while of lying beneath a lovely warm quilt of security I heard a knock on the door. 'Yeah?'

'Can I come in?'

It was Dad. 'Sure,' I said.

The door opened and he popped his head in, 'You want to come for breakfast?'

'Yeah. Great.'

'Ten minutes?'

'Right.'

'Ok.'

The door shut again. I don't know who'd felt more awkward, me or him. Him, I think. I got up, pulled on my jeans and left my bedroom. I had to shower and get ready. Thirty minutes later we were climbing into his car. 'Your hair's still wet,' he said.

'It's getting dryer,' I said.

I fastened my seatbelt as he started the car, and we pulled away into the main road. 'Thought we'd go down the coast,' he said. 'Home. There's a café sells breakfast.' He glanced at me, 'You're not like, a vegan or anything?'

'No.'

'You go to church?'

I burst out laughing and he glanced at me, smiling, 'What did I say?'

'It's just a funny thing to ask.'

'There's no guide book for what to ask,' he said. 'Believe me, I checked.'

I leaned over and plugged my old iPod into the dash, fiddled with the knobs, 'You did research on how to be a long-lost dad?' I asked.

'Sure. Googled it.'

'I suppose there aren't many guides,' I said.

'Actually, there are,' he said, 'But they're useless.'

'And actually, I do go to church,' I added, 'just lately, but it's nothing formal. I just go for a chat with God.'

He flicked the indicator and the car slid up onto the motorway ramp. 'And what does he say?'

'Mostly he just listens.'

He nodded.

'I'm not religious or anything,' I said, 'It's just nice to talk to someone who's not a professional do-gooder.'

'God's not a do-gooder?'

'Well, no,' I said. 'To be honest, the church is just a place that was open one time, when it was raining.'

It was his turn to laugh.

I pressed a button on the dashboard and the music from the iPod came on. Zero 7. Mam's favourite. I sat back on the leather seat and closed my eyes. I could hardly hear the engine, it was so quiet, though when I opened them at one point we seemed to be doing about ninety-five so I closed them again, relaxed. The next time I opened them we were parking on a cobbled lane up above the river Wear, right by the entrance to the docks, and I could see herring gulls wheeling. 'Come on,' he said, getting out. I unplugged the music, jammed it into my pocket and followed him along an old lane until we crossed a footbridge and reached a café that seemed to have been built into the side of a warehouse. The walls were made of layers and layers of very thin, soot-blackened bricks, the entire wall seeming to bow slightly in the middle. There was a jaunty sign in the window that said 'All day breakfasts.'

He opened the door and went in, and we stood looking at the menu written on a chalkboard while all around us came the smells and sounds of a busy cafe. 'Full English,' he said, 'What about you?' and when I said, the same he gave me a twenty and told me to order while he snagged a window table, where a couple were just leaving. I went to the counter and ordered breakfast. The lady behind the counter said, 'I'll bring it over. You sitting over there with your dad?'

'Yes,' I said, and the feeling I got from that single word was just magic.

When it arrived we sat and ate, not saying much but after a while he said, 'My dad, your granddad, was a fisherman, and he used to come to this café for breakfast, three in the morning sometimes, depending on the tide.'

I'd never thought of my Dad having a dad. There didn't seem room to fit that person in my head. But now, it was like he was unfurling a carpet, laying out a family history I'd never been aware of. He went on, 'I couldn't face doing that, to be honest. But the fishing industry was dying out anyway, all the boats getting burnt by Europe, fishermen paid off. I joined the army when I was sixteen, met your mam, left the army when I was twenty, had you two…'

'Why'd you leave the army?' I asked, which was not the question I wanted to ask but it'd do for starters.

'I got shot,' he said.

'Oh.'

He looked at me for a long moment then winked, and I wasn't sure what to say. He said, 'We had Laura quick, then you, three years later. I'd left the army, I had a job…' he paused.

'Then you left.'

He nodded. 'The job was destroying me. Sucking up to a boss I didn't respect, selling stuff I didn't like, to people I didn't care for… so I decided to have a change of career.'

'Another one.'

'Yeah,' a rueful smile, 'Soldier, salesman…'

'Criminal,' I finished his sentence.

'Yes.'

He sliced his last rasher of bacon, ate it, then took a long gulp of tea. 'The tea here is the best in the world.'

'Who told you that?'

'My Dad.'

'Dad's are not always right.'

'Fair point.' He put down his cup, looked at me. 'You've got questions.'

It wasn't a question.

I said, 'I've got sixteen years of questions.'

He sat quiet.

I said, 'I can't take it all in. Just tell me why you left.'

He used his napkin to wipe his mouth, though there was nothing there to wipe, and then he picked up mine, reached over and carefully wiped my mouth. 'I haven't wiped your chin since you were a baby.' Then he put down the napkin and said, 'I found I was good at crime. I developed a niche.'

'What sort of niche?'

'I extort criminals. They're never going to the police. Oh, they'll grass you up, as soon as look at you, if they have something on you, but they won't actually go and complain. I discovered that I could rob criminals and so long as I scared them more than they scared me, it'd be fine. So I put a squad together.'

We were interrupted by the lady coming to clean away our dishes. Dad stayed silent; when she'd gone he said, 'You did something very similar.'

'You know?'

'I've been back in the area a few months. I kept an eye on you.'

'But why did you leave?' I asked again. There were so many questions to be answered, but this was the big one. 'Why'd you leave *us*?'

He looked at me, coolly, 'You were my one weakness. My vulnerability. If I had a family, I could be got at. So I left.'

'You could have given up your life of crime. Most people would have.'

He shook his head, 'I couldn't not be who I was. Who I am.'

'I don't know who I am,' I said.

'Neither did I when I was your age.'

'You got shot?' I said, changing the subject. 'Really?'

He nodded. 'Through the left lung, just missed my heart,' he patted his chest softly, 'I was three months recovering. Then rehab.' He looked away, stared out toward the point where the river met the sea.

'It damaged you?'

'Physically? Not much in the long run. But it enlightened me. It showed me the truth. And then when I left the army, I was with your mother, had Laura and you, I tried to ignore it, but it kept speaking to me.'

'The truth?'

A nod.

'So what is the truth?'

'An inch to the left and I'd be dead. That's the truth. The guy who shot me was a hundred yards away; if he'd twitched a tenth of a millimetre, I wouldn't be here.'

'I don't get it though. You nearly died, so you left us?'

'No. I lived, and that set me free. Free of anything that I didn't want to do, or be. It gave me licence.'

He could see I wasn't quite getting it, so he said, 'I had a friend when I was at school, a lovely lad. He committed suicide when he was fifteen because he was gay, and his parents, well, he thought his parents wouldn't forgive him. They might not have, they were very religious.'

'What was he called? Your friend.'

'Naser. He was lovely. Funny, kind. Gentle. I knew he was gay when he was five, it was obvious, and no one cared. He was just Naser. But he couldn't face it, he couldn't face the shame, and he committed suicide.' He took a sharp intake of breath, 'The thing is, what I'm trying to say is, at that point, before he put that noose around his neck, before he stepped off that chair, I wish I could have spoken to him. I would have said, if it's that bad Nas, if the feeling you have is that terrible, if the dread is upon you so heavy, then all bets are off. If you are prepared to give up on life, then life has given up on you. Then there is no obligation, there is no debt, you don't have to continue to play the hand that life has dealt you. Nothing makes sense, so you can stop trying to make sense of it. You can just shed the feelings. Shed it all, like a weight you don't have to carry. And you can start again from new.'

I thought about this. 'So life gave you freedom to be you, because you were so close to losing it, it lost its claim on you.'

'Pretty much.'

'So you left us.'

Another nod.

'It changed you. Being shot.'

'It focused me. Took a while for me to realise, but when I did, it was obvious.'

'What's it like?' I asked. 'To be so ruthless and cold. To do whatever you want to do. To not care about anyone or anything.'

He looked up from his cup and at me, eyes steady and calm.

'It's the best thing,' he said. 'It's the best thing in the world.'

After we left the café, we drove to the far south side of the docks, parked up and took a walk beneath a railway bridge and along the beach. I'd never been here; it was out of the way, hidden behind derelict factories and the ruins of warehouses whose smashed windows stared sad-eyed from above. We walked for a mile or so and we came to a place where the sand was patched with tussocky grass and rose into dunes. He said, 'I'm not planning to die until I'm eighty-four.'

'Eighty-four?'

'No. But when I do. Scatter my ashes here.'

'Why?'

'It's where my dad took me fishing when I was a boy. This little beach has a spot reserved for my soul.'

'You're being maudlin.'

'Just making sure, is all.'

'Ok.'

I looked around. The wind was constant and buffering. Most of the buildings were hidden now by ruined trees, thorn bushes and dunes. The sea was grey, the sand dirty yellow, the waves licking the shore without any enthusiasm. It was desolate. I felt desolate. I didn't understand him. Not at all. 'Ok,' I said again.

When we got back in the apartment, a couple of hours later, Lisa was on the phone and she glanced up at us, at Dad, then me, and she put her hand over the phone and whispered to him, 'Have you been freaking the boy out?'

'He has,' I told her.

I looked at him and he winked. 'I have,' he said, and she went back to her conversation. He said, 'I have to go to a meeting. I thought you might want to see what I'm doing. How I do it. The whole enterprise.'

'That'd be good,' I said.

'Give me a couple of hours,' he said, and left me there, went straight back out. He hadn't even taken off his coat. I went to the window and looked out until I saw him leaving the building, walking to his car.

'So what did you talk about?' Lisa asked, putting down her phone, her conversation over.

'He told me about his life. Why he does what he does. Why he left.'

'And how do you feel about it all?'

'I don't know how I feel,' I said.

'You two seem so alike, but….'

I nodded. 'Same ingredients…'

'…different recipe,' she finished for me, smiling.

'Do you love him?' I asked. Then I said, 'Sorry, it's not my business.'

'It's ok,' she said. 'I do.'

'Does he love you?'

'I don't know. He can tell me everything, and still leave me with no clue as to what he is thinking or feeling.'

'He's good at what he does.' I watched his car pull out of the parking space, gliding smoothly toward the main road. Being him is what he does, I thought.

Nothing else.

A couple of days later, Dad and me were sitting on a bench on

the quayside, near his apartment, just chatting. He said, 'How

I work is, I persuade people to give me stuff, and often they

don't want to give me it, so I use leverage.'

'Give me a big enough lever and I can move the world,' I said.

'Archimedes. Right,' he said, and he smiled to himself. 'Well, if you give me the right lever I can persuade anyone to give me stuff.' He stared across the river for a while. 'There was this guy, back when I started off. A real old school gangster. Proper hard case, and he just couldn't be physically scared; couldn't be frightened into line. He had an iron hand.'

'Like the Terminator?'

He chuckled. 'No, like someone who'd had an industrial accident when he was just a kid. I suspect the accident, the trauma of it, I think it created him.'

'Like it did you, being shot?'

'Yes, if your industry is being a soldier.' He smiled, distant, remembering something. 'This guy, he was fearless; this kid who'd lost his hand at seventeen, he had become a man fearless, scared of nothing. He wore that injury like a badge. A shield. By the age of twenty-five he owned six clubs, he ran dealers across town,' he paused and looked at me, 'Now he was in his forties, hard as granite, smart as a fox, absolutely relentless. And I wanted to take him down.'

I shivered.

'Cold?'

'No, I'm fine,' I said.

said, 'I went to see him at his office, early one Monday morning, and I told him my business plan. Which was to take over his business.'

'How did he react?'

'He just laughed at me. Well, jeered more like. Gave me a quick resume of his extremely interesting life, and a summary of what he'd do if I didn't leave right there and then.'

We watched as the red and white swing bridge swung open, letting a dredger past, letting it move upriver.

'So I told him I was serious,' Dad said. 'On his desk was a paper knife. One of those mild steel things people use to open letters. Not sharp or anything, just a blunt edge and a piss-poor point. I picked it up and he laughed and said, "Are you going to try and stab me with that?" and I said 'No. I'm going to show you that I am serious, and what I will do when I'm serious. I took out a handkerchief and laid on the table, then I placed the palm of my hand flat on the table, on top of the handkerchief, and I put the tip of the blade against the back of my hand, and I pushed it through, very slowly. Just like that. Then I pulled it out, slowly, and I cleaned the blade on the handkerchief. He looked a bit shocked.' Dad gave me a look, to see if I understood, and said, 'I told him I'd put a knife through myself to prove a point, which was that I was prepared to do anything it took, and that if he didn't sell up today, at this very moment, I'd arrange for him to lose his other hand. And besides, I was bleeding all over his expensive oak table, which I intended to keep for myself, so I'd appreciate his signature quickly.'

He smiled. 'I thought he was going to faint.'

'Didn't it hurt?'

'The trick,' he said, 'is not to mind.'

'TE Lawrence.'

He looked at me in some surprise. 'I forget, you read a lot.'

'You do too?'

A nod.

I glanced at the back of his hand, which bore no scar, and then I grinned at him, 'You are *such* a storyteller, Dad.'

He broke into a smile. 'It helped that I had two big lads come through the door at that point with shotguns. And one of them had a cleaver sticking out of his pocket. But the point stands, you have to use leverage, threaten to take away something that's valuable to them, or offer to give them something they value highly. I told him I'd take his other hand, and he saw that I was serious. That I had purpose.'

His fingernails tapped the arm of the bench we were sitting on, 'Besides, you were looking at the wrong hand,' and he held up his left hand and I could clearly see a white scar, about a half-inch long, on the back of his hand. He turned it over and there was a smaller scar dead centre of his palm. 'Leverage,' he said. 'And commitment. It's an unstoppable combination.'

And two big lads with shotguns, I thought.

I guess he was showing me his way. I think maybe he was apologising for stuff too. Looking back, I don't think he ever intended me to be like him, I think he knew we were made different. But he was saying, 'This is me,' and letting me in, deeper and quicker than he'd ever let anyone in. Lisa said more than once, he never told her what he was thinking. But he told me. As best as he could, he told me everything. Just told me stuff. Lots of stuff. He'd spend an hour detailing a plan or a scam or a threat or an act, or something he'd done before we met up, not out of bravado but just to inform me. Here I am, he was saying to me. This is what I do. And what I took from that was that I was not, and never would be, anything like him.

Not to say I didn't try.

Dad said, 'In the glove compartment is a Glock 26. It doesn't have a safety catch, but so long as you don't pull the trigger it's not going to do any damage.' He glanced across at me as we rounded Hall Bend, past the big old house where some famous person used to live. I couldn't remember his name.

'Before we get out I want you to put it in your pocket. And don't take it out until I tell you.'

I nodded.

We drove through Seaham and I looked down on the waves crashing against the harbour wall. We drove for another mile and pulled into a car park right on the clifftops, the suspension of the M5kicked as we went over the speed bumps. Dad got out and I followed. He said, 'The guy we're meeting is a councillor. I give him money, he does what I ask, when it comes to planning permission.'

'Fair trade,' I said. 'But you're not really planning on building anything.'

'Not really, but I need permission so the plans are legitimate. Then we get the big compensation.'

'Ok.'

'But now he's saying he wants more. Double.'

'How much is that?'

'Ten K.'

'Pay him,' I said.

He shook his head. 'There's a principle at stake.'

'There's a deal to close,' I said.

He glanced at me then. A question forming, then he smiled, amused. We continued our walk along the path and as we did we passed a red Citroen, Dad slowed and tapped on the passenger door window with his knuckles, but we kept walking until the path ended. I glanced back and saw a fat man climbing out of the car. Dad pointed out over the cliffs, 'Look at that.'

The sea was raging.

The fat man caught up.

Dad said, 'Councillor.'

The councillor said, 'Did we have to come out to this neck end? Just for a five-minute chat?'

'We're not there yet,' Dad said and began walking down a step muddy slope toward the Blast. The councillor looked at me and asked, 'Who's he?'

'Work experience.'

Dad had to raise his voice as the sound of the sea almost snatched away his words. I scrambled after him, the councillor in between us as we worked our way down onto the dark cindery beach. Dad said to me, 'See how this part of the beach is raised up bout six or seven feet?'

'Yeah.'

'And the sand isn't sand, it's black slag. Iron ore slag. This used to be the place where the blast furnace emptied the sludge and clinker.'

I looked at a pool of water beneath the cliff edge. It was red. Dad turned to the councillor, 'The slag is eight hundred metres long, and forty-five metres wide, and two meters deep.' He paused as the wind whipped at his coat, mussed up his hair, and the sea crashed onto the sandy beach beyond and below. 'How many cubic metres of this waste do you think are on this beach?' But the councillor was brushing mud from his pants where he'd slipped and didn't answer. I knew what Dad was doing. In the distance I saw two men digging for worms. Fishermen. 'Seventy-two thousand cubic metres,' I said, and Dad looked at me with some pride. 'Correct, he said.

'Is there a point to this?' The councillor asked, clearly uncomfortable.

'Five thousand points,' Dad said. 'Possibly ten thousand.'

'So finally, we get to the heart of the matter,' the councillor said. Voice smug, standing, metaphorically at least, on firm ground now.

'We're businessmen,' Dad said. 'And my work experience lad here says it's a fair trade, and I listen to his advice.' From his pocket he took out a fat envelope. 'But I like to do this sort of thing away from prying eyes. '

'Can't get much further away than this,' the councillor said. We'd walked half the beach by this time, Dad forging ahead. Me slightly behind the councillor, who glanced back at me like I was an alien. But he licked his lips, because he liked the money. We walked on. The sea grew louder; the tide was coming in. Dad turned and said, 'They filmed parts of Alien 3 here. This beach, it's like a moonscape. Like some forgotten planet.'

We were closer to the fishermen now and I thought, why are they digging in the iron clinker for worms? But as we passed them Dad paused and turned, pointed. 'See that hole?' he asked. I looked at the two men. They'd been digging a trench, not digging for worms. They were wrapped in heavy coats and hats, but I recognized Teez. They both held shovels.

Dad turned to me and said, 'Take out your gun and if he moves, shoot him,' pointing at the councillor, whose face had turned a similar grey to colour of the sky. I took out the gun. Pointed it at the councillor. He got even paler. His skin as grey as the clouds that were tumbling across the sky.

Dad stepped a little closer to the councillor and said, 'What is going to happen now is this: we are going to wrap you in chicken wire,' Teez grinned, and helpfully pointed at a roll of mesh that lay by the edge of the trench. Dad said, 'Then we

are going to put you in that hole and bury you. The tide

doesn't quite reach this far but the slag gets saturated. It

becomes a sort of thick iron soup.' His voice was cold, far

colder than the North Sea fifty yards to our left. 'You will

drown,' he told the councillor. 'You'll try not to, but you will.

You might survive ten or fifteen minutes. You might survive

an hour. But if the weight of the slag doesn't crush you first,

you will drown.' He gave a sad smile. 'And the saturation

from the waves will flatten out the marks of digging.' He

turned away from the councillor, stared out to sea. I said, 'Can

I shoot him?'

Purely for dramatic effect.

'Who *is* he?' the councillor asked, nodding toward me, his face

ashen.

'Work experience,' I said. 'Let me shoot him,' I said to Dad.

The councillor's legs gave way and he sat down heavily on the

wet slag. Like a tired sack; a devil sick of sin. Dad shook his head. 'No shooting unless he tries to run.' The councillor said something then, but the wind swept it away, lost in the roar of waves and tide. Dad said, 'What?' and the councillor looked up, repeated his words, 'What do you want?', his eyes pleading. Dad said, 'I want to bury you in the slag, wrapped in chicken wire. Is that too difficult for you to understand?' I stared at the man sitting there on the damp, gritty slag. I stared at Dad, and Teez and whoever else was standing there beside him wrapped in a hoody and a scarf. I thought, this is awful; this is not play-acting. They're like school bullies, and they're picking on the fat kid. Dad said, 'But my *intern* there,' and he winked at me, 'suggested we try something else.' He motioned toward the hole, said, 'Get in.'

The councillor stumbled to his feet and walked to the trench, legs flopping like heavy rope. I think half of him did not believe anything would happen. The other half knew that it would. I thought, this is how mass murder happens. People just fold. They give in. They submit. The councillor sat down on his bum again, slid heavily into the trench, hands all smeared. Dad asked, 'Does it fit?'

'Don't,' he said. 'Please.' He was crying now.

'Maybe we should break his legs before we bury him,' Teez said. 'Like in that movie.'

'Please don't.'

'Can I shoot him first?' I said.

I couldn't help myself.

Dad squatted down at the edge of the trench. 'Are we reaching an understanding, councillor?'

Then the gun went off in my hand.

Bang!

The bullet skipping off the hard-packed surface a foot away from the councillor's head and he gave a cry and fell down into the trench.

'Oops,' I said.

Dad looked at me, then back to the councillor like I hadn't just accidentally fired a gun three feet from his face, as though it was part of a plan. 'Are we reaching an *accord* councillor?'

I heard the whimpering *yes*, that came from the trench. I found myself both excited and sickened by what I as taking part in. Dad said to him, 'You'll get your ten k, councillor. But if I were you I'd clean yourself off before you get back in your car.' He straightened up, smoothed down his coat and without another word he walked back the way we'd come. As he passed me he took the gun from my hand and gave me a look as though to say *What the…?* But when we got back to the car ten minutes later he didn't mention anything that had happened, he just got in, waited for me to fasten my seat belt, fired up the engine and drove us home.

As we passed back through Seaham I looked back down at the waves crashing against the docks and I thought, it's unremarkable, to him, this thing we've just done. To me, it's insane; it's like a pantomime, but instead of a wicked witch and a couple of ugly sisters there are real villains. So what does that make me I thought? A carnival clown maybe, acting out a part? Or does comes too easily to be an act? Maybe it *is* me. I pondered for a while then glanced at Dad. To him it's just business. To me though, I'd always thought I was basically a good guy, that inside I was really a hero, trying to get out and be heroic.

But I wasn't.

I was one of the bad guys.

'That crazy act...?' Dad said after a few minutes.

'It didn't work for me,' I said.

'I don't know. It seemed to come natural.'

I nodded. 'It does.' Then I said, 'It fits, but it's not me.'

'It *was* effective,' he admitted, and smiled to himself, glanced in the mirror as he drove, 'but maybe you're right.' He looked over. 'It gave Teez a shock. Not many people can do that.'

'I couldn't tell.'

'I could.'

'He's got a face like stone.'

'Like a gargoyle; but I know him better than you.'

As we passed Seaham Hall again I remembered something.

'Lord Byron,' I said.

'Byron?'

'He stayed there a lot.' I pointed. 'He was a regular visitor. Then he went away to fight in Greece.'

'We really should compare reading lists,' Dad said, and reached over, ruffled my hair.

'Yeah,' I said, and I thought, you could have been a normal dad, and we'd have had a great relationship, really great. You'd be the cool dad all my friends thought was smart and interesting. You could have done anything you wanted; you're so smart. And because you hadn't left her alone when she was little, Laura wouldn't have had that vacant space in her soul that can never be properly filled. And Mam, she would have been content and happy.

And.

And.

And shit, really.

Just dreams.

I looked out of the window.

I still called home every day or two, just to check on Laura, and little by little the days turned into weeks. IGCSEs contacted Oscar after the first month and confirmed I was disbanding the outfit, because what I was learning from Dad was that really, despite the crazy bravado, I was not up to snuff, I wasn't going to make it in the big time so, as the philosopher said, if you're going to lose, lose early, that sort of thing. But Oscar'd sort of

guessed by my four-week absence that was the case he said,

and Andy had stopped arriving with the goods anyhow.

In fact, Andy had disappeared, he said.

Which I knew already.

The crew had gone back to school, the school rugby team was

now on a winning streak, and Oscar reeled off the stats of who

scored what, in what minute, and who got injured and how

many minutes it took the ambulance to arrive when someone

got a leg broke, and how many miles they'd travelled in the

school minibus donated by a mysterious benefactor, and I

thought, well, every cloud, and all that. But school didn't

figure in my plans. Four months before my GCSEs and all I

could think of was Mark Twain saying *I never let school*

interfere with my education.

Well, me neither.

In fact, the next few weeks were a whirl of following Dad

from meeting to meeting, sitting listening to him as he

explained how business worked – all business is about leverage and contracts he said, and in that he reminded me of Shylock, the contracts thing, but not really in any other way, mostly he was quiet and worked behind the scenes, twisting people to his will, striving toward his ultimate aim – the big pay-off - more like Iago, I guess, though he was not Shakespearian my old man. Not at all. There was nothing theatrical about him.

But he was thoughtful.

He worked things through in his mind. One time we were sitting in his car and the traffic had stopped for some sort of road accident. We watched as the blue lights of an ambulance flashed past. Dad said, 'See this? The roads, the ambulance, the police, see all this infrastructure?'

'Yes,' I said.

'People think this will last forever. They think they have a divine right to this, because it is here, now. They think having means deserving.' We paused to watch as two police motorcycles glided through the traffic like dolphins through choppy waves.

'We don't deserve what we have?' I asked.

He went on. 'You know your history?'

'Some.'

'Back when the English were living in thatched huts, the middle-east was the centre of civilisation. It had been civilised for five thousand years. They had knowledge, they had culture, they had writing, science, mathematics; they had commerce that linked China with Europe. The entire world passed through the middle-east. They had trade.' He paused before continuing as the car edged a few feet further forward in the queue. 'Then the Mongols arrived, and within a few decades two thirds of the population were dead. Everything they'd worked for destroyed. Every certainty they believed in had been put to the sword.' He glanced at me, the car moved forward a few feet. I saw the ambulance parked up on the verge. He said, 'There was a city called Merv, a metropolis.

Imagine London, crossed with Aladdin's cave, a city filled

with a mix of races and cultures and it was a commercial hub,

traders came from thousands of miles to buy and sell.

Perfumes, spices, slaves, gold, silver, they bought and sold

everything that could be bought or sold.'

He went on, 'Merv had a population of about a million people

when the Mongols besieged it. And this city of trade and light

and education surrendered to the barbarians, even though

they had thirty-feet high walls, because they were traders, not

fighters.'

We pulled level with a police car.

Dad said, 'After they surrendered, the Mongols led every

them out into the desert. The entire population. And they

killed them all. Every single one of them. A million people.'

I took a deep breath.

'Nothing lasts forever, Mickey,' he said. 'You think it will, you

want it to, but it can't. The people of Merv thought that they could reason with fate. They thought their wealth and their knowledge could deflect swords.'

'So what's the point of even trying?' I said.

We drove slowly past the accident now, a jumble of bashed-in cars and crinkle glass scattered about the road, a medic was performing CPR on a bloke lying on the grass verge while a policeman stood by. Slowly, we slid past this scene, Dad's car smooth and almost silent, then, after following directions from a motorbike cop, we began to speed up as the road ahead cleared. He said, 'The point is to live while you can, live well, appreciate the good things, but don't depend on it all lasting forever.'

I looked back at the scene of the crash.

'You're not big on comforting words,' I said.

'I enjoy life,' he said, 'It's a feast, and you have to take your fill, when you can. But you, Mickey, you look for certainty. You look for an island, a refuge, when you should be swimming with the current.'

'I don't know about a feast,' I said, 'but you mix your metaphors like they're an all-you-can-eat a buffet,' and he looked across and grinned at me.

'All I mean is, you can't expect certainty.'

I thought, not with you as a dad I can't.

He glanced across at me as though he'd read my mind, then he looked back to the road.

I spent a lot of time with Lisa too. She told me the plans she had for Dad and her, and this involved children, and I think she was pleased to be able to sound me out because on that topic my Dad had a poor track record. 'It's different now,' she said, 'We'll be leaving this life soon and we'll settle down, find a little town...' it sounded like the lyrics of a pop song to me, and just as believable.

But I liked Lisa a lot and it was her faith in my Dad that kept me grounded, kept me from believing the rot he fed me, the lies and the packaged violence that she wrapped around herself like a promise, a quilt to keep her warm. He was a criminal, and watching him at work was like watching a shark circling in a kiddie's playpool. It didn't give me a good feeling. On the other hand I have to admit, it was nice, really nice, not to have to worry about anything. It was nice not to be the one responsible.

One of the first things I did after I'd moved in with Dad was tell Laura where my stash was, and to make sure that whoever Mam was living with this week, they didn't get to know about it. 'Nothing flash,' I said, 'Just pay the bills and we'll save the rest until I can officially leave school.'

'Then what?' she asked, it was during one of our twice-weekly phone calls. I let the silence hang for a while, then I said, 'Maybe we'll get out of town. Go somewhere warm?'

I could hear her nod. 'I'll have to chase up your passport,' she said.

'How's work?' I asked, meaning, are you using again, and she said, 'Work is fine, they've asked me to do more hours, talking about making me a shift manager. And no I'm not using, in case you're wondering.'

Mind reader, Laura. Always has been. But not always as truthful as I thought, it turned out. 'Ok,' I said. 'I'll call in a couple of days.'

'Mickey,' she said, 'Are you coming over soon?'

'Yeah, I guess.'

'This last year, it hasn't been so bad, has it?'

'It's been good.'

'K, call soon.'

I put down the phone.

As usual, Lisa had left me alone when I called home, and Dad was out at some meeting. But this time, when he came home, about half nine, he had blood on his shirt and his knuckles, and on his shoes too. He looked exhausted, like he'd taken a beating as well as given one. I watched as Lisa went into care-overdrive, fussing him, but quietly, making him take off his clothes and take a shower, then a bath, not asking him what happened but working out from his tone, and me too, that whatever had happened wasn't going to be discussed, and when Lisa left the apartment twenty minutes later with a sportsbag containing Dad's bloodied clothing and expensive shoes I wasn't too surprised that when she returned a half hour after that she was empty-handed. In between, Dad came out of the shower wearing only a towel round his waist and he sat chatting quietly on a phone I'd never seen before and never saw again either, a disposable, a burner phone, I guessed, I recognised the brand, and as he sat discussing whatever, with whoever, I saw bruises around his waist, like he'd been in a minor car crash or had been kicked, and he had a contusion across his upper arm. And I saw a small ragged scar just below his nipple. It was where a bullet had torn into his chest, almost killing him. That was done before I was even born. An inch to the left and I'd never have existed. I went to my room just so I could glance back at the scar made by the exit wound, hoping that if I understood his wounds I might better understand his crimes, and I saw it, about half the size of my palm, star-shaped. I could see the muscle working below the thin translucent skin as he switched hands, he turned to me as he spoke on the phone, looking quizzical, and I noticed his knuckles were bruised and cut too. Old and new scars marked his body, like the story of his life told in physical relief. I gave him an Everything Is Alright smile and went into my room. Picked up a book and read for a while.

Stories are my escape route, Laura says, and she's right.

The next day, it was like nothing had happened. Dad walked

a little stiffly, like he'd hurt something, pulled a muscle. But

after a quiet watchful breakfast, watchful on my part and on

Lisa's, not his, he left the apartment, giving me a wink before

he slammed the door. This might sound strange, but I can't

tell you how good it felt, my old man, some sort of outlaw,

acknowledging me as he left. Mainly it was the growing realisation that I didn't have to be that person. For the first time in years I didn't have to be the outlaw; I could let someone else take charge. Then, just after lunch he returned and said to me, 'Want to come for a walk?'

'Sure.' I wanted to ask where, but then I thought, it'd be a surprise. I was enjoying the feeling of just bobbing on the tide, besides I knew how he worked now, he'd tell me in his own good time. We left the apartment, went down to his car, got in and drove the twelve miles into Sunderland. We came to a quiet spot near the river. He liked his rivers, my old fella. He parked up in an empty lane and we got out. 'Your gran went to school there,' he said, pointing at an empty space with walls on two sides and a rusting barrier on the others. 'This entire area was industry. There were two huge cooling towers there,' and he pointed, 'and the ships used to berth down there and load coal from the mines.'

'There's nothing there now.'

'No.'

We looked at the cinder path and the rough grass. There were bricked up doorways leading into the sides of the bank, between which the path led down to the river. To one side were some ancient gravestones. 'That graveyard was there even before the industry came,' he said. 'Surprised it survived.'

It hadn't really. They'd moved the gravestones so they were all stood up against a high wall. 'City of culture,' I said. 'That's what we are.'

'That's right,' he said with a crooked smile.

'Why did you bring me here?' I asked.

'Let's walk down there,' he said, and I followed him down a cinder path until we reached the rotting staithes where the industry used to be. 'You afraid of heights?' he asked?

I shook my head.

'I am,' he said, 'I can't swim either. Hate water.'

And with that he stepped lightly onto the rotting, slippery corpse of an old boat that had sunk into the mud decades ago and had sat there ever since. He inched his way out along the rotting planks until he was standing on a single spar over the heavy flowing river. He looked at me and then turned around to stare out across the water, where gulls flew and the wind murmured and moved his coat. I looked down at the muddy water flowing beneath him. He turned, 'I really am scared of heights. And water.'

'You'd never have made a paratrooper then. Or a marine,' I said.

He laughed. 'PBI,' he said. 'Poor bloody infantry, that was me.' He stepped off the plank and onto a cross beam, his foot skidded for a millisecond then he righted himself, his coat fluttering in disapproval, I could see his face was pale and realised he really didn't like it out there on the rotting boat, fifteen or twenty feet above the dirty, flowing river. He really was scared. 'Why you doing this?' I shouted, because the wind was picking up and I had to shout to be heard, then wait

'til he reached the next plank, where he could plant both feet.

He turned and looked at me and shouted back, 'Because I'm

scared.' He stepped down onto a cross-spar, and walked

lightly back to where I was, back on firm ground. He

shuddered, 'I am *really* scared of water,' he said.

I shook my head, bemused.

'You're not impressed?'

'No.'

'That's ok,' he said, 'I didn't do it for you.'

We clambered up the short slope and back onto the cinder

path. We walked back into town, past the Vaults, past the Uni.

'I thought I'd tell you my plans,' he said. 'I've got two final

things to sort out, then it's all done.'

'Ok.'

'I thought that maybe you could see if there are any holes in

the plan. Be a sort of trouble-shooter.'

'You mean be a smartarse and a nitpicker.'

'Pretty much.'

'I can do that,' I said. 'But why tell me? I'm just a kid.'

'You're blood,' he said. 'I can trust you in a way I can't trust anyone else.'

'Not even Lisa?'

'I keep Lisa out of it. She has an idea, I have her sign things sometimes, but I don't go through my plans with her.'

'The others?'

'You're blood,' he repeated. 'The others I trust, but …'

'No one's got your back,' I said. 'Not really.'

'Not really, no.'

We cut up by the Minster, then walked through the Bridges, then down Blandford Street. I counted four pawnbrokers offering to buy my used jewellery, four charity shops offering to sell me second-hand clothes, and three others, boarded up. Seagulls were eating from discarded wrappers. People riding benefit-chariots with shopping bags on the back. City of Culture, I thought. Then I thought about what Dad had said.

'Ok,' I said to him. 'Fire away.'

And he did.

He laid out his plans to me, in detail: events, timescales, costs, risks, collateral damage, everything. As he talked we walked out through the other side of town and up by the Civic Centre. He laid out his plans cold, and some of it was really cold, brutal stuff, and as he went through it I asked questions, some were stupid, some, well most really, he'd thought of already, but one or two made him think. At least, I like to think they did.

We walked all the way to Backhouse Park, and round it, twice. It felt good, being with Dad, being trusted like that. I didn't have his ruthlessness or his vision, but I somehow felt safer too, because he was ruthless and had vision, and he had a complete grasp of what he was about. He reminded me of a wolf in human clothing, and I was his cub, which made me feel safe even though I wasn't, not really. Because Dad was a complete predator, and that's not safe to be around. And with his gang they were more like locusts, descending on a town and stripping it bare of profit. Locusts who only preyed on other locusts. Some they sent to hospital, one guy, Dad said, they sent on a cruise, he even took his wife. Imagine that, one day you're the Tony Soprano of your council estate, you're making a tidy fortune, you're strutting your stuff on the criminal stage, and the next day you're visited by some gangsters, they show you photos of what they do to people who don't give it up, and they bundle you and your wife onto a mini cruise, take your phone, tell you to enjoy yourself, and a week later when you get back – nothing's left. Everything you owned has gone. They'd even sent a minder with the guy on the cruise, while they completed the transactions. That was just one example. But cruises aside, mostly they put just people in the hospital, cleaned them out while they recovered. More than that, I'm not saying.

I don't think he told me all this because he loved me, or because he had a need to tell someone, anyone. I think he really did tell me just because he wanted to know if there were any holes in the plan, and I was blood, so I could be trusted. It was a simple equation: I was his cub, I was part of his pack. He could trust me. As we talked and walked for a couple of hours or more, and I could have walked like that all day, with Dad just talking and me mostly listening. It'd have been nice if we were talking about football, or me how my studies were going or the possibility of me getting an apprenticeship or something, but discussing organised crime was better than nothing. We got back in the car and he gave a small cough, 'I've talked to you more than anyone I can remember,' he said. It felt good.

'Hey Lisa,' I said, feeling tired but cheerful when we got back to Newcastle, but Lisa was just coming off the phone and she looked serious. She said to me, 'Where you been?' And to Dad she said, 'I've been calling you.'
'I switched off my phone.'

She looked at me. 'You need to call home,' she said, and by her expression I knew something was wrong. My blood was running cold as I picked up the phone and watched absently while the phone rang at the other end as Lisa motioned Dad to follow her into the kitchen where they could speak privately.

'Laura?' I asked, when the phone was picked up.

'It's Martin.'

'Where's Laura?'

'She's been arrested,' he said, the sneer heavy in his voice. 'She's been charged with possession and dealing. They found a stack of drugs.' He just couldn't keep that sneer from his voice. I loathed that sneer. 'And we both know who they came from, don't we, little Mickey?

'The amount they found, she'll be looking at seven to fourteen years inside.'

I could hear Martin chewing as he spoke, he disgusted me, and the barely hidden contempt he had for me in return dripped from every word he spoke. I put the phone down and turned to find that Dad was next to me. 'Lift home?' he said quietly.

I nodded. 'Laura's been arrested.'

He nodded; I think Lisa had told him while I was talking to Martin. 'Tell me in the car.'

We drove in silence back home.

'Nice street,' Dad said as he parked the car. Double yellow lines, but I doubt parking tickets worried him. It *was* a nice street. Edwardian. Mostly flats now but still a semblance of what it once was. 'You pay for it all?' he asked me.

'Yes.'

He checked his mirror, and we got out, I hurried to gate, almost ran up the path and then paused to stare at the front door, which was basically smashed into pieces. There was a man standing just inside the door that I vaguely remembered as the landlord, he was about to say something when Dad intervened, and I walked straight past him to find out what was going on.

'Where's Mam?' I asked Martin, finding him, feet up on the sofa in the living room. He'd got noticeably fatter in the weeks I'd been gone. He looked up, spoke loud and slow, as though to an invisible crowd, emphasizing his words for dramatic effect, 'Everyone relax, Super Mickey has returned to rescue the maiden in distress and kill the fire breathing dragon!'

I repeated, 'Where's *Mam*?' and he sort of rolled of the sofa, still chewing something, I noticed, and there was an empty pizza box on the carpet next to him. I went back out to the hall where Dad was placating the landlord, 'I'll pay for everything,' he was saying in his quiet, insistent voice.

'Who are you again?' the landlord asked.

'I'm the father.'

The landlord glanced at me, then behind me to where Martin had emerged from the room, 'Well, who..?'

'We're estranged,' Dad told him, 'But I'll pay for everything.'

And he took out his wallet and peeled off what I can only

estimate at around a thousand pounds in twenties. 'This should cover everything,' he said.

'Ah, yes.'

The landlord wasn't happy, but he took the money, still looking troubled and a mite confused, so Dad said, 'There's been some sort of mix-up. You come back tomorrow; same time and I'll ensure everything is fixed by then. Ok?'

'The police said there were drugs…' Dad turned to stare at Martin and the landlord followed his gaze. 'Don't look at me,' Martin said, and I jumped in, 'He's not even supposed to be here' – this to the landlord – 'it's Mam's scuzzy boyfriend,' which made Martin growl something which in turn made the landlord back off a little and turn to Dad, who seemed adult and reasonable in comparison. He muttered, 'I'll come back tomorrow.'

Dad nodded, 'Please do, and in the meantime I'll sort everything out.'

The landlord said, 'I hope there's no more trouble.'

'There won't be.'

'Thankyou, Mr,…'

'Hall. Michael Hall,' and the landlord smiled, pocketed the money and left. Dad turned to me and said, 'Is your mam here?'

'No.'

He took out his phone, 'I'll find out where she is.'

'And Laura.'

A nod.

'Oh!' Martin sneered, 'Is this the other returning hero?'

I watched Dad scroll through a list of numbers til he found the right one, 'Yeah, it's me,' he said to someone on the phone. 'Can you find out the gen on a girl, just been arrested, drugs charges I think. Laura, Laura Hall, she'll be eighteen…'

'Seventeen,' I said.

'She's seventeen.' A nod. 'Yes, still a minor. Find out where she is, what the charges are and who her state-appointed is.'

'You think you can waltz in here and take over?' Martin said, still trying to insert himself into the conversation as Dad finished his call. Dad ignored him like he wasn't there, looked at me. 'We'll go out to the car, should get a text in the next couple of minutes.' He handed me his phone.

Martin pushed in between us, grabbed Dad by the shoulder, 'Hey, arsehole. Absent-*dad*. Hey you, you *fucker*! I'm talking to you!' Martin was almost as tall as Dad, but much heavier set, and he had a meaty paw on Dad's expensive coat. Much of his size was beerfat though, and I'd seen his puny white legs one time when he dashed from the shower to his bedroom wrapped in only a towel, so I figured in a tussle it would be a close-run thing.

But I wasn't expecting Dad to move so fast.

In the time it takes to say *Dad don't!* he'd grabbed Martin by the throat and pinned him up against the wall, holding him there with some sort of hidden but ferocious strength, his left hand gripping his throat while out of nowhere he'd produced a wicked-looking curved knife, the blade all serrated and it

was in his right hand, hovering over Martin's eyeball, 'Pick an

eye, fat boy,' Dad whispered, leaning in close, face to face.

'What?' a coughing gurgle as Martin tried to breath properly.

'Dad, you're choking him,' I said.

'Pick an eye,' Dad repeated, ignoring me. 'Left. Or right,'

'*Wha*?' Martin said again, his voice a gargle, struggling to

speak as Dad's fierce grip tightened on his throat.

Dad said, 'I'm coming back here tomorrow to get the place

fixed up, and if you're still here mouthing off, *you* get to lose

an eyeball.' He leaned closer, so they were nose to nose, and

Dad's voice just a whisper, and more scary for that, 'Now I'm

happy if you choose, but if you don't, I will, so. Pick. An. Eye.'

'*Please*. I'll go. I'll go.' Martin begged, though it sounded more

like, 'Plagh, agh gagh, agh gagh'. His voice was hoarse now,

and when Dad relaxed his grip and pushed him toward the

floor he gave a mighty retching cough, bent double, gagging

spit. Dad turned back to me like nothing had happened. The

knife had gone. 'Let's go to the car,' he said, leaving Martin kneeling against the wall, moaning. As we cleared the broken down door, Dad paused and said to Martin. 'If I notice your fat corpse again, I *will* take one of your eyes.' Martin flinched at the words. 'Do you believe me?' Dad asked, his voice quiet but insistent. The reply was a sobbing, snotty nod. I almost felt sorry for Martin. The school bully taking on someone who was out of his league.

'Say it,' Dad said.

'I believe you,' Martin said, his throat hoarse.

'Keep out of family business.'

'She's not yours,' Martin blurted out, finding his voice, and for a moment I was scared Dad was going to do something really bad, and Martin obviously felt the same cos he flinched, but Dad said quietly, 'No, you're right. But he is.' Pointing at me. 'And so is Laura. And we're all going to have a conversation, and when we do they'll probably tell me some stories about you, Martin Hinde, and if I hear anything bad then I'll come looking for you.' He leaned in closer, voice a whisper, 'And you won't believe what happens after that. Even while it's happening.' Dad stared at him, beating him down with his eyes, and Martin just quailed like a scared dog, his arms reflexively rising like he was warding off a blow.

Dad turned and walked out.

I followed, 'How'd you know his name?' I asked, but Dad just said, 'Has that text come through yet?' as he unlocked the car. We got in and he drove through town towards god-knows-where and then I felt the phone vibrate.

'Read it,' he said, glancing at me.

'She's up at Farringdon. Charged with possession, dealing, possession of a dangerous dog, Christ that'll be Maximus' I said.

'Your dog?'

'Yes. I hope he's alright.'

'They'll have him at the pound. What's the rest of the text say?'

'No brief yet.'

He took the phone from me and began to dial a number.

'Dad,' I said, and when he looked at me I said, 'I know a lawyer.'

'A solicitor?'

'No, a barrister.'

'You keep him on a retainer?' A smile playing on his lips. I shook my head, took the phone from him and began dialling as we drove to the police station.

'Call him,' Dad said.

We met Karl's dad on the street opposite the police station an hour later. Dad's idea, he seemed to have an instinctive aversion to police stations, or maybe his criminal super-powers met their kryptonite once he was inside the doors. Either way, we decided to go to the MaccyDs opposite. 'I'll fill you both in over a coffee,' he said.

'You've got some information?' Dad asked as we went to the counter.

'Yes,' they're going to interview her in a half hour, I've got word to her that you're here Mickey, and I'll be her counsel in the interview.' He looked at Dad, 'I don't think we've been introduced properly.'

'Michael Hall.'

'James Greener.'

They shook hands formally, and for a millisecond I saw an older version of me and Karl, one bluff and friendly and quietly intelligent, the other lean and quick and guarded. But they seemed to hit it off when Dad said, 'I'll cover all the costs,' and Karl's dad said, 'No, this is pro bono, Mickey's been like family for years.' Just then the door opened and a younger man approached as we sat down at the table, 'Thought I might find you here,' he said, approaching us.

'This is Tom,' Karl's dad said, and Tom sat down with a breezy *Hello* to all. 'Don't let the youthful appearance fool you,

Tom is my own personal pitbull,' he said. Tom shrugged and grinned at me. He was about thirty with a thatch of blonde hair, pink, ruddy skin and a long, seemingly boneless body that slouched across a chair. 'What I suggest is that you and Tom,' he spoke to me at this point, 'Go down to the pound and rescue that mutt of yours, while your dad and I get Laura out of chokey, huh?'

'Will you get her out?'

A nod. 'I will.'

'Ok,' I said, then asked, 'Where's Mam?'

'She's inside the station.'

'I want to see her first.'

Karl's dad checked his phone for messages and said, 'She knows we're here and is going to come over.' Tom said, 'We need to be quick if we want to save your dog. The cops don't like their dogs getting beat up in a fight.'

'Maximus beat up the police dogs?' It seemed to me that everyone set their dogs on Max, but Max always survived.

Tom held up his phone, 'Got a police scanner app on this baby. Followed it in real time, even before I knew we were involved. Better than Netflix. I'm hoping to get an app that hacks into police body cams…'

Karl's dad coughed, as though to say, I don't want to hear this. 'Save the dog tales for later,' and Tom just grinned at me like a naughty boy. I liked him already. Then the thing happened that I'd wished for my whole life.

Mam came in and said hello to Dad.

I made some space and she sat next to me, facing him. 'Hello, Mike,' she said, her face looking crumpled and sad, but beautiful too in a way I'd never seen before and I thought, she still loves him, even after all this time, she still *loves* him. Then Dad reached over the table and took her hand, rubbed the empty space on her ring finger, 'Hello Janie,' a wistful smile on his face and I thought, Christ, he still loves her too. I looked at Tom, baffled by this turn of events, and he took my cue and said, 'Right, we're off to rescue a dog.' We stood, said quick

goodbyes, I got a hug off Mam, and we left.

'Car's just over there,' he said when we were outside, pointing

toward an old Impreza STi, in rally colours of mid blue with

gold wheels, with a big wing spoiler and a huge exhaust.

'That's yours?' I was impressed.

It was parked crookedly on the yellow lines outside the police

station. 'You like it?'

'Yes.' I said. 'I like it very much.'

Tom unlocked the deadlocks and we got in. He started the

engine using a switch beneath the dash, 'Gift from a client,' he

told me. 'He can't use it for the next five years.'

'It's awesome,' I said as the car burbled into life.

'Let's go get your dog.'

'Right,' I said.

The dog pound was at the back of Gill Bridge Avenue police station. Tom told me they kept a few cages for dogs that had to be held for one reason or another as we walked in. He went to the desk and asked to speak to the duty sergeant, who duly arrived and looked less than impressed when Tom showed him his credentials. 'You've come for the dog? That big beast?

Naah,' the sergeant said. 'He's getting put down in the morning.'

Tom put out a restraining hand to calm me down and leaned a little closer, 'What grounds do you have for that, sergeant.'

'It attacked three of my dogs.'

'I think it was more a case that your dogs attacked it. The dog is a family pet that was in its own home when your lot smashed down the door and your beasts attacked it.'

'Says who?'

'Says me when we sue you and your chief inspector. And with the publicity we'll get behind us we'll win. This country is a nation of animal lovers.'

'It was a legitimate call, we had information there was a drug dealer there, and we were right.'

'An alleged drug dealer. You're not a prosecutor.'

'And you are?'

'I'm counsel for the defendant. In this case Maximus Hall, a Dogue de Bordeaux, aged four, illegally removed from his home after being illegally attacked in an unprovoked assault by four police dogs.'

'Three police dogs, and he near damn killed one of them.'

'Wouldn't you fight to protect your family?'

'Well yes, but that's…'

Tom cut him off, 'Well, I'm glad we agree on something.'

'We found drugs.'

'If I was able to look around, I guess I'd find drugs on these premises too,' Tom said, 'But that doesn't make you a drug dealer, and it wouldn't give me the right to put down the police dogs you keep in the back.'

The sergeant straightened up, 'Look, you can't have the dog, sir. It reacted badly, very badly, and it needs to be dealt with.'

'You send four slavering Land Sharks into a house and expect the owner's dog to *not* react?'

It needed to be dealt with, *sir*.' The sergeant was getting pissed at Tom's persistence. 'And it was three dogs.'

Tom took out a pen and asked the sergeant for a piece of paper. He wrote down the sergeant's badge number, repeated it to himself, then took out his phone and began filming the sergeant, handing off the camera to me. In a stage voice he said, 'Maximus is a family pet and you're going to destroy him for defending his home?'

'Turn off the camera sir, or I'll be forced to take it from you.'

'On what grounds?'

'Behaviour liable to lead to a breach of the peace.'

'Really? You're threatening to arrest a family lawyer while he's trying to save the life of an innocent dog?' I kept filming. Tom said, 'All we are asking for is the return of the family pet.'

'It's a dangerous animal.'

'Only if you smash down the door and send five German shepherds in to attack it.'

'We had word there was a pitbull type dog in the house. And there were only three police dogs.'

'First, it's not a pitbull, so your intelligence was way off.

Secondly, do you always attack first? Is that the way the police

conduct their business around here?'

He turned to me. 'Turn the camera off, sir.'

'I'm minded to deliver a writ of *habeus caninus*,' Tom mused.

'A what?' the sergeant asked, clearly nonplussed.

Tom paused as though he'd thought of something, but really I

knew that the direct approach wasn't working, and so did

Tom, as he stood staring at some distant spot and nodding to

himself. 'Wait there,' he said to the sergeant, as if the sergeant

was about to do a runner, 'I'm just going to make a phone

call,' and he checked the details he'd written down on the slip

of paper, took the phone from me, dialed a number, walking

outside as he began to speak.

The sergeant looked at me, 'Is he always like this?'

'Dunno, first time I met him.'

'He's like Tigger. With ADHD.'

I laughed at this.

The sergeant looked at me, 'So who are *you*, exactly?'

'Work experience,' I said quickly, 'My name's John Hopper.' I

held out my hand and he sighed, gave it a brief shake. His

palm was clammy, despite the calm exterior. 'You planning on

being a lawyer John?'

'No,' I shook my head.

'Good decision,' he said.

Tom walked back in, looking triumphant. At the same time

the desk phone rang and the sergeant picked it up, spoke,

listened, nodded sadly and replaced the phone. After a

moment, he stood, said, 'Right. Let's go get the bloody dog.'

Tom leaned over and whispered to me, 'It's not what you

know, it's who…'

We arrived triumphantly back at the station where Laura was

being held, I got out of the car and spotted Mam talking to

Karl's dad, ran over and gave her a hug, 'Hey, what's all this,' she said, laughing and hugged me back. 'Sometimes,' I told her, 'I forget you're a real person.'

She squeezed me tighter, 'You think I stopped being a person when I became your mother.'

'Yes,' I said, my head buried in her shoulder. She hugged me tighter still, until I let go. I asked Karl's dad, 'What's happening with Laura?'

'She's out on bail,' he said, looking up from stroking Maximus.

'Where is she?'

'Over the road having a coffee with her dad.' He looked at Tom and said, 'Look, we'll get away, leave you four to sort things out. We have to return tomorrow at half nine so how's about we meet here about quarter to?'

'Right,' I said.

He patted me on the shoulder, Tom fist-bumped me and they walked away toward separate cars. Mam said, 'He's a nice bloke.'

'He's a top bloke,' I said. 'He's going to help us sort everything out.'

'Tom seems nice too.'

'He rescued Max. Sorted it out, called the Chief Inspector and told him he was going to call the Daily Mail.'

She looked pensive, '*We* need to sort everything out, Mickey. You, your Dad…'

'I know.'

'You think he's a hero, and god knows I still love him, but he's a bad man.'

I nodded, 'I know, Mam.' I thought of Laura's comment from years ago. 'He's stern.'

'Stern,' she laughed a little. 'That's the least of it. Being with your Dad and having children, it was like walking around waiting for a bomb to go off. I've seen him do things.' She paused, and I could only guess at the sort of memory that had sprung to mind. 'We can't be together,' she said finally.

'No.'

'Let's get a taxi home, leave them to talk a bit?'

I looked across the road to MaccyDs where Laura was sitting

at a window table, facing Dad. He said something, reached

forward and pushed her hair away from her face. I wished I

could hear what they were saying. I wished… she laughed at

something he said, a real wide smile on her face… I wished it

was me sitting there.

'Fathers and daughters,' Mam said, reading my mind,

placating me with a smile.

'Yeah,' I said, 'Let's go get a taxi home.'

'Mothers and sons too,' she said, grinning, knuckling my hair

in arare moment of affection as we walked along the road

toward the lights of the taxi rank. Maximus rumbled

something deep in his stomach. I think he was agreeing with

us.

When we got home there was already a guy there, fixing the

door. I stood and chatted to him for a bit while Mam was

inside talking to Martin, and God knows what story he was trying to spin her. I heard raised voices, but it was mainly Mam's doing the raising, and as I stood chatting to the joiner, stroking Maximus' fur, I paused to consider what the hell was going on with my life.

How had it come to this point? Here I was with my former-drug dealer's attack-dog-turned-family-pet, there was a guy replacing the door smashed in by police who'd arrested my sister for having drugs that belonged to me, a sister who was at this very moment having a chat with my criminal Dad…

Drugs.

That was the common denominator. Drugs. You can blame me; you can blame Laura I guess, or maybe the bloke who gave her first ever syringe of heroin at an age when she should have been sharing pictures of pop stars with her mates. You could blame Dad. Or Mam. Fact is, it didn't matter. All I had was a broken-into-pieces family, and the common thread was drugs.

Leaving the joiner to continue fixing the door, I went down to my room and began tidying the awful mess the police had made. Drawers were out, clothes strewn, cupboards emptied onto the floor. Listlessly I began to tidy up.

Then I picked up my phone without thinking.

I called Emily.

It was a weird conversation, didn't last too long. I don't know what I was trying to achieve, firstly cos we'd barely spoken for months, not since I'd blanked her when she came to see me when I was dealing, and secondly because we weren't in the first flush or anything, all we had was a back-story and some memories. I was tentative and she was holding back. We chatted for a while and then we hung up, there was none of this 'you hang up first' malarkey, we just hung up. It was just a crap call. A few minutes later there was a tap on the door, it was the joiner. 'Finished,' he said, holding out the keys, 'Your dad said to give these to you.'

'Thanks.'

'No worries,' he said. 'I've done work for your dad before. Long time ago. Solid bloke.' We walked up the stairs to the front door, he showed me, 'I've replaced the door, fixed the frame where the hinges came off, and the lock is really strong.'

'Great,' I said. 'I really appreciate it, you coming out at this time.'

'It's all good,' he said, and gave me his business card. 'Tell your old man to give me a call.'

'Will do.'

'One more thing, your dad said not to give a key to that, well, the guy in there.'

'Martin? No. He's not getting one.'

'Right then,' he picked up his tool bag, swung the door back and forward a couple of times. 'Any problems, let me know and I'll come straight out.'

'Thanks again.'

I watched him go, and then just stood in the doorway watching the streetlamps, listening to the wind, the traffic in the distant main road, smelled the takeaway shop a block away, the smell of fresh wood only inches away. If my life hadn't been such a disaster it would have been a lovely evening. Maybe it was anyway. Maybe the trick was just to be grateful for having a doorway to stand in and a night-sky to look at.

For about half an hour I stood at the door, watching the world go by, hoping that I might see Martin storm past with his bags packed, or maybe Dad would drive Laura home and they'd both come into the kitchen with me for a chat like a proper family, but nothing happened, the place was just quiet. But it was lovely. I started to feel the cold after a while so I took Max downstairs, and got back to tidying up the mess the police had left me.

The next morning, Max came ambling through the door pushing it wide with his thick snout. 'Hey boy,' I said, surveying his recently acquired war-wounds and then climbing groggily out of bed, 'You want to go for a walk?' Maximus grunted, and when I rubbed his ear, he sighed, both of which I took as signs of assent so, a quick shower, a slice of toast and half a cup of tea later, we were out the front door and heading toward the park.

We must have spent a good hour there. We stopped at the kiosk, and I bought Max an ice cream cone, extra-large, and he ate it in eleven seconds. I had myself a coke and we watched the ducklings on the pond being shepherded by their mam. I sat there and thought it through, though I didn't need to, and I knew exactly what I had to do. They were my drugs, not Laura's, and I couldn't let her take the blame. I had to go to the police and tell them it was my fault. I could do time, I knew I could. But not Laura. Drugs are easy to get in jail, and I didn't think she could spend five years in prison without getting back into drugs again. It was my crime; I'd do the time.

I patted Max's big head, 'Come on,' I said, 'Let's get you home. I've got some things to do.' He dragged a bit at first, stood his ground, all stubborn, and I think he wanted another cone so I bought him another, complete with monkey's blood sauce all over the top of the cone, and then, eventually I had him trundling home with his big slobbery chops dripping melted vanilla ice cream. I'd made up my mind and I knew what had to be done. We didn't rush back though, I needed time to get my thoughts in order, sort everything out so there were no mix-ups.

I walked up the steps to the flat and let myself in. I could smell tea and toast in the kitchen so went back there to see if Laura was back from her visit to the station. Instead, Mam was sitting there with another woman. Mam looked up, 'Hi son,' she said, her face looking strange, her eyes flickering to the woman who sat opposite her at the kitchen table who turned to me and stood up. Not a social worker, I thought, so that leaves…

'Hello Mickey,' she said. 'I'm DCI Sandra Steabler. I'm with the regional crime squad.' She flashed her credentials at me, though to be honest, I wouldn't have been able to tell the difference between a warrant card and a free-ride membership of the Euro-Disney. I pulled up a seat at the end of the table, and she sat back down 'You come to arrest me?' I asked.

'No,' she said.

'It wasn't Laura who had the drugs,' I said, 'They were mine.'

She looked at me, 'I haven't come about that. Not exactly. So for the moment I'll pretend I didn't hear you say that.'

I sat back, 'Oh,' racking my brains as to what it could be. Just then Martin popped his head round the kitchen door and I looked at him, 'Martin,' I said, realisation dawning, 'What have you done?'

He leered, 'Don't come all high and mighty. There's only one criminal in this house, and I'm looking at him.'

It had dawned on me. 'You grassed Laura up.'

He glanced at Mam, who couldn't look at him, her expression fixed at some point past the police officer and out the window.

'It must run in the family,' he said, 'First your dad, then Laura, then you. All crims.'

'Get out!'

It was Mam's voice.

'Get out before I throw you out!' she told him, her face both furious and implacable, neither of which I'd seen before. The police inspector just looked at him and spoke smoothly, but with authority, 'Leave us alone, Mr. Hindes, or I'll arrest you for interfering with an investigation.'

He muttered something about gratitude, but closed the door as he left, and I heard a bark, Maximus sending him on his way. This made me smile to myself, but then I looked back at Mam, and then DCI Steabler, and my smile faded. I took a deep breath, let it go. 'Alright then, give me the bad news.'

She nodded slowly, as though she'd been waiting for my full attention before she started, reached down and took a creased folder from a battered suitcase, opened the folder and took out some notes. Then she began to speak in an even, almost friendly tone. But she wasn't my friend.

That quickly became clear.

It turns out she had quite a simple deal for me. Laura was looking at a possible seven-year sentence for possession, more for dealing, and if they added in the gun they found in sealed bag in the toilet cistern they could take that to ten years minimum. I knew that was bogus, Laura had never touched it, and if anyone's prints or DNA were on it it'd be mine; the police inspector was simply showing me they were serious. But they didn't want Laura.

Nor did they want me - my attempt to confess had fallen on stony ground because they didn't want to hear it.

They wanted Dad.

See, the regional crime squad aren't interested in teenage drug dealers, they're interested in professional criminals who live beyond the law and turn over millions in tax-free profit. Criminals who extort from other criminals or, as happened most recently, extort land from mostly ordinary people in order to sell it at a huge profit to town councillors who are themselves desperate to spend money on a bridge just to show just how forward thinking they really are. The regional crime squad wanted to catch criminals who were smart and ruthless and brutal enough to properly need taking down.

They wanted Dad.

And they wanted me to tell them everything that I knew: they wanted details, dates, locations, everything. They wanted me to give them Dad on a plate. They already had someone undercover working for Dad (and I found out later it was Teez who was the undercover cop, which was a surprise to all concerned) but no one had all the information. People knew bits of this or that, but no one knew every part of the puzzle ('uncorroborated evidence', she called it).

No one, that is, except me.

They somehow knew he'd told me stuff and, it seemed, they knew I had a really good memory, that I'd even offered him advice on how to do things better. Criminal things. So there was no one else, they thought, who could join all the dots. Just me. There was no one who Dad had taken into the full confidence. Except me. The police officer laid this all out in her smooth, agreeable tone, and she made me an offer worthy of a tragic hero in a Greek drama. It was easy to say, but not easy to do. They'd drop all charges against Laura, and all I had to do tell them everything I knew about Dad.

So.

Laura.

Or Dad.

That's what they offered me.

'She's a bundle of joy,' Mam said after she'd left.

'She was ok. Doing her job. Keeping the streets safe.'

At that moment Martin emerged from the living room, 'Has Juliet Bravo gone then?'

I looked at him and decided there and then that I'd finally ran out of patience with him. I said, 'Here's the thing, Martin, if you so much as look at me again, never mind speak to me, I will call the police and say you've been raping me.' Mam gave a start at this but I continued. 'Then I will set my dog on you, and when it tears off your private parts, that's assuming he can find them, I'll call it self-defence. Do you understand, fat boy?'

For a moment Martin looked like he was going to give me a clip, and it began to dawn on me that I really had grown taller in the last few months, and put on a bit of weight, that I was taller than him now, maybe not tougher, but big enough to not be a walkover, and I think it had dawned on him too, but still he looked like he might try. Then a rumble from Max who was standing just behind him, changed his mind on that. 'You,' he said, 'You're just like your old man. Criminal scum.' He stomped back to the living room and his TV, slammed the door. I looked at Mam, momentarily at a loss for what to say.

'He *is* getting fat,' she said.

I had some serious thinking to do.

It felt like I was on my own again, with no one to turn to, and

the only person I could have discussed it with was the person

I was being asked betray. I reached into my pocket, took out

the card that Inspector Steabler had left me and studied it.

Then I closed my eyes, took some slow deep breaths and

thought it through. I felt like I wanted to go and speak to Mam,

and get her advice, but I knew she was too deep into our

world to give anything like a considered opinion. I wanted to

text Emily to say I had a problem, that I needed advice, and I

had no one to turn to and could she call me after school for a

chat. But I couldn't do that either. It wouldn't be fair on her.

Most of all, I wanted to speak to Laura but she was now down

at the police station and would stay there until I made my

decision. Fact is I couldn't speak to anyone. Like my birthday

card had said, no one's got your back. But then again, as I sat there, eyes closed, thinking it through, I realised I didn't need to.

I knew exactly what I had to do.

At half past two I walked into the police station and asked to speak to Inspector Steabler. She appeared a few minutes later.

'You didn't take long,' she said.

'There's nothing to consider,' I said.

'We'll need to book an interview room but before that I'll need to get you a social worker.'

'Before we do any of that, I want your agreement that Laura walks out without any charges.'

'Agreed.'

'In writing.'

For a moment she looked a bit narked, but she mentally swept that aside, eye on a bigger prize than some a snotty-nosed kid heading for a minor drug dealing charge. She considered me for a moment, and I saw exactly what she thought of me written across her face. I was vermin. I was nothing. Just bait to catch something bigger. I saw her calculating the various permutations for a few moments. 'In writing,' she agreed, finally.

She motioned for me to sit down and wait while she went to make some calls. So I sat down and waited, knowing what I'd just agreed to. Knowing what I'd just done. I felt grubby. Of all the things I'd ever done, this was the worst. Everything else, all the dealing, all the running around doing errands for other dealers, all the money I'd made from illegal activities, that had all been done with willing partners, willing customers. I hadn't forced anyone to do anything, I hadn't given away loss-leaders to try and make more addicts, I hadn't sold to little'uns, and I hadn't had people 'disappeared' or anything.

I'm not trying to justify my actions, but selling skunk to an end-of-term teachers' party, or delivering cocaine and Viagra to town councillors at a taxpayer-funded political rally, while funny on many levels, wasn't evil. At least, not in my book it wasn't. And delivering it all in the handlebars of a BMX bike was just ironic.

But this.

This was a grubby little deal.

It was sordid.

Just then a door opened and I looked up, and it was Laura, accompanied by a large policewoman. My heart lit up and I smiled, 'Hey sis. They letting you go?' She flung her arms around me, hugged me tight, a wide grin on her face. 'Mickey. I was so scared, but they're not going to press charges…' she was about to continue but Inspector Steabler appeared just behind her, with a mannish little woman in a suit, the social worker, I guessed. Laura looked at them, then back at me, a question forming on her face. I said, quickly, 'Go home. Don't tell Mam. Or anyone. Not about this.'

'Mickey,' she said, 'What's going on?'

I followed the police inspector and the dour little social worker toward a door, turned and said again to Laura, 'Go home. I'll call you when this is done. Don't tell anyone.' As I spoke, the armoured glass door closed between us. I turned and followed the inspector and the social worker toward the interview room.

The courtroom was full. But it was quiet. Attentive. The clerk

said, 'Please give your name.'

'Michael Hall.'

'Address.'

I told him.

'Date of birth.'

Ditto.

I was wearing a brand-new school uniform, my hair was cut and combed flat, almost, and I stood in the witness box waiting to speak. Until this moment it had been a whirl of police interviews, statement writing, signatures, followed by a few weeks of waiting for the trial. And here it was, the big day. My starring moment. I could barely focus, I was so nervous; I had tunnel vision. My heart was beating so hard I thought I'd faint. The clerk of court had approached me a few moments earlier. 'Nervous?'

I nodded.

'Just imagine the judge in his pyjamas,' he said quietly, with a wink, and I glanced across at the man in the wig on the raised seat. 'Paisley pattern,' he added.

'I was thinking baby blue,' I said.

'Only on capital cases, which this is not.'

'I'm quaking,' I said. 'Seriously.'

'You'll do fine,' he said, and handed me a book, then stepped back. 'As you are legally a minor, you have a social worker should you feel you need advice or support,' and he nodded toward the do-gooder sitting alongside my lawyer, but I didn't look across. A social worker was just extra complication to me, another voice demanding attention, another layer of white noise to ignore, an irrelevance. 'Thanks,' I said, knowing that social workers had not really done me any good in the past and weren't likely to do me any good now, and then we got all business-like. I swore my oath on the bible to tell the truth, the whole truth and nothing but the truth. And after I'd given the basic facts the judge leaned forward and asked me, 'You are aware of the serious nature of this case, Michael?'

'Yes sir,' I said.

The clerk coughed and said to me quietly, 'Call him Your Honour.'

I nodded. 'I'm aware of the serious nature of the case, Your Honour.'

'If found guilty, your father could be facing a life sentence.'

I looked over at my Dad, sitting at a large table on the other side of the courtroom with his lawyer and a couple of other legal types, and he looked back at me without expression, like he was staring at the horizon, and then I turned back to the judge, 'Yes, your honour.'

'But you are not here to convict your father, or acquit him. You are here to tell the truth. You are here to simply answer the questions put to you, and answer them clearly, truthfully and thoroughly. The jury will decide on issues of guilt or innocence. Do you understand?'

'Yes, Your Honour,' I said again.

The judge nodded, turned to the prosecution team and said, 'You may proceed, Mr Rooks.'

Mr Rooks was the prosecutor. The man who could put my Dad away for life, if the conspiracy to murder charges were proven, or put him away for eighteen years if the slightly lesser charges of extortion and violence were proven. He was also the man who could sentence my sister to seven to ten fourteen for possession of Class A drugs with intent to sell, if I didn't testify against my Dad. All of a sudden, I felt a tide of doubt and terror rising inside me. I couldn't win. There's no way anyone in my family can win. We are all going to lose. We always lose.

Who decided that we always lose?, I thought. Whose idea was that? Was I to blame for everything? Was Dad? Mam? Was it a group thing, we'd all screwed up and now we were going to pay? Probably, I thought. I thought back to my trips to the church and my attempts to talk with God. Maybe would have worked better if I hadn't been selling drugs between conversations.

Mr Rooks stepped up and faced me. 'Michael,' he said, 'You are a vital witness in the case against your father, and I know that you are torn between family loyalty on the one hand, and doing the right thing on the other. Please remember that you are under oath and, I trust, you will ensure that you simply tell the court the truth. All you are required to do, in fact, is tell the truth. Tell us what happened in your own words, and not leave anything out.'

Waffle, I thought, glancing across at my Dad who was sitting by his lawyer. Whose truth will we be telling? is what I wanted to ask. Mine? Unlikely. Dad's truth would need to include a 7.62 full metal jacket through the right lung, and that was unlikely to appear in the court transcript.

But I stayed quiet.

I looked back at Dad, caught his eye this time, and he held my gaze for a moment, then gave me the tiniest of winks. I looked back at Wiseman who said, 'I'm going to ask you a series of questions about your father and the time you spent with him, and I am going to ask you about what you know about his business affairs, what you saw and what you heard. You will have to answer fully and honestly.'

Or my sister goes to prison I thought. We had it on paper, the deal, but that depended on me standing here and saying what I had to say.

'You understand what you must do?' he asked.

I nodded, 'Yes.'

I understood alright. A simple choice: Dad or Laura. One deserving, the other undeserving. But both were family. I glanced across the people who were sitting in the courtroom watching proceedings and spotted Laura and Mam sitting near the doors at the back, their heads were together and they were whispering quietly. I looked away. It was all down to me. Whatever happened, whatever had happened in the past, our collective family history had all funnelled down to this moment.

And me.

I took a deep breath, exhaled slowly, and then I smiled to myself. Bugger these guys, I thought, I'm for family and I'm not playing their game.

I had other plans.

Sometimes the only way to not lose is to make yourself so unimportant that you stop being the focus, you just make yourself fade away.

I learned that early, always going to new schools, having to deal with school bullies every time. You do it by making other things more important. That's how I'd discovered my listening thing. My trick, as Karl called it. By doing that you take the focus off you and putting it on someone else, and I'd sort of done that now.

It began shortly after my first interview with the police, when I realised the depth of information I'd collected on Dad in our short time together, and I realised too late that Dad had been telling me all this stuff in a weird way because he wanted to be closer to me. I realised that they were going to use that information to destroy him. After the first four-hour interview in a small stuffy room, recorded on video of course, followed by a lunch break of crappy tea and a dry-ish burger, and then another two hours of interview, recorded on video all accompanied by a social worker siting silently facing a police officer, a lawyer and someone taking notes, I'd been allowed to go home.

The house was quiet.

Mam was sitting reading the Daily Mail, her online tabloid of choice since I'd bought her an iPad with my drug profits. I glanced at it, the usual horror stories of people being caught out, people screwing up, people found out, being morons, or just a bit embarrassing. The usual check-list of desperate, failed celebrities, corrupt officials and ordinary people who'd become, for a day or two, objects of hate or derision due to some trivial error of judgement or rash decision.

People like me.

'How many people do you think read that?' I asked her.

She swiped to Google without looking up, 'Hold on…' did a quick search and then said, 'says here, over two hundred million views a month. Why?'

'I can't believe there are two hundred million mugs in the country, that's all.'

'Probably only two million mugs, everyone reading a hundred times.'

'Probably,' I said.

'Mugs like me?'

I grinned, 'Probably,' and she threw a cushion at me as I left the room to go down to the basement. I checked my messages to find Oscar had called. I rang back and he picked up on the seventh ring, as always. 'You rang me, Mr Genius!' I said.

'Don't call me that,' he told me. 'I'm aspergic and I have an eidetic memory, but I'm not a genius.'

'Hello Oscar,' I said.

'Hi Mickey,' he said, like he'd just picked up.

There was a few moments of dead air while I waited for Oscar to tell me why he'd rang. I could hear him breathing slowly on the other end of the line, so I gave up waiting, 'Why did you call, Oscar?'

'I wondered if you wanted the database. Mum said I had to get rid of it.'

'Database?'

'Of our sales.'

'You kept a database of our sales?'

'Sure.'

'All the money we earned?'

'Yes. I've got the spreadsheet. I recorded the data in terms of date, product, customer, costs, retail price, profit... I did it right, didn't I? I didn't make a mistake?'

He sounded worried for a moment, like he really was never sure if what he was doing what was people expected him to be doing.

'You did good Oscar,' I said, keeping myself calm to keep him sweet, but to be honest my head was spinning with this new information. I needed time to think, so I said, 'I definitely want that information, Oscar. Give me a minute and I'll call you back.'

Without a word he hung up, and I just sat there cradling the phone. I thought for a long while, trying to turn this to my advantage. This was better than I'd dared imagine and an idea was already budding. He hadn't just kept a record of the profits. He'd kept a record of everything. An idea was quickly flowering, in fact it was attracting bees and cross-pollenating with other ideas, metaphorically speaking. I called him back. 'Everything?' I said, just to be sure, 'You kept everything?' I couldn't keep the excitement from my voice. 'Including names, people?'

'Sure. I said I did.'

'Did you keep addresses too?'

Silence. I said, 'Are you nodding, Oscar?'

'Sorry, yes, names and addresses. I kept everything. I *keep* everything. I don't forget anything.'

'When did you do it?' I asked. 'I mean, I used to see you write down the money we'd taken, but that's all.'

'I only wrote that stuff down for you,' he said, 'So you would know how much we made. But every night when I got home I recorded everything else on the spreadsheet. I recorded all the details of what we had done. I included the location, the weather…'

'The weather?'

'I thought that it might affect sales.' His tone changed. 'That cake shop got raided you know, the real one, Bakeaway.'

'I know.'

'It was a real shop,' Oscar said. 'We shouldn't have used their pictures.'

'I just stole the images and the logo for FaceBook.'

'Are they in jail, do you think?' Oscar sounded concerned.

'No. I heard they're suing the police for damages. The police wrecked their shop.'

A quiet moment. 'We wrecked their shop, Mickey,' he said.

It was my turn to nod silently. 'Listen, can you send me a copy of your spreadsheet?'

'Yes. Now?'

'Now would be good.'

'K,' Oscar said, and hung up without further discussion.

A moment later the email came through, and I opened the attachment. I scanned through the details and it was all there. From the moment I'd employed Oscar as book-keeper he'd recorded everything: names, dates, drugs of preference, streets, weather…he'd even recorded the buses that passed as we stood on street corners selling our wares. Of course, he didn't have the name of every schoolie who'd bought an eighth of dope, he didn't know all their names, but he had recorded their school, gender, hair colour, estimate of age, and while he didn't have the name of every body-builder who'd pulled up in a pickup truck and bought some horse-steroids either, he had recorded their licence plate, clothes, hair colour (usually shaved, I discovered, reading the various descriptions) and so on. But for the bigger sales, for parties and things, he had even more info.

A whole lot more.

I remembered he'd ask me about those times when I'd rode my BMX to drop off a score with some punters, and at the time I thought he was just being literal, his demanding every detail, that he had no ability to imagine. Now I know he was being exactly that, literal. He'd transcribed every word I'd said about every drop-off, and from reading back those notes I could begin to recall more and more details myself. I quickly saved a copy of the database under a different name, emailed it to myself so that I couldn't lose it, and I added more details to the records where I could remember; extra details I hadn't told him. By the time I was feeling tired it was after three in the morning and I was still only a third of the way through.

I woke early, my plan fully formed.

I went online, googled 'what to do if you have a story to sell' and then, when it told me, I began searching for media agents. After fifteen minutes I'd come up with a few I liked the sound of, emailed them and waited. Within an hour two of them had called me back. After a discussion with both I went with an agent called Ben who sounded young and enthusiastic and promised me he could sell my story for a small fortune. Within two hours he called back, 'The Daily Mail said they'd pay a hundred thousand, if the information is legit. They'll need the names of all the councillors, police, teachers and so on. '

'Not enough,' I said.

'You're an unknown,' Ben said.

'Try the Telegraph, the Times and the Guardian,' I said. 'Tell the Daily Mail what we're doing.'

'An auction?' Ben mused. 'Good idea. I'm on it.'

And then quite suddenly my mind was back in court.

My heart had slowed almost to normal, my vision became clear, and I gave a little smile. It was going to be alright, I thought. It was going to be easy. The bad side of me was laughing, thinking, this is going to be fun.

The barrister, Rooks, asked me the first question, just general background stuff about my life, my absent dad and that sort of thing, trying to make him out to be a feckless stayaway criminal, which he actually was. I answered it as best I could, describing our life of crappy bedsits, temporary dads, unpaid bills, and hoped I wouldn't humiliate Mam too much. And then I added some added more information, like the time we spent three months living with the hells angels at the clubhouse, and I paid my way by repairing and cleaning all their bikes, which wasn't true. Or the time I'd accompanied Goldfinger when he went debt collecting with his gun, which also wasn't true.

But I was just getting warmed up.

I added more, like telling them about the time I delivered drugs using a drone. Totally untrue. And then I added even more. Outrageous stuff. Unbelievable stuff. I took basic facts and elaborated them into mosaics of unproveable lies and vaguely believable half-truths. I went on adding details until the barrister asked me to stop.

He went back to his notes, read something for a moment or two then turned back to me and asked me another question, this time about how I met Dad when he came back. And I did the same thing again. I invented a whole novel's worth of extraneous material that added to, coloured and completely distorted the truth of what I was saying. No, I hadn't been driven away in a black 5 series, I said, it'd been a gold-plated Humvee. I wasn't carrying an old revolver; it was a Desert Eagle .50 cal, complete with silencer and full auto capacity. Dad had a crew of about eighty guys, they all wore black, even black backpacks, they were tooled up with M4s, and waiting in a row of mini-buses…I'd dug around on the internet to find the right information on the sort of guns carried by criminal gangs and based most of the details in my answer on a few famous heist movies.

Mr Rooks kept checking his notes to try and work out where my agreed statement ended and my 'colour' began. For each true word I spoke that appeared on my statement there must have been a dozen totally fictional ones. He was beginning to look confused, was good old Mr Rooks. After about ten minutes, as I was mid-lie, you might say, I saw a messenger enter the courtroom and approach the prosecution table. He whispered something to another barrister sitting there behind piles of post-it noted files and sheets of paper. With the outlandish details I was giving, Mr Rooks me was looking more and more disconcerted, but not totally concerned, not yet, in fact I think he was blaming himself for missing something. He kept asking more questions, checking his notes, then cutting me short when I went into random-information and bullshit-storytelling mode. I think it was when I described Dad's harem of seven Russian supermodels, one for every day of the week, all of them called Svetlana for ease of communication, that it began to dawn on him what I was doing, and at the same time the guy at the table was doing his best to catch his eye.

Another question.

Another completely random, massively embellished to the point of irrelevance answer, definitely containing a tiny grain of truth, but a grain of truth on a beach-worth of insane, made-up nonsense. Again the guy at the table desperately tried to catch Rooks' eye without annoying the judge. Eventually though, as I was describing Dad's underground lair, complete with massive steel gun-safe and IT facilities that hacked straight into NASA and the CIA, the judge coughed loudly and said, 'As entertaining as this is, I suspect you need to speak to your associates, Mr Rooks, who have been attempting to gain your attention for a while now.' He looked at me and said, 'May I suggest we take a fifteen-minute break?' then he gestured to the clerk, who came over to the stand and told me to go back out into the hall. I noticed the clerk's eyes were watering, whether tears of sadness or silent mirth, I couldn't tell. Dad stayed at the defendant's table though, he was still under arrest, looking down at the table he was sat behind, handcuffed, and I could tell he was trying desperately to suppress a grin.

As I left the courtroom Laura caught my arm, 'What's happening?' nodding toward the barristers, who were now furiously speed-reading something on a computer, swiping through page after page. 'Hear that noise?' I said, and she shook her head, so I explained: 'That's the sound of the shit hitting the fan.'

I'd sold my story to the tabloids.

In doing so I'd also earned myself £150,000 - minus fifteen per cent for the agent and forty per cent for the government, so really I'd earned a little over £70,000. All held in my agent's company account until I'm old enough to claim it, as per the original deal I'd worked out. That way it can't be taken away from me by the legal system or by Mam or Martin or whichever boyfriend she has when I get out of jail. Just in case my performance in court hadn't already done so, the newspaper article had completely destroyed my own credibility as a witness. The headline was I WAS A TEENAGE DRUG DEALER which, by the way, was the first completely true thing I'd said all day.

But I wasn't stupid, and neither was the Daily Mail.

We'd steered clear of any mention of Dad's trial, and I didn't name the crew, but I named everyone else: the teachers, the doctors, the city councillors, the businessmen, the odd high-up police officer... Oscar's eidetic memory had meshed perfectly with my enthusiastic sales pitch so that not only had we sold to virtually everyone of any importance in the town we had amassed a record of every drug sale we ever made. And in retrospect, my customers seemed to have gone crazy with the stuff. I hadn't realised how mad for drugs people were in this would-be City of Culture. But partially that was because, just like with my statements in court, I'd added extra information into the mix. Once I had a name, a date and a buy, I could add more detail. I could ramp up the colour. Those blokes, and they were mainly blokes, they could hardly say, 'Yes I *did* buy an ounce of cocaine from a teenage school-truant drug-king, but you know, I really *didn't* buy four ounces, and I only bought it twice, not every fortnight for a year. And the horse tranquiliser? That's simply not true!'

That wasn't really much of a defence in the court of public opinion. Twitter almost caught fire with the self-righteous anger that was burning from every tweet. Midway through the first morning of my court testimony, the prosecution had discovered that I'd released the names, addresses and chemical preferences of many, *many* important people to the Daily Mail, complete with lots of random information for 'colour' as Ben, my agent, put it.

'They like the personal side of things,' he explained. So I told them. How Norman 'Nocky' Lloyd, the dapper, loud-mouthed chief councillor who was always in the paper sounding off about the poor and the downtrodden, and who'd helped close down the local libraries, thereby depriving me of my auto-didactic literary education while claiming a fortune in expenses for himself and his cronies, how he'd been wearing only a leopard-skin thong and tassled nipple-pasties when he answered the door to fetch the cocaine I'd delivered.

He had actually been wearing a suit, though he *had* bought the cocaine. And six Viagra tablets.

I also explained how I'd spotted Assistant Chief Inspector Joseph Weaver, the current acting police chief, wearing devil's horns and a leather apron when I'd arrived at Echo24 one evening to deliver ecstasy and acid to a party. He was still in uniform, I added, which made the accessories looking even more incongruous. Basically, a lot of people who would have much preferred their names to stay out of the newspapers had details of their criminal activities splashed across the tabloids, and were showed up for being the hypocrites they were. And while a lot of the 'colour' might have been at least partially faked, the dates, the addresses, the names and, crucially, the drugs, were real and could be cross-checked. Over the coming weeks, heads rolled. And by lunchtime on the second day I'd pretty much been scrapped as a competent witness in Dad's trial.

The following day, two high powered lawyers acting for the Daily Mail had been called to appear in front of the judge and explain why they had interfered with an ongoing trial. But they argued the series of articles, for it was a series, not just a one-off, had no relation to the trial of Michael Hall senior, being all about the exploits of Michael Hall junior and involving, as it did, many upstanding members of the community. It was a public interest story they said, and reluctantly, the judge agreed.

Mam's phone was ringing off the hook. Then the Guardian ran an article on me, and all of a sudden I was a "poster boy for the underclass" (their words) – a smart, articulate, drug dealer with a back-story worthy of tears on the X-Factor or a punch up on the Jeremy Kyle show.

I was symbol of the wasted youth to be found on every street corner and every housing estate in the country. I was held up as proof that the government and/or the opposition/society/whoever were all wrong in their approach to education/crime/families and everything else you'd care to name. Even the Green Party waded in, arguing that it was the breakdown of the cultural village that had led to this tidal wave of crime amongst disaffected youth. Something to do with nuclear power and a corrupt, white, cis male, racist establishment.

It was all bollocks really.

I was just trying to survive.

Of course, it blew Dad's case out of the water. They still had him, but not on the major stuff I'd been the star witness for. In the final meeting I had with the prosecuting barristers, accompanied by a social worker, of course, and Karl's dad, who was still acting as my legal counsel, I pleaded ignorance of the articles, a barefaced lie and they knew it, and then I offered to spill whatever else they wanted spilling, I said that I'd even make things up, I'd lie to help the prosecution if they wanted me to, which made them recoil in horror, but by the end of that short meeting I had found myself with a sort of invisible force-field around me, and none of the prosecution came anywhere near.

Not ever again.

Which was quite nice, actually.

This took a few days to play out. All I knew on that first Monday of the trial was that the brown sticky stuff had hit the whirly thing and everyone was getting a coating. For the first couple of days, until everything really got into gear, I still had to go to court and give testimony, and the lurid web of truth-infused lies was spinning bigger and bigger until, by the Wednesday, Mr. Rooks and DCI Steabler met me and Mam at court and took us aside and told us they wouldn't be needing me on the stand for the foreseeable future. I'd still have to attend every day just in case, but short of something major developing, I wouldn't be required to stand as a witness. I noticed that in one of the folders Mr. Rooks' was holding there was a copy of the Daily Mail. And the Daily Mirror. And the Star. And the Sun. I checked later and all were running my story. It turned out that my agent Ben had sold my tale to the other tabloids too, and a couple of magazines. The Telegraph was running a big spread on local government corruption. In total, after tax and agents' fees, I was looking at over a profit of hundred thousand pounds.

Nice work, and all that.

Better than dealing drugs.

For the next couple of days I had a sort-of ringside seat outside the courtroom. As a possible witness I wasn't allowed inside but I could sit and watch everyone hurry about trying to rescue the case, enjoying the expressions of barely contained panic on the faces of people who, on Monday morning, had been smug and arrogant.

I'm not naturally a system-smasher, not an anarchist or anything, but I really enjoyed tearing down this small piece of the establishment. By Friday, accompanied by a silent social worker, I was just sitting reading a book in the café next to the court. Mam had stopped coming after the first day, and Laura too, though she texted me every day to check what was going on. I think they'd both overdosed on Dad, the sweetest honey being loathsome to the taste, and all that malarkey. Friday afternoon I was told not to bother returning on Monday. Job done, I thought, and I went home feeling very pleased with myself.

You'd think, by now, I'd have learned not to be smug. You'd think I'd have learned not to be complacent, not to be so self-satisfied, not to be over-pleased with my ability to destroy things.

It was life, you see. Life had me in its sights again, and it had already pulled the trigger.

And someone else had got caught in the crossfire.

'Laura,' I shouted as I closed the door. 'Hey sis, it's all over!'

And for once, I thought, we *had* won. Our family, who never won anything, had won.

I was grinning as I listened for a reply but none came so, still smiling, I went down to my room looking for Max. He wasn't there, so I went back up and through to the kitchen, checked the back yard. No Max there either. I shouted his name, maybe she had taken him for a walk, something she never did, I thought, and then a heard a whimper.

'Max?'

I went back through to the living room and Max was there, sitting beside Laura, who was lying on the settee. Quite still.

Her skin was waxy and white, her lips a shade of palest blue, a needle on the floor beside her.

She wasn't breathing.

She lay as still as those plaster statues that decorated the walls in St. Ignatius. Max looked at me, whimpering, and I knew. I totally knew without having to check. She was dead. She was gone, and this time, there'd be no saving, there'd be no ambulance, no flashing lights and sirens and men in scrubs to save her, no doctors to infuse fresh clean blood into her system. I sat down on the chair next to her, took her hand, which was cool and soft and lifeless. 'Aww sis,' I said, feeling so low I couldn't even grasp it. Just numb. 'Aww, Laura.'

There was no coming back from this. Not for me, not for Mam, or Dad. And not for Laura.

Not for ever.

Turns out that while I'd been keeping my eye on the trial and on Dad and on my business empire, I'd forgotten to keep an eye on my big sister.

Turns out that she was more fragile than I'd ever realised, and without anyone to keep an eye on her, she'd decided to go back to the thing she loved and hated in equal measure. The thing she *needed*. The thing that comforted her when she was low. See, when I'm low, my thing was, I looked out for Laura, but when she was low, and I wasn't there, she looked for the needle. And meeting up with Dad, the trial, everything, she'd got low and I was busy, and so she'd reached back. It was the classic returner's OD that I'd read about (one of my many diversions in the library): she'd taken her usual dose, but after months off the stuff her system wasn't used to it anymore and she crashed. Alone. And me, her parachute, I'd failed to open. I wasn't there, and she'd died as a result.

But that realisation came later. For now I just sat with her and held her hand, my big sister, the focal point of my life, the one living human being I could always rely on, and life had completely burned away for me. It was all over.

I was numb.

There was nothing now.

I sat for ages. Just sat next to her. For a while I even slept. I dreamt we were holding hands, holding hands and walking backwards down the middle of a busy road, and every time a car approached, we floated backwards over the top of it, laughing. She turned to me and smiled at me and I woke, smiling back at her. Then I remembered, I looked down at her still, peaceful face, her pale skin, and something inside me went cold, something froze. There are parts of me still, all this time later, that don't feel things the way I should.

Not any more.

Martin found us, sometime later. It was dark, and he came in his usual loud, obnoxious self, I didn't even look up at him, just sat and held Laura's hand. But then he did something unexpected: he reacted as an adult. He didn't even ask, he just called the ambulance and the cops, then called Karl's dad to intercept Mam, who'd was visiting Dad.

Then he went and got a blanket and covered her.

'Not her face,' I said, as he tucked the blanket in around her,

took her hand from me and tucked it inside the blanket, gently,

quietly, like she was a sleeping child.

Then the ambulance came and the cops and the social workers

arrived and all that shit, and everything went mental. I think

he saw that I was about to either blow, or collapse, and people

were asking me questions, and he said, 'I think the lad's had

enough for now,' taking me by the arm and outside, for a

walk, a long walk, and the weird thing, as we walked he held

my hand like I was a kid too, didn't even try to make small

talk, he just walked with me, and we ended up in the park

sitting on a bench, him sitting with his head bowed slightly,

me staring up at the stars, wondering which one was Laura.

The next few days passed in a sort of numb blur. I think

Martin made most of the arrangements: Mam was in a state

and I didn't know what to do. Dad was in jail. So Martin

sorted everything out. Maybe he wasn't such a twat after all.

The funeral was short, we aren't the most religious of people, though I asked the priest from Ignatius to do a ceremony for us and he did. Dad's a catholic, I discovered, so that made it ok but the priest said he'd have done it anyway. The last ever time I saw Mam and Dad together, they were sitting side-by-side on the pew as the curtain closed and Laura's body went into the fire. Dad was handcuffed, a police officer on the other side of him. I was sitting in the next row with a social worker, Martin next to me. I watched Mam. She was just destroyed. This is just bad, I thought. We're the worst fucking family in the world. We're not even funny. We're not even quaint. We are just vermin. Useless.

The priest was really kind though and the words he spoke were generous and true. I suspected he had a soft spot for me because of my regular visits, he thought I was a repenting sinner. Or maybe he appreciated the money I'd been donating on the sly. I hoped it would get Laura well in with God, get her a star to sit on so she could ride through the skies every night. Laura had been pregnant too, we'd discovered. No one even knew she had a boyfriend or anything, and I realised there was so much about her I didn't know, so much of her life I wasn't a part of. Her friends from the supermarket came to the funeral, plus old school friends, even her old English teacher, and they were all in floods too. She was well-liked. Emily was there, as was Karl and his dad, they stood quietly at the back. I'd been holding it together until then, and afterwards, outside, I went to Karl and he put his arms around me and held me while I shuddered silently, forcing myself not to cry. He was saying 'It's ok bruv, it's ok,' and I heard Laura's voice in his as I fought back the sobs that threatened to engulf me, and knew it would be ok, sometime in the future it would be ok, even if now it wasn't now, the world would turn and eventually, I heard her say through Karl's voice, it would be alright. *It's ok Bruv*, she whispered to me. And it was then that I really knew she was gone. Then it was all over and Dad went back to jail. Mam and Martin and me went back to the empty house. We didn't hold a wake.

I sat in the empty living room for a bit and then, quietly, I let myself out and walked back toward town. It was growing dark already, the streetlamps were on and the shops had their lights blazing, and those shops that were permanently closed, their shutters seemed to reflect the light back onto the street too. I reached the Wearmouth bridge, walked out onto it and looked over the edge, pulled off the tie I'd been wearing for the funeral, and threw it over the side, watched it flutter down into the darkness. I looked out along the river, saw the arc lights from the cranes unloading a cargo ship onto the south dock.

Across the river the university campus seemed to twinkle, lit by a thousand bright windows. Cars passed me, the beams raking across me and leaving me in shade. I refused to cry because when you cry, you say goodbye, and I wasn't ready to leave her yet. And anyway, how many tears do you shed for someone who is at the centre of your life? How many tears is a person worth? And when you eventually stop crying, you think, is that it? She was worth an hour, a day, a week or tears? That's the measure? That's all? I couldn't allow myself to measure her in grief. I couldn't put a price on her, not even a price in tears.

Without thinking I turned and began clambering up the curve of the bridge structure, until I got to the iron platform fringed with steel spikes, designed to stop people climbing any higher, but I easily clambered past and scrambled further up and up, the curve of the bridge flattening off as it reached the top. Eventually I reached the apex where the broad spans flattened out. Unlike my old man, I was never afraid of heights. I reached the point where the two curved spans met in the middle, and I stepped lightly across the gap and then turned to look out past the river toward the inky grey North Sea. This high, the wind had picked up, buffeting me a little, and I closed my eyes, raised my arms, stretched them out like wings;

I felt weightless, in the darkness it was like I was flying, and I could have stayed like that forever, above the light, above the people, above everything and everyone, just alone and weightless. Then someone driving a truck below me blew on their air-horn and the shock nearly made me fall off the bridge. Heart hammering, I gathered my balance and decided that, yes, maybe it would be wise to at least be careful of heights, maybe it would be smart to acknowledge that I really didn't want to fall three hundred feet into the cold, dark river below. So, more careful now, I scrambled back down the ever-steepening rivet-studded girders, sliding the last ten feet onto the platform, then monkeyed round the spikes and down onto the street below. I felt my heart beating hard inside my chest, my breathing was fast, the adrenaline coursing through my veins, and I felt so wobbly I had to steady myself against the railings for a moment.

What was I doing? I thought.

Back home, I let myself in and went straight downstairs to my room, took off my dark suit, white shirt, dark socks and polished black shoes, threw them all in the bottom of the wardrobe, pulled on a cheap t-shirt, an old pair of jeans and my Converse on bare feet, then I lay down on the bed, having decided I was never going to leave this room again.

I felt burned. Raw. Numbed.

My heart had slowed after the bridge thing, but the adrenaline was still lurking, making me feel unpleasant. I lay staring up into the darkness, expecting nothing back from it, and getting nothing back either.

Just darkness.

I lay on the bed but I still couldn't let myself cry.

It must have been toward midnight when I heard someone at the front door. Martin's voice, and someone else; I ignored it. A minute or two later though, someone tapped lightly at my bedroom door. I ignored it. Go away, I thought. I couldn't even be bothered to speak. Just go away.

Then another tap.

I waited a few minutes, but I sensed whoever it was still standing outside, so I got up and opened the door, saying 'Go away,' but when I saw who it was, the words froze in my mouth.

Emily.

'Hi,' she said, her voice low.

'Hi,' I said.

'I thought you might need some company,' she said.

Emily.

It was like being lost in a Grimm Fairy Tale forest and spending years struggling through dark undergrowth and following treacherous paths, and then suddenly seeing a single light, far away, shining clear and bright.

I woke up early the following morning and turned over in bed, and there she was, next to me. She opened her eyes, 'Hey,' she murmured. She looked more beautiful than ever. I remembered the night before; how she'd stood there looking vulnerable, and so sad. How she had reached up and stroked my face with the tips of her fingers. 'I'm sorry, Mickey,' she said. 'I am *so* sorry.'

How I'd taken her fingertips in mine. 'It was my fault,' I said, 'I neglected you.'

'I've missed you,' she'd told me. 'I've never stopped missing you.'

'I missed you too,' I told her. 'All the time.'

'I'm so sorry about Laura,' she whispered. 'It's so unfair…' her voice faded and we stood like that for a moment until I felt my body begin to shudder, felt some valve releasing all the pent-up emotion, and all the hurt and despair I'd suppressed, all the bad *shitty* things that had happened, it all suddenly flooded to the surface and for the first time my tears began to flow, and I began to sob uncontrollably, and she flung her arms around me, and I threw mine around her, and she kissed me, and I kissed her too as I cried and cried and cried in her arms.

After I'd cried for what seemed like a lifetime, I felt all mushy inside, like the hurt had softened into something I could live with. We kissed, for what seemed like another lifetime, until I said, 'How long can you stay?' and she whispered, 'I think you need me here with you all night.'

'You sure?' I said, barely able to speak.

'Yes.'

'Won't you..?' I said.

'No.'

'You mean..?'

'Yes.'

'What about..?'

'It's over. Long over. It was only ever you.'

We were sitting on the bed by this point and she stood up and closed my bedroom door and then came and sat beside me again. 'This is not the time for opening old wounds,' she said, 'or going over old ground. I'm here to look after you. You need someone with you tonight.'

She was right.

I hadn't realised how lonely I felt, how desolate, how empty my life had become after Laura had passed, until now. I'd switched off, embraced the darkness. Embraced my own cold heart. And here was Emily carrying a flame, and that flame was herself, to bring me light and make me warm again. A lifetime's worry, two weeks of terrible, bleak grief, and now a girl who loved me had come to make my life, or at least a small part of my life, alright again. Something inside me fell apart at that moment. For the first time I could remember, the cold, watchful centre of my heart thawed and it floated up and away like a kite on a breezy summer's evening.

We kissed some more.

World, I thought, just shut your mouth.

Don't. Even. Start.

And now, here in my room, we were together and for a short while the world was perfect. For an entire night the world was a better place than I'd ever known it to be and everything that had happened before was made bearable. I don't know if soulmates exist, but for that one night our souls were connected. Being with her was like being in a church lit by a thousand candles, each one flickering bright and alive, just for me. But the candles grew too bright, my eyes opened and it was the sun shining through the gaps in the curtains. It was morning, and life was intruding at the edges of my perfection. 'Morning,' I replied, kissing her nose, determined to keep real life at bay for as long as it was possible. Which was not possible, as I discovered when Mam opened the door a few minutes later and brought us in a tray of tea and biscuits. 'Morning!' she said, pasting the Hall-family-patented

Everything Is Alright smile, though I could see her grief etched plain behind her smile. I looked at Emily who just said, 'Morning,' back, sat up and gave my Mam a hug and a smile.

'I was up earlier,' she explained, when Mam left the room. 'You were sound asleep and I thought I'd better announce my presence.'

'Right,' I said.

'Pour me a cup of tea,' she said. 'I need to get ready.'

'Ready for what?'

'School, silly.'

Oh, right. School.

I poured us both a cup of tea. School. It'd been so long since I'd been there I'd forgotten I was supposed to go. It meant nothing to me, was just a word, a random sound.

Balancing my cup of tea, I watched as Emily dressed, thinking I would never see anything so perfect in my life ever again as Emily after we'd spent our first night together, wishing I could halt time at that very moment, just stop the clock from moving forward. I didn't want to see the day: the darkness of the night before had belonged to us; the warmth, the hidden secrets, it was ours, like we were the first people on earth, and afterwards we'd talked and talked, and though I knew, I think we *both* knew, somehow, on some deep level, that this was where our paths divided, that the night we'd spent together signalled the end of something, but somehow it didn't matter, what we'd shared was eternal and if it ended now or next week or next year, it ended on our terms.

She told me how she felt, and I told her, and we talked for hours, sometime during the night we held each other and just cried and cried, and then took turns in crying, and comforting, and then laughing and then, well, some stuff is private, obviously, but despite what had happened before between us, it was a wonderful night. And the thought of school had never intruded. I watched her putting on her uniform. I cleared my throat and she glanced round, 'What?'

'Last night, you know, was I..?' my voice dried. She looked puzzled for a moment then laughed, 'Oh that? Yes, you were. Very.' And she leaned across the bed and kissed me one more time.

I grinned at that, relieved, and said, 'You did ok too,' and she slapped my shoulder laughing, 'Ok? Just OK?' until I told her she was the best I'd ever experienced and she said something like, *really?* and I could tell that straight-A, quietly competitive Emily *really* wanted to know what I thought of how she'd been last night. 'It's just,' I said, 'I know I'm supposed to know stuff, me being a bad boy and all that, but that was my first time.'

I felt myself blushing.

She paused, fastening her blouse, a smile blossoming on her face. 'It was mine too.'

Oh.

Right.

I wanted to ask about Karl but I didn't need to. She said, 'Karl was a nice boy but, well, he wasn't you.' I watched her pull her blazer from a large bag she'd carried into my room the night before. She tugged it on, fastened the buttons, looked at me, 'Not even first base,' she said primly. Then she turned to the mirror to re-touch her hair, whispering half to herself, 'God I look a mess. Like I've been dragged through a bed backwards.'

After a few moments of what I can only describe as improving on perfection she stepped back and said, 'Right,' picked up her bag and turned to me, 'School calls.'

'Come back again,' I said.

'I will,' she said, 'Maybe not tonight, but I will.'

I went to get out of bed but she pushed me back, 'Stay like that,' she said opening her eyes wide as though to take a photograph. 'The thought of you like that will sustain me through a dire day of double sociology, maths, English and Biology.'

'You'll ace biology,' I said.

'I've got the best teacher,' she said and gave me a bad attempt

at a wink that made me laugh.

She laughed too.

Strange as it sounds, it was a time for laughter. It was a time

for making love and celebrating life and watching pretty girls

dress and being in love and...

...and then she was gone.

A few weeks after the funeral, and despite my sabotage, Dad

was sentenced to 10 years for extortion and other related

crimes. It was later reduced to seven years on appeal, though

we didn't know that when they led him downstairs to the cells.

Curiously, my lurid testimony seemed to go for my Dad

rather than against him. The sight of a teenage boy driven to testify against his father in order to protect his sister from prosecution by the Crown Prosecution Service, was seen by the jury and the press as heavy-handed. Crass, I think a local newspaper called it. And then of course, my story had already splashed in the nationals.

The whole tabloid-crazy soap-opera story of a teenage drug dealer selling drugs to teachers, police chiefs and city aldermen. If it hadn't been about me, Mam would have loved it, would have followed every development with rapt attention and then given me the highlights every morning over breakfast. I wasn't exactly seen as a hero, but I was described in the one article as "plucky and protective, if misguided" which, I guess, was true enough. Piers Morgan described me as the ugly face of capitalism, which was also true, and then offered me a spot on his new show, which I declined. For a week or two the thing caught fire and everyone wanted details. The national crime squad got back on my case and I had to give more statements, but not about Dad now.

About everyone else.

Oscar's spreadsheet helped a lot, a whole lot, and the heat had completely gone out of Dad's case. In the grand scheme of things, his trial became less important to them, and I think it showed. They were working on the fly now, backtracking, scrambling round the hole in their strategy where my testimony would have sat. In parallel, a different group of crown prosecutors were pumping me for information related to Oscar's database, and that info I was happy to give for free. But for every single, provable fact, I added two or three made-up ones. Colour, as I've explained. They were in a frenzy, the police and the lawyers, knowing some of what I was saying was provably true, but suspecting much of it to be completely false, and the worst thing was their not being able to tell the difference.

After a couple of weeks of intense questioning though, I'd had enough so I played my trump card. That night as I sat in my room eating pizza, after I'd texted Emily the day's news, I called my lawyer, well, Karl's dad, and I told him in a level, serious tone that I felt suicidal. He quickly made some calls and the interviews stopped in their tracks. The police left me alone. As Karl's dad said, they had a copy of the database (a partial copy, if I'm honest, I kept some back as insurance) and the rest was up to them to investigate. It was untrue, to be honest, the suicide thing, but if nothing else I know how to play the social care system, so mental health, "every child matters" and all that social-work nonsense kicked in, they backed off, terrified that if I killed myself they'd all be in worse trouble than they were already. Still, I couldn't fix everything.

Laura wasn't coming back.

At the end of his trial, Dad was still facing ten years, though after the re-sentencing, and with time served and time off for good behaviour, he'll serve just over three. He wrote to me and told me he still plans to retire, just not with the same package as he'd expected. I don't believe he will but I'm glad he wrote to me, I'm glad he said it.

It was a proper letter too, slotted inside a card. He said that I'd had to make some tough choices, and he thought that overall, I'd made the right ones, that he'd have done the same. And he was pleased at the metaphorical wasps' nest I'd kicked across the courtroom floor. The bad-dad part of him enjoyed the idea of all those good people being tainted and condemned. I wasn't sure this level of glee was appropriate for a parent, but I'm no expert, so I let it slide. He said he wanted to keep in touch when he got out. I'm not sure if I want to, but I've still got another couple of years to decide.

I was arrested on the court steps immediately after the verdict on Dad; they wanted me to spill all the gen, but I spilled more than they bargained for, and they hated me for the trouble I'd caused them. I'd asked them if they'd wait until we were somewhere quiet, not to embarrass Mam, but the way I altered my testimony, the way things had snowballed out of all control, the fallout from the newspaper articles, it had made them very angry. Though I hadn't exactly gone against our deal, I'd testified as they asked, after all, and given them the facts they'd asked me to give, but I'd stretched the truth, and their patience, beyond the limit. So they cuffed me and read me my rights in front of Mam took me direct to the cells where for a few more hours, ironically, I was only a few dozen feet from my old man.

I was charged with possession of class A drugs with intent to supply, supplying class A drugs, supplying class B drugs to minors, possession of a firearm and failure to control a dog in a public area, amongst other things, though my trial was eventually postponed after they agreed to let me finish school and take my exams. You see, Mam had been taken to court for failure to send me to school and fined £500 - they basically threw the book at us - but it meant they had to let me go back to school.

I ended up living back at the flat with Mam, Max and Martin, wearing an ankle tag so they could keep track of me, and I was looking at a future consisting of exams, followed by a few years in a Young Offenders Institute. If you look at my school attendance record though, you'd realise I had no intention of doing either – to my 'don't do homework' rule I'd added 'don't do school' and was about to add 'don't do three years in a YOI.

You'll be unsurprised to hear that I had a plan.

A few of weeks after Laura's funeral I'd done one of those

things people do when they're miserable: I'd cleaned my room.

First, I unplugged all the toys that the drug money had

bought: the PlayStation, the iPad, the Samsung, none of them

had good memories and, besides, I rarely used them. Then I

threw most of the expensive clothes Dad had bought me into a charity bag, along with the suit I'd worn to the trial and the funeral. Let some poor kid in Romania wear them.

Amongst the clothes, in a drawer, I found a hair bobble that I remembered had belonged to Laura, it must have got mixed up with my stuff when Mam was doing the washing, it still had a couple of her hairs clinging to it, and I slipped it onto my wrist as I worked.

Maximus trotted down the stairs and lay watching me as I emptied the wardrobe of everything that I didn't need, which was most of it, and then I did the same with the drawers. I kept the underwear, socks and a few t-shirts, couple of pairs of jeans, kept the bare minimum. I kept just enough to keep me warm, and clean, but everything else went into a charity bag. In a bottom drawer I found my old Berghaus rucksack and I stacked that by the door feeling like I was almost done cleaning, but not feeling any better. There was a buzzing in my head, like something needed to break, some kind of a storm was needed to wash away the heaviness I felt inside, but I couldn't find out what it was; I needed to reboot but I couldn't find the right keys to press. I sat down on the bed for a moment thinking, after everything I'd done, all my efforts to fix things, to make them right and all I had to show was an empty room and a calendar of a Greek Island.

I felt low.

More, I felt wiped out. Like I had almost ceased to exist.

Standing again, I went to the calendar and studied it, saw that someone had scribbled on it the corner of it **Future Plans**.

Laura. I recognised her handwriting.

'I need to take this down, sis,' I said. 'There's no future plan. There's just nothing. I'm all out of ideas.'

I reached up and took hold of the corner of the calendar where it was held to the wall by blu-tac and I peeled it away, careful not to tear it, and as I did I saw something behind the poster that made me frown, then slowly, it made me smile. There was a gap in the wall, behind the poster, a hole about six inches square cut neatly into the plasterboard wall, and behind it was the grimy and dust-covered shelving of the original alcove that had been boarded over years ago. But it was what was sitting on the shelf that caught my eye. Neatly stacked bundles of cash in vacuum-packed polythene bags. Cash. Lots and lots of cash. All piled up. I reached in and took down one of the bundles from the top, brushing off the thin layer of grime, looked at it, turned it over. Twenties. I took down another bundle. Tens. Each bundle was in a plastic bag on which was printed '£500' and there were lots of them. Attached to one bundle with an elastic band was the passport Laura had sorted for me ages ago. I hadn't even realised she'd completed it. And there was an envelope beneath the passport, and inside this were details of a bank account in my name, for a bank I'd never heard of, something called EFG, from Luxembourg, which sounded impressive. Inside the envelope was a bank card too, wrapped in a post-it note that contained a PIN, and there was a statement, which I read, and then reread. The cash in the alcove wasn't the half of it. I never kept track of quite how much money I'd earned in my year of behaving badly.

Apparently, Laura had.

I sat back down on the bed, dazed, thinking, I don't know about my scheming or Dad's ruthlessness, but Laura won the prize for secrecy. How had she done it? I thought back to one day when I'd seen her wearing overalls, covered in dust, coming out of my room with the vacuum cleaner and she'd said something about spring cleaning, and I thought about her getting me to take a picture of myself for the passport application form, and I thought of all the times I'd left cash in piles, never thinking to check if it was all there when I went for it later while, it turns out, she'd been quietly siphoning of a large chunk of it.

I knew, I suddenly knew, that she'd been taking care of my future for a time when she might not be around. All the time I thought I was looking out for her, she'd been doing the same for me.

'Oh, sis,' I whispered, wiping away fresh tears with the back of my hand, 'What have you done?'

Carefully, I put back the cash and stuck the calendar to the wall, just to give me time to think, but really I'd already decided what I was going to do. Laura knew too, she'd known way back, before it all kicked off, and she'd made me this insurance plan. I put the envelope with the bank details in my pocket and took the charity bags filled with my old stuff upstairs, opened the front door and left them on the step, looking around to see if anyone was watching me, I felt nervous and excited, closed the door quietly, and went back down to my room to use the iPad one last time to do some online research into how to take off an ankle tag without alerting the authorities. It only took five minutes to find out how, and about two minutes to actually do it, and then I did some fact-checking online too, checked out timetables, routes, that sort of thing, didn't write anything down though. When I'd finished I switched off the iPad, unscrewed the back and took out the hard drive, slipped it onto my pocket to throw away later; I wasn't going to leave a trail of electronic breadcrumbs for anyone to follow. Then I took down the calendar one last time and packed my Berghaus with what lay on the dusty shelf behind it, filled a third of it with the bundles of cash, and topped it off with spare underwear, socks and t-shirts, slipped the passport into a side pocket. 'Max!' I went to the door and shouted, wondering where he'd gone, and after a couple of minutes he came ambling back down to my room. I squatted down and petted him, stroked his muzzle, scratched the inside of his ears, which he loved. I got face to face with him, took his big head in my hands. 'I have to go, Max,' I said, forcing a smile on my face, 'There's nothing for me here.' His big eyes looked sad, and I thought, he *knows*, he might not have words like me, but he knows a farewell when he hears one. 'I'll write.' I promised, 'and I'll tell Mam to read out the letters to you, cos I know you'll understand.' I hugged him, 'And maybe when everything dies down, when I'm in the clear, maybe you can come out to wherever I am and we can have a nice quiet life together, how's that sound?' He gave a little growl and then yawned. I stroked his muzzle, hugged his sturdy frame one more time, then stood up, hefted the rucksack and looked round the room, saying a silent farewell to my old life, to my old self. I tapped the little bobble I was wearing on my wrist for good luck, and left my room, left Max, who was still standing watching me, went upstairs and opened the front door, stepped over the charity bags, and out into the street.

I'd write to Mam later, I decided, she wouldn't miss me for a day or so, and by then I'd be far away. I knew where I was going and for the first in my life, I think, I had a plan, I had a long-term plan. I wasn't just reacting, or desperately chasing something I couldn't catch, like the dreams I had of running after the kite that had flown away from me.

For the first time in my life I knew where I was going. Knew it with absolute clarity. I stepped out into the street, laughing to myself at the madness of it all, the sudden certainty of what I was doing, and I headed toward town, toward the station. I cut through the park as the sun came out from behind the clouds, shining down on me as I walked past the monument to some dead Victorian robber baron, past the library, the only one left in town, past the pubs that opened at eight every morning and were filled all day with people drinking their lives away. I walked past the social workers' offices, the city's only growth industry. Walked through the grimy streets, below rusting street signs. I passed tattoo parlours, I passed boarded-up shop windows and signs offering to buy people's jewellery. A solicitor's office had an advert telling me to make a claim, because someone was to blame. I passed a poster telling me I lived in the City of Culture on which someone had graffiti'd *Justice for Chelsey.*

I'm done with all this, I thought to myself as I went into the station and bought a ticket at the machine, walked down the concrete steps and onto the platform, dropping a pound coin into the lap of a homeless guy as I stepped over him. I'm done with everything I ever knew. It's time to start over. It's time to be a better person, time to live a better life. I sat down on a bench and waited for the train that was going to take me somewhere different, somewhere that wasn't here.

I thought of Laura, and I knew that Dad was wrong because, all that time, someone had my back, someone was looking out for me, and I heard her voice again, the mix of pride and sadness when she'd seen me in my new clothes after I first moved in with Dad, 'Look at you, Mickey, 'she'd said, 'You're all new.'

I am, Laura, I thought, as I waited for the train that would take me to a new life.

I'm all new.

James Ross' new novel **Shoreline Gold** is due for release in 2020

www.jamesross.media